Praise for The Other Man

"My heart raced from the first page, every word in this sinfully exhilarating romance making me forget the world around me and immerse myself blissfully in yet another scorching R.K. Lilley story.

~Natasha is a Book Junkie

"SCORCHING — a deliciously hot page turner full of intrigue and angst."

~Vilma's Book Blog

"Absolutely 5 stars. RK really outdid herself. Heath was all kinds of dangerous and dark and sexy. BRAVO!!!!! Another spectacular read by R.K. Lilley, possible her best yet."

~Ana's Attic Book Blog

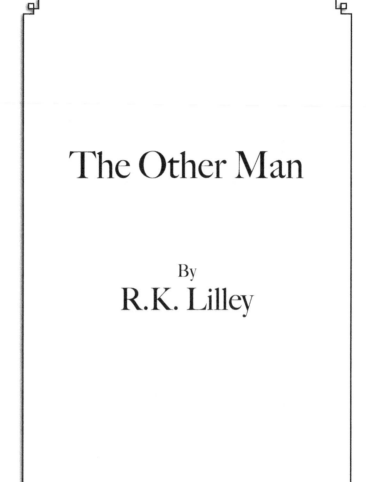

The Other Man

By
R.K. Lilley

The Other Man

ISBN-13: 978-1-62878-034-5
ISBN-10: 1-62878-034-7

Interior design by Warkitten Formatting!

www.rklilley.com

Give feedback on the book at:
Authorrklilley@gmail.com

Twitter: @authorrklilley

Instagram: Authorrklilley

Facebook.com/RkLilley

First Edition

Printed in the U.S.A

This book is dedicated to my mother. You've been to hell and back and lived to tell the story. You've come so far, endured so much, and at this stage of your life, to be doing better than ever, it's both moving and inspiring. Thank you for not giving up, but instead kicking ass.

You know it means the world to me.

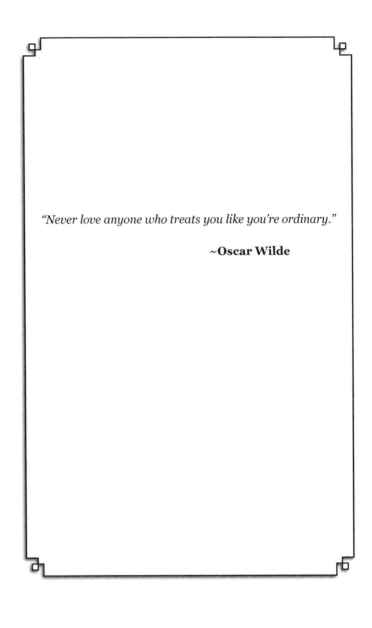

"Never love anyone who treats you like you're ordinary."

~Oscar Wilde

CHAPTER
ONE

LOURDES

I felt eyes on me all through the grocery store. I had good instincts, so when I turned and saw no one, I was surprised.

It was a quick run, mainly for fresh produce and meat, so I was in and out quickly, my mind on Dair.

He was hot. Tall, with a body to die for. Huge arms, a rock hard chest. And the rest was just as nice, with messy brown hair and kind eyes that always made me feel like I was with an old friend.

Hot, successful, and almost too easy to talk to. I found myself spilling my guts to him practically every time we spent any time together.

Still, we seemed destined to stay in the friend zone, and even I couldn't have said why.

I collected my organic Swiss chard, spinach, kale, tomatoes, zucchini, onions, leeks, just grabbing the usual—no specific meal in mind. I was a vegetable junky, so I'd find something to do with it all, and force as much of it on my boys as I could when they came over for dinner. Cooking healthy and feeding it to them was a compulsion for me at this point.

They were great sports about it and rarely complained. They were such good boys.

My pride and joy.

My divorce had been ugly, but so had my marriage, and over a year later I found myself in a strange place. I loved my work, my children were grown and thriving, and I was enjoying life more than I could ever remember. There wasn't much romance in my life, but there hadn't been much even when I'd been married, so it still felt like a clear turn for the better.

Perhaps I was one of those women that were just better off alone.

Certainly, I was happier.

I collected some fresh organic chicken and some grass-fed beef, enough for one small woman and two large men. I still cooked family sized portions, as my boys often showed up for dinner. I hoped that would never change.

They were so good to me. They were as busy as I was, but always made time to check in with their mother. I couldn't ask for more.

I was in the checkout line and had just finished piling my items onto the belt when I felt eyes so intently on me that I had to check again.

I glanced behind me and found my eyes meeting icy blue ones.

I quickly looked away. The eye contact had been uncomfortably intense.

I waited a beat, then looked again, assuming the large blond man would have had his fill staring at me by then.

He didn't, meeting my eyes even more brazenly the second time.

My eyes darted away again, but I'd had enough of a look, with my photographer's eye, to take inventory.

Tall, blond, tan, big, and muscular. Gray T-shirt, dark gray jeans.

Hard jaw, harder eyes.

Smoking hot.

He could have been any age from twenty to thirty going by his mean, unlined face. The scruff on his hard jaw and his aged blue eyes made it impossible to say.

I instantly wanted to photograph him. If he wasn't a model, he should be. There was just so much character in his face. And so much to read in his hard expression.

Aggressive and a touch of something else. Something akin to hostile, though I couldn't imagine it was directed at me. Just a restless man that hated standing in line for even five minutes, I figured.

I glanced furtively at his single item on the belt, my eyes snapping away, face flushing when I saw that it was a twelve-pack of magnum condoms.

Well, shit. Why did that turn me on? It shouldn't have. The guy was probably a jerk and off to have sex with what I assumed would be a random woman. Men that intensely good-looking buying condoms generally were.

Tell that to my libido.

We were waiting forever for an old, white hippie lady to count out exact change, and I didn't last long before checking him out again. This time my eyes wandered below his belt, the magnum thing making it impossible not to be curious.

I flushed as I looked away again. His jeans weren't tight, but I'd made out enough of a bulge to embarrass myself.

What was wrong with me? I was not turned on by strangers. Even the idea was ludicrous. I needed more than looks to even consider getting physical with a man.

Finally I paid for my things and carried them out toward my car.

I was nearly there when the sound of something hitting with a splat onto the pavement had me whipping around.

I blinked up at the big blond stranger, who had apparently been following close behind me, then glanced down at the single tomato that had managed to fall from one of my bags onto the ground.

I lifted the paper bag, brows drawing together at the very neat hole in the corner. It looked like it had been cut, but that was impossible.

"Let me carry that for you, before anything else manages to fall out," a deep, gravelly voice said to me.

I looked at the stranger.

He was offering to do something nice and polite, but his tone wasn't even remotely friendly.

It was odd.

"No, that's all right," I told him with a shake of my head, balancing both of my bags into one arm, and bending down to collect the ruined tomato, then straightening when I saw that was clearly pointless. It was a goner.

My hair had fallen over an eye when I'd bent down, and without missing a beat, brazen as you please, the stranger reached a hand over and stroked it away from my face, then let it linger there, in my hair, bold as you please.

I just stared at him, a bit shocked. I couldn't remember a time in my life running into such an aggressive stranger.

His mouth shaped into the barest shadow of a smile as he gripped a light handful of hair at my nape, his big body shifting closer.

He didn't say a word, but as his eyes moved over the masses of my hair, I felt and knew that he was clearly admiring it.

He didn't *have* to say a word. His eyes were the compliment.

"I insist," he finally said, taking both bags out of my arms before I could protest. His box of condoms (not in a bag) was held, shameless as you please, in the hand of the arm he shifted my bags to.

My slack jaw snapped shut, and I turned on my heel, heading to my car. I'd thought I knew how to handle every kind of man, but this one left me baffled.

I would let him load my bags into my trunk and politely send him on his way. As far as I was concerned, that was the easiest and best thing to do.

I opened my trunk for him, then watched him and his Mack truck arms, as he shifted both bags into my car.

He straightened and stepped close to me.

He let his eyes run over me, top to bottom, and I just stared up, struck dumb by his unapologetic boldness.

This man had a strange effect on me. I really needed to get a handle on it.

Finally, the once-over stopped, lingering on my cleavage. I was dressed up a bit in a sexy white dress that had been meant for another man, one who was not a bold stranger, but this one seemed to appreciate it more than I'd ever intended. Certainly Dair never would have admired my breasts so openly.

My chest swelled in a shocked breath as he brought a big hand up to lightly finger my collar. It was wide and cut from my neck down to the lowest point of the opening, right between my pushed together cleavage.

"You're a very beautiful woman," his gravelly voice mused idly, as though he was talking to himself more than me.

His eyes returned to mine as he addressed me directly, "But then, you know that, don't you?"

I shook my head, at a loss.

"I'm Heath," he told me, like this was all perfectly normal. "And you?"

"Lourdes," I told him breathlessly.

His touch was light but very deliberate as he let his knuckles brush directly over my nipple. It swelled and hardened instantly, as though it was trying to return his touch, with or without my consent.

With a ghost of a smile, he pulled his hand away and stepped back.

"I'll see you around," he said, tipping an imaginary cap at me.

Without another word, he turned on his heel and strode away.

I watched him walk away, fascinated with the way he moved, fast and purposeful, with complete confidence.

And that was that.

Or it should have been. If things were normal and life was still sane, it would have been.

But something had shifted, and it wasn't a subtle shift.

I'd come to the attention of a man who didn't play by any normal rules, and my life was about to get very interesting.

CHAPTER
TWO

I was at the dog park the next morning. It was a brisk fifteen-minute walk from my house. I was letting my blue Great Dane, Tato, run in the park. This was a daily ritual, even in the worst of the Vegas heat. My great beast of a dog needed the exercise.

I threw Tato's slobbery tennis ball as far as I could for the umpteenth time, and he took off after it with great bounding strides.

"Morning, Lourdes," a gravelly voice said just behind me.

I jumped about a foot.

I knew that voice, but what the hell?

I turned, letting my face show how perturbed I was by his unexpected presence.

I wasn't wearing a scrap of makeup, and my heavy hair was in a thick, messy braid that I was sure couldn't have been my best look, not to mention that I was wearing baggy sweats.

Yes, my first thought was vanity. Of course it was. This guy was sex on a stick.

"What are you doing here?" I asked him, my tone bordering on hostile.

He smiled; the first full smile I'd ever seen on him.

He liked me hostile. It was twisted.

He indicated the sweats and running shoes he was wearing. "I was jogging. Imagine my surprise when I spotted you. Nice dog."

I supposed it kind of added up. The store where I'd met him was pretty close by.

He must live nearby, I decided.

But to be sure . . . "Do you live around here?"

"Not too far," he said, and didn't elaborate.

Tato returned with his slobbery tennis ball, and I threw it again.

"What's your dog's name?"

"Tato." I caught his look. "Short for couch potato. My kids named him."

"How many kids do you have?"

"Two. Well, they aren't kids anymore. Now they're grown men, but my youngest was twelve when we got Tato, and he named him."

"Both boys?"

"Yes."

"How old are they now?"

"Twenty-one and eighteen."

Even his stoic face couldn't hide his surprise. "Did you have them when you were *twelve?*"

I laughed, flattered and a touch chagrined, though I got this a lot. "No. I had my oldest at twenty. I'm forty-one."

I laughed again when I saw his eyes widen. "What, did you think you were hitting on someone closer to your own age?"

Something in his expression changed, something worrisome that made his nostrils flare. "I never thought about it."

I let him off the hook. "Don't worry. I'm not a cougar."

"Oh, trust me, I'm not worried. Let me walk you home."

What did that mean? And how insane would it be if I let this strange man walk me home?

"I don't know you that well," I told him warily.

"So get to know me. Let me walk you home, make me a cup of coffee, and we'll talk. I'm harmless." He smiled a sharp smile that clearly illustrated that he just might be the least harmless person I'd ever met.

Why did that harmful smile make me wet?

"You're not harmless," I pointed out wryly.

"To you, I am. And look, Tato thinks I'm all right."

As he spoke, my traitorous dog was nudging Heath's hand with his nose.

I watched for a minute as he crouched down, petting my dog until he had him on his back, completely submissive.

That was when I decided to let him walk me home. Why not?

Was it dangerous? Yes. But going by my suddenly throbbing body, my tingling thighs, my aching breasts, perhaps I needed a touch of danger in my life.

It had been so long since I'd felt desire like this.

It wasn't something I wanted to disregard.

It was something I wanted to explore. Thoroughly.

I put Tato on his leash and started to leave the park.

Heath took my arm like it was the most natural thing in the world.

It didn't feel natural. It did, however, feel good.

I found myself leaning into him. Even with that small contact, the back of my arm against his chest, I noticed that he felt amazing, so hard and big.

I'd been married young and never in my life so much as considered having a one-night stand. That seemed suddenly like an oversight. Perhaps I needed to do it once, just to try it out. And Heath was a man who seemed more than capable of making it worth my while.

Rough, dirty, sheet-clawing sex fairly radiated off him.

And I wasn't forgetting for even one millisecond about those magnum condoms.

"Don't make me regret this," I told him quietly, stealing a glance at his face.

His mouth quirked up. I was already learning things about him, and one was that he *never* smiled with his eyes.

They stayed cold, always.

I should have been more worried about that.

"You won't," he assured me, voice quiet and steady. "And you won't forget it, either."

I took a deep breath, looking ahead, blinking rapidly. He was arrogant. Why did that turn me on so much?

"What do you do for a living?" I asked him, figuring I should know *something* about him.

"I work in security."

That could have meant anything, really. "Care to be more specific?" I prodded.

"Not particularly."

Well, that was to the point.

"What do you do for a living?" he shot back.

"I'm a photographer."

"Care to be more specific?"

I almost smiled. "Specifically, I photograph *everything*. People, places, things. I'm freelance, and I basically work with whatever catches my eye."

"You could say I'm freelance, as well. See how much we have in common?"

Not one thing. Still, it didn't make me want to turn around.

Or if it did, the slow burn that had started low in my belly overshadowed it too completely for me to linger on it.

Hopefully this sudden desire I had for a bit of strange wouldn't blow up in my face.

Something occurred to me. "Maybe we should go to your place instead."

It seemed wiser not to let him know where I lived.

Another humorless smile. "It's not big enough for that dog of yours. Let's drop him off at your house first."

I chewed on that for a bit, but I decided that it didn't really matter.

More than anything, he seemed like the kind of guy that you had to worry about never seeing again, the opposite of the kind you couldn't keep from staying away.

"How long have you lived in Vegas?" I asked him, still grasping for a bit of common ground.

"Not long at all. What about you?"

"I've always traveled a lot for work, but I've had a house here for over a decade. I only started staying here fulltime in the last year or so, though. Been taking a break from traveling, but it won't last forever."

I was babbling. Why was I telling him so much? He clearly wasn't going to reciprocate, and he likely didn't care about anything I was saying.

"Why were you taking a break?" he asked, as though he *was* interested.

I'd have figured he was just being polite, but I already knew him well enough to understand that he was *never* polite.

"I . . . went through an ugly divorce, over a year ago, and I decided to stay in one place for a bit, get my head on straight."

"Vegas is an interesting place to stay to try to get your head on straight."

That made me laugh because it was very true. Still, somehow it worked for me. "My boys enjoy it, and they enjoy staying in one place. I took them everywhere with me when they were kids."

"Do they live with you?"

"No, but they live close and visit often."

"So now they hate to travel?"

"No, I think they still love it, I just think they're more well-rounded than I am. What about you?"

"I enjoy traveling, and I've done a fair amount of it."

That was it, nothing else. He wasn't a sharer.

"Where did you live before Vegas?"

"Here and there."

"Which was your favorite? Here or there?"

I got a slightly bigger smile for that one. "Here. Right here. Do you have any other pets?"

Hello, random. "No. Just Tator here. How about you?"

"No pets. No kids."

I'd figured. He didn't seem the type to have any attachments at all, let alone *dependents*.

I turned my head slightly and found his eyes on me, full of a disconcerting razor-sharp focus.

It was so disconcerting, in fact, that I began to question what I was doing. This wasn't me. I'd felt a surprising surge of lust and let it temporarily cloud my judgement.

"Knock it off," he said lightly, or as lightly as he could with that gravelly, bar brawler voice of his. "Quit thinking so hard. I told you, you won't regret this. You might be too sore to walk without a limp tomorrow, but you'll be happy about it."

Something heady and electrifying shot through me.

My nostrils flared, and my breath grew short.

He'd guessed what I was thinking. That, and all of the sexy, arrogant things he'd just spouted, had me back to being too turned on to think properly.

A man that knew how to read a woman. That combined with his knockout body and those magnums, well, I couldn't help it, expectations were getting very unrealistic.

This was not good. It'd been too long for me, and it had just occurred to me that I was a bit desperate.

I missed penis. I liked penis, and this sexy creature apparently had an impressive one. The inner hussy that I never knew I had wanted badly to see it. See it, and a lot of other things that flashed through my head quite vividly.

Beyond my impeccable instincts and against my better judgement, I kept right on walking with him, all the way to my front door.

I let him into my house, and he prowled inside.

I followed him, letting Tato off his leash.

Tato bolted straight for the kitchen, then out his oversized doggy door into the backyard.

Acutely aware of the eyes burning holes into my back, I went into the kitchen, washed up, and got a pot of coffee brewing.

When I turned to look at him, Heath was leaning against my counter, bulging arms crossed over his chest. It didn't even feel like my kitchen anymore with him in it.

The man staked his claim on everything. He owned whatever space he occupied.

That sparked a visual that made me shiver, head to toe.

He just watched me, eyes way too intense, not even a hint of a smile on his mouth.

"Come here," he said, voice low and guttural.

The most unnerving shock went through me, but I went.

I was standing almost close enough for our chests to touch when he reached up with one hand, gripped my thick braid, and began to wrap it around his heavy fist. He did this until his knuckles were digging into my scalp and then he pulled a little harder.

It stung, but it wasn't the sort of pain you wanted to shy away from. Not at all. It was the kind you wanted to lean into, to explore to its fullest, because you knew that just on the other side of that pain was intense pleasure.

"How rough can you take it, Lourdes?" he asked, bringing his mouth very close to mine.

I was trying not to pant. "I don't know," I replied honestly. "Why don't you show me what you got?"

He smiled, and this time, it very nearly reached his eyes. "You asked for it."

CHAPTER
THREE

I thought he was going to kiss me. I wanted him to. I wanted that and more. But he didn't, not then.

Instead, he let me go, and stepped back, nodding his head at the coffee pot that had just finished brewing. "I know better than to come between a woman and her morning caffeine."

I smiled wryly, but as I prepared us both a cup, my hands were shaking so hard that I wondered if I should even drink it. I was already wound up too tight to contain.

"How do you take it?" I asked, my back to him, my shaking hand on the creamer.

Before he even touched me, I felt him getting closer. I shivered as he pressed his chest against my back, his taller form folding over me until his hands braced on either side of mine, gripping the counter's edge.

"I'd rather show you than tell you," his gravelly voice rasped into my ear.

I gasped, then silently cursed at myself. This was not me. Men did not make me nervous. "I was referring to the coffee," I said archly. "Cream and sugar?"

"Just cream," he responded. "No sugar. I'm sweet enough."

That forced a hard laugh out of me, because we both knew that he was about as sweet as a pit bull.

I finished mixing our coffees, him pressed to me all the while, his body dominating mine before he'd ever even kissed me.

He took his cup and moved away. I was equal parts relieved and disappointed. I was having a hard time knowing what I was feeling, what I wanted, where he was concerned. I knew this was moving too fast, was certain of that, but at the same time I wanted more, wanted it to move faster, to go forward with no brakes.

I took a few breaths, then turned to look at him, leaning back to brace my hip against the counter as we both took our first drink.

"How do you feel about restraints?" he asked casually.

I nearly choked on the hot liquid pouring down my throat.

Of course he's into kink, I thought to myself, eyes narrowed on him. Any man that young and good looking *would* have some quirks.

"Like handcuffs?" I asked when I'd finally recovered from the fit of coughing that he had caused.

His arched brow just arched higher, the corner of his lip lifting up in what I thought was amusement.

I shook my head. "No. Sorry, *no*. I don't know you that well." I set my coffee down, done with it. I was already too wired.

He set his down, too, and in spite of everything, all I could concentrate on was how his muscles moved under his tight shirt with every movement.

He moved to me slowly, and I had to consciously make an effort not to hold my breath.

"Fair enough," he told me. "We'll work on getting to know each other better. But in the meantime . . . " His hands reached down, grabbing both of my wrists.

I watched those hands. They were so big. I never saw myself as particularly delicate or small. I was slender and fit, but not tiny. But as he grabbed my wrists, circling them with his fingers, I became hyperaware of just how delicate I was compared to him. How fragile.

A strange thrill moved through me. Strange because it wasn't only desire I was feeling. Mixed in there somewhere was a definite thread of fear.

Why did that only enhance the desire? I almost didn't even want to investigate it. Yes, it was perverse. But it was also exhilarating. Exhilarating and so much more.

Exciting.

Compelling.

Intoxicating.

Electrifying.

So many things I hadn't felt in too long to name, and I didn't want to pass on any of them.

He squeezed my wrists. Not to the point of pain, but with just enough pressure to let me know his strength, which was formidable.

"I won't use restraints," he said quietly. "Not until you're ready. But I will hold you down. Can you handle that?"

I found myself nodding jerkily, even as I wondered if I really could.

I didn't know why I just agreed to that, just like I didn't know why I was about to have sex with a perfect stranger in the middle of the morning on a Tuesday.

It felt dangerous, yet completely necessary.

It was a while before I could look away from my captive hands and up into his cold stare.

"Any other quirks of yours that you want to tell me about upfront?" I managed to ask him in a somewhat steady voice.

He smiled, and it was colder than ever. "Not particularly."

Well hell, that was far from reassuring.

He took a step back, still holding my wrists. "I don't even know where to start with you," he said, voice low, eyes on my body.

That wasn't reassuring either, but going by my body's reaction to every alarming thing that came out of his mouth, it was becoming clear to me that maybe I didn't want to be reassured.

He moved closer again, took one captive hand and pulled it, palm first, to cup him. I moaned at the feel of him. The hardness of him, the foreign largeness. I rubbed him over his sweats, my heavy-lidded eyes on his cold ones.

I suddenly found myself grabbing a handful of bare cock.

I glanced down. He'd shifted his waistband down, exposing himself.

My jaw nearly dropped, eyes going wide. He was fully aroused and huge.

Holy shit, I thought. Oh no, I hadn't thought that. I'd said it *aloud.*

He seemed to get a kick out of it, which I didn't think was good. This guy did not need any more strokes to his ego.

"I take it your ex-husband didn't measure up," he said. Arrogant bastard.

"I don't think many men measure up to *that*," just sort of slipped out of me. But fuck it all, it was only the truth.

I ringed my fingers around his girth experimentally, licking my lips. My fingers couldn't touch. I let him go, watching his heavy cock bob down heavily as I did it.

I've always considered myself to be a passionate, sensual woman. I've enjoyed sex, not just the physical release but the intimacy of it, but this was something else entirely, like some new person was suddenly sharing space in my body.

Never in my life before that moment had I felt a *need* like this. It was so acute it made my teeth ache.

Never had I felt like a bitch in heat, but I did then. I stared at that cock, and I *wanted* it. Wanted to drop to my knees and beg him for it, any way I could get it, anywhere.

"Your turn," he said, his rough voice drawing my eyes back to his face.

I licked my lips, mind gone blank, no concept of what he was asking or why. "E-excuse me?"

He smiled his cold smile and pushed my hand back to his cock. "I took something off. Now it's your turn. You take something off."

I glanced down at his sweatpants, hand feeling at him, memorizing his length with hungry fingers. I tugged at my other arm, but he held it fast, still gripping my wrist.

"You didn't take anything off," I pointed out. "You just pulled something out."

He chuckled, and I glanced up at his face. I wasn't sure if I was disappointed, or more fascinated than ever, that even when he laughed it didn't reach those eyes of his.

He pushed my hand away, dragging it behind my back, along with the other, gripping both of my wrists in one massive hand. The other went to my braid, twisting again, wrapping it around his fist, tilting my head back.

My lips parted, eyes closing as I realized that he was *finally* going to kiss me.

It wasn't what I expected, that kiss. After all of his blunt statements, I'd expected him to be rough, to ravage from the start. He did not. Instead, his lips were soft, coaxing, easing mine open for the shockingly tender onslaught of his tongue.

His body shifted, crowding mine against the counter, his hardness digging into my leg.

I moved against him, impatient for more contact.

He deepened the kiss until I was moaning. I tasted and sucked at his driving tongue as it plunged repeatedly to mate with mine.

He groaned, shoving his enormous erection hard, hard, *harder* into my thigh. So hard I wondered if I'd have an oversized boner shaped bruise there tomorrow.

He ripped his mouth away from mine, gasping. "Bedroom," he said curtly, taking his hands off me and pulling away.

I nodded, then began to move on unsteady legs toward my room. I could feel him at my back, his breath on my neck every drugging step of the way.

I paused in the doorway to my bedroom, but his hard body nudged me all of the way into the room. That made me shoot him a glance over my shoulder.

Every line in his face read unapologetic, so I knew it had been deliberate.

"Raise your arms over your head," he ordered me.

I raised a brow at him, but did it, holding them high, arching my back, my aching breasts thrusting forward.

His nostrils flared, and he stepped close behind me, so close I could no longer crane to see his face.

His big hands settled on my hips, gripping into the fleshy part, testing it in a way that made me tremble.

My arms started to lower, but a rough, "No, keep them up," in my ear stayed them.

His hands started skimming under my shirt, teasing at my belly.

Abruptly he pulled it up and over my head.

A muscle quivered in my stomach as the skin of my abdomen was bared.

My shoulders drew up tight as, with rather impressive speed, he unsnapped my bra and tore it off my arms, tossing it carelessly to the ground.

His hands ran from my shoulders to my fingertips with a feather light touch. I could hear my own breath panting out of me as he folded my wrists behind my head, held together close to my nape.

He used that hold to nudge me, moving me closer to the bed.

"All this needs is a bag over my head, and we'd have a perp walk," I said, my wry tone spoiled by the fact that I couldn't seem to breathe properly.

He liked that, I could hear it in his voice as he responded, "If this is a perp walk, I need to do a better job of patting you down." As he spoke, he shifted my wrists to one hand.

I sucked in a breath as his free hand moved to my collarbone. I glanced down to watch as he slid it over my skin until it held my breast, watched it move with the rapid rise and fall of my chest. He ran a rough thumb over my nipple.

"You're trembling," he rasped into my ear, making me tremble all the more. "Fear or excitement?"

I licked my lips and gave him the truth. "Both."

"Are you wet?" he asked, hand snaking down my body, pushing into the waistband of my pants and going unerringly, aggressively, for my sex.

"Yes," I gasped, though he'd already answered his own question, his fingers rubbing over my slick folds.

"You don't normally do things like this, do you?"

"Bring strange men home and lead them to my bedroom? Um, *no*. This is not a habit of mine."

"I'll be sure to make it worth your while, then."

Somehow, impossibly, I believed that he would.

CHAPTER
FOUR

A bruptly, he released my wrists, and I turned to look at him.

He backed away, one step, and then another, his eyes on my breasts as his hands went to the bottom of his T-shirt. He shrugged it off, the material straining to the point I thought it'd rip as he dragged it off his shoulders.

I sucked in a shocked breath as I took in the hard flesh he'd exposed.

Scars were painted all across his granite torso. I don't know why, I think it may have been his face, which was so handsome and young, and unscarred, but those markings caught me completely off guard. They were all shapes and sizes, ranging from several little round ones (two of which were still fresh and pink) to long jagged cuts, the worst being a particularly big one that drew up along his side in a way that made it look like someone had literally tried to gut him with a knife.

Somehow, I knew not to ask him the first question that popped into my head, which was, *What happened to you?*

Instead I studied him for a long time, his cold eyes on me, his jaw held hard as he studied me back. Finally I settled for, "You've been shot recently." It was an understatement. He'd been shot many times, and knifed, and if I had to guess what some of those marks were, he'd even been branded and burned.

Tortured, I realized.

This man, who was much younger than I was, had been brutally tortured. Repeatedly.

Something inside of me, my strong maternal side I was sure, went soft for him.

"Yes, I've been shot a time or two," he grumbled out, sounding pissed. "Is that a problem?"

I shook my head, even while I wondered if it was. Was he a criminal? He didn't strike me as a cop, so what was the alternative?

He seemed to see something in my face, utter shock perhaps, that had him reassuring me in a soft tone I'd never heard him use before, but I loved it and craved more as soon as I heard it. "I've lived a violent life. But, Lourdes, listen very carefully, because this is a promise: I'd never hurt *you.* Okay?"

I nodded jerkily.

"Aside from rough sex, that is," he felt the need to add.

I licked my lips and nodded again.

"Very rough," he continued. "But you won't mind that. In fact, unless my instincts are wrong about you, soon you'll be *begging* me for it." As he spoke, he reached into one of his pockets and pulled out a handful of condoms, of the magnum variety.

He was pushing his sweatpants down impatiently when he said, "Get on the bed. On your back. Arms above your head."

I went liquid even as I managed to comply.

He tossed the condoms on the bed by my hip, leaning over me, arms bracing on either side of my ribs, eyes running over my body.

He bit his lip appealingly, blinking languorously. "Your body . . . " he began and trailed off.

He shut his eyes, shook his head, and when he opened them again, whatever had come over him, whatever he'd been about to say, seemed to have passed.

I didn't worry about it for long as his hands flew to the waistband of my pants and started pulling, dragging my sweats and panties down at the same time, taking my socks off as well when he reached my ankles.

He became preoccupied for a moment when he'd freed me from my bottoms. I squirmed a bit as he separated my lacy panties from my sweats, studying them.

He held up the tiny scrap of material, arching a brow at me. "This is what you wear under *sweats*?"

I just nodded. I didn't want to talk about my underwear or anything else, really. Action was required. Words? Not so much.

He shook his head, and, as though that settled the matter, he tossed my panties over his shoulder, eyes moving back to my body.

"Spread your legs," he said gruffly.

I did it, eyes on his cock, wondering how much longer I'd have to wait before I had *that* inside of me.

He let out a small string of curses, but that didn't make me stiffen. On the contrary, it made me melt, each profanity washing over me, because I knew that he was only perturbed because he wanted me.

To the degree that I wanted him. And that was saying something.

"Any requests before we do this?" he asked. "I'll warn you now, there'll be no stopping once I start." As he said this, his eyes moved up my body to devour my chest, taking in my full, straining breasts.

I took them in too, looking down at myself, watching in fascination as my back arched, erect nipples seeking him.

I licked my lower lip, watching how every tiny movement I made seemed to capture him. "Another kiss would be nice," I said softly.

His nostrils flared, and he moved to climb on top of me, straddling my hips, his hands holding my wrists firmly above my head.

He bent his face to mine, angling his head as he took my lips.

His kiss was different this time, more like what I'd expected from the first kiss, his tongue demanding, invading, greedy, like he couldn't get enough, like he wanted to devour me.

I gave him everything he asked for, lips surrendering, body submitting, my hips bucking in reflexive anticipation.

I moaned out a protest when he took his mouth away, but not for long as it stayed attached to my body, moving down along my jaw, then to my neck, licking, sucking, biting as it went.

When his hot mouth reached my breasts, it was like a voltage of electricity to my chest, my back bowing, teeth gritting as he licked and sucked, pushing the ripe globes together to nuzzle from one to the other, then fastening like a suction to my nipple.

I could've gotten off just from the sound of his mouth feasting hungrily on my flesh, I was *that* primed.

Luckily, he was just as primed, and so it didn't come to that. There wasn't time.

Foreplay was not the order of the day.

This was about fucking. It was that simple. His cock inside of my cunt, the faster the better.

He tore his mouth away from my skin and reached for a condom. He ripped the foil on the packet with one hand and his teeth, keeping my wrists captive all the while. He even rolled it on one-handed, which was rather impressive considering the size of him.

Practice made perfect, I supposed. And I tried to linger on *that* as little as possible.

He moved down my body, shoving my legs wide apart to accommodate his hips, and lined us up, breast to groin.

I craned my neck forward to watch as his tip found my entrance, and he nudged in that first delicious inch.

It's been way too fucking long, I thought to myself.

And that was my last coherent thought for a very long time.

He shoved in, slowly at first, shifting his hips to work himself against my soft flesh. I heard the noises that left my throat as though they were coming out of somebody else as my soft flesh welcomed him inch by slow inch.

It took forever for him to push inside of me, but I wouldn't have rushed that part if I could, watching as each delicious centimeter of his shaft disappeared into my sex.

I clenched around him, my cunt sucking him in so earnestly and intensely that he cursed and praised me in equal parts every second that he progressed.

It was a shock as he finally, at last, *about fucking time*, shoved fully into me, buried to the root.

The air punched hard out of my lungs at the brutal impact as he hit home.

I'd never been so full. That was a fact.

I took in this new foreign fullness with great heaving breaths that brought my sensitive chest up to rub against his slick hard one, then drop down and away again with each rough inhale, exhale.

"What in the *holy fuck*," he muttered succinctly.

I wasn't sure if that was a question or a statement, but regardless, I had nothing to add. That summed it up for me, as well.

And then, *then, oh my God, then*, he started to move, dragging out of me with big, jagged pulls, it taking a few of those pulls to have only the tip of him inside of me again.

He paused briefly there, at just the point where I felt so helpless that I lost it.

Just lost it. Sobbing, pleading, begging him to move, to come back inside of me, to fill me up entirely.

And he was no sadist, thank God. He obliged right away, ramming back in with one long heave, then yanking out again, faster now, smoother with every movement as my body learned to accommodate his size, accepting the length and girth of him like it'd been made for just this purpose.

There was something so simple and profound about that first mating. He occupied an empty place inside of me, literally and figuratively, a lonely space that I hadn't known needed filling.

It was beautiful and riveting. I didn't want it to end, but had to fight not to finish too quickly.

He drove into me, again and again, his thrusts rough to the point of brutal.

I'd never been into rough sex.

Well, I'd never tried it, but I hadn't thought I was into it.

I'd thought *wrong*.

How could I be so wrong about myself? How could I not know about a need like that until it was given to me in its entirety?

And that need, *that need*, it swallowed me whole.

I needed this like I needed air. Needed someone to fill me so acutely, so completely, mercilessly invading me, over and over, pounding me into the mattress, taking absolute, indisputable ownership of my body until I couldn't say where he began and I ended.

Needed it so much, I couldn't stop begging for it.

Loudly.

Repeatedly.

And he gave it to me, everything I begged for and more, rutting into me with mindless abandon, pounding in and out, in and out, faster and faster, harder, and still, impossibly, *harder*, until screaming, I burst.

My orgasm didn't just surprise me. It *assaulted* me. Tore through me and broke me into a million twitching pieces.

One big hand clawing at my hips, he pumped into me four, five more times, then planted himself deep, to the root and came.

I watched as the chill at last left his eyes. So many things rushed in to replace that consuming coldness of his.

Wonderful things.

Addictive things that let me know somewhere deep down he was as affected as I was.

Hunger. Admiration. Desperation. Lust. Wonder. Need. Abandon. Madness.

It was beautiful to watch, the way he changed in those brief moments of bliss.

Beautiful and dangerous.

I'd do a lot to watch him change like that, to get even the briefest glimpse of that other side of him. The need was powerful to the point of self-destructive, especially considering the fact that I barely knew him, and what I did know only seemed to point toward the fact that he was a wild thing that was not even close to being tamed.

CHAPTER
FIVE

I was still reeling, still completely caught up in what had happened mere seconds ago, but not him. He was up, standing, peeling off the used condom, tossing it into the closest wastebasket, then pacing the floor at the foot of my bed, eyes intense on my limp form.

No, wait, not pacing . . .

Stalking.

Prowling.

Like a lion, his narrowed eyes on me.

I was his prey, and he was ready to pounce.

Again.

"Is everything all right?" I asked him, my voice hoarse like I'd been screaming.

Had I been screaming? Had he literally made me scream?

Oh yeah. *Shit*, he had.

It was an embarrassing thought, and I let my mind shy away from it, even as the sound of those desperate cries still echoed in my mind.

"All right?" he mused, his tone low, voice more road-worn gravelly and rough than ever. "Yeah, I'm *all right.*"

I blinked at the way he said it, though I couldn't read him well enough to know what to make of it.

His lip curled up like he was annoyed. He reached an arm up, running it impatiently over his short-cropped hair.

Why did every move he made turn me on? Every minuscule shift of his body made mine respond, breasts tightening, sex clenching.

He elicited reaction without trying, controlled me without even touching.

My eyes ran down his ripped to within an inch of its life body, moving over each mark and scar. I found those marks to be fascinating and beautiful. He didn't wear them like they were flaws, and so they weren't. If it wasn't so obvious what they were, I thought I could have been convinced that he'd been born with them all.

I knew better than to ask, I knew the answer, but I'd have loved to photograph him.

The artistry of his hard, massive, tortured body needed to be captured, even if its owner never could be.

I shook off the thought. I couldn't think things like that. I barely knew this man, so why on earth would I want to capture him?

He'd never be mine. I knew it instinctively, and so I didn't let myself even wish for it.

My eyes widened as they finally made it down to his spent cock.

No, not spent. Hard and getting harder, though I knew he'd gotten off when I had.

That was when I really started to appreciate the younger man thing.

My husband hadn't taken good care of himself for a good decade before we'd split, and the softer he got, the softer his dick had gotten with him.

It's funny how sometimes you don't realize how much you need a thing before it's right in front of you. And suddenly, I needed that hard, tireless, randy, young cock like you wouldn't believe.

I licked my lips.

"How old are you?" my mouth asked him, even while my brain didn't actually want to know.

I mean, it was a little late for regrets.

He scowled, like really scowled, and on him that was a scary thing. He was intimidating enough when he smiled.

When he scowled he looked like he wanted to kill someone, and I didn't doubt for a second that he was a man who got what he wanted.

"Who cares?" he shot back. This was clearly as sore a subject for him as it was for me.

"I care," I answered softly, but more because I thought I should care, thought I should ask, thought I should *need* to know.

Really, though, I'd have just as soon avoided knowing. My level of cougardom on this felt pretty irrelevant at that moment, all things considered.

"Twenty-five," he said, tone abrupt.

I winced.

I'd been hoping for a higher number. The higher the better, really.

"Not much older than my firstborn," I said tightly.

He didn't like that, as in *really* didn't like it, going by the sudden and mean twist to his mouth.

Well, I didn't like it either, but it was still the truth.

"What the fuck does that matter?" he asked.

It mattered, of course it did, but I didn't have a chance to vocalize an answer, as it was clearly a rhetorical question, because he was on me, kissing me again, fisting a condom on and fucking me again, between one gasp and the next.

Good. Even though I'd brought it up, I didn't want to talk about it or think about it any time soon. We clearly had better things to do.

I took his weight on me, his hardness in me, with a soft, needy moan. It felt so fucking good, like the first time hadn't even happened, like I was as hungry for him as I had been not an hour before, with over a year's worth of celibacy under my belt.

He was holding my wrists above my head again, needing only one hand to do so, the other palming my breasts, assaulting the soft flesh of my chest with his hand while his cock assaulted the soft flesh of my cunt in desperate earnest.

It was faster that time, as though he'd used all of his patience with the first mating. He sucked the tip of one straining tit into his mouth while his free hand snaked down and started working my clit, bringing me over so fast that it caught me off guard, my breath sobbing out in one long, "Heeeaaaath."

He growled like a wild animal into my skin, planted himself inside me, stayed planted, and I felt his thick cock twitching, bucking out his seed.

I said his name again, faster, wanting, *needing* to watch his face, and he lifted from my chest, eyes meeting mine, giving me that look again, the one that replaced the coldness.

More than any crave-able thing about him, I craved that brief, unguarded moment when he lost himself inside me.

I was lying on my bed, flat on my back, completely naked, covered only by a sheet.

My head was still spinning.

What the hell had just happened?

I'd never, never, NEVER had my body, my *world*, rocked like that before. Heath fucked like a force of nature—fierce, powerful, unstoppable.

I knew I was good in bed. I was fit, flexible, and adventurous, but with Heath, all I'd managed to do was hold on for the ride. And come. Repeatedly.

The force of nature I was currently worrying over had gone into the shower exactly one second after he'd finished getting us both off. He apparently didn't like to wear his sex around, not even to sleep.

Would he even stay to sleep? It was barely noon. I guessed he'd be leaving as soon as he was done with his shower.

I could expect nothing else from this whole crazy thing, but I felt tender (not just my body) about it all. I'd never done casual sex.

It was perhaps an acquired taste. One I wasn't planning to acquire.

I was still lying there (nearly exactly how he'd left me after fucking my brains out) when he came back out of my bathroom, wearing nothing but a towel, his mind-boggling body still slightly damp.

The look on his face had me losing my breath.

He dropped the towel.

My mind was on a very specific part of him, one that should not be looking quite so eager after our earlier activities, as he approached the bottom of the bed.

Without a word, he bent, grabbing my sheet, and pulling it slowly.

It surprised me enough that I made an embarrassing little noise and tried to hold onto my only covering.

"Let go," he growled.

God, he was scary. Why did that do such delicious things to my body?

I dropped the sheet.

He tugged it off, then snagged first one of my ankles, then the other, his shoulders and arms flexing as he dragged me down the bed. When he'd finished dragging, he started spreading, pulling my legs wide apart.

He just stared at my sex for the longest time, his gaze so hot that my hips started squirming restlessly.

I glanced down at him. He was fully aroused, his heavy cock pulsing.

Sore or not, sated or not, I wanted it again more desperately than ever.

Finally, he let go of my ankles, grabbing my wrists instead and pulling me to sit up, my splayed legs jolting together. He perched a foot snug at my hip, burying both of his hands in my hair.

I licked my lips and stared. He'd brought me within a few inches of his eager cock. I didn't have to guess what he wanted.

I leaned forward, looked up to meet his eyes boldly, and tongued his tip.

He cursed and surged against me.

Keeping solid eye contact, I sucked his thick, plush head between my lips.

I had to break eye contact soon enough as he pushed deeper, and his jagged breaths became the only thing in the room louder than the sounds of my busy, sucking mouth and my milking, stroking hands.

There was no polite conversation about whether or not I swallowed, but as I felt his balls draw up tight, his orgasm close, I pushed back to suck at his tip, hands working him, my eyes on his face.

That was one thing that had stood out to me from the last few rounds. I loved to watch his face as his eyes went unfocused and wild, all of the coldness leaving them. I watched it happen again, relishing the sight.

He stroked my hair after he'd finished, my tongue still laving his tip, his eyes directed on me again, cold again, but admiring, at least.

After he finally pulled away, I lay back on the bed, not sure if I wanted to get off or pass out.

Without a word, he moved to my dresser across the room, unerringly going for my hidden vibrator, knowing which drawer it was in, exactly as though he knew just where to look, like he'd done it before.

My aroused, smitten brain didn't linger on that, focused more on him and what he was about to do to me than on the things about him that should trouble me.

As he pulled the thing out, though, I managed to find my voice for something, at least, "Not that," I said faintly. It was an intense toy. "I'm a little sore *for that.*"

He raised his brows, looking fascinated by the notion. He dropped the vibrator back in the drawer, hand going for his randy cock. He was already semi-hard again and looked in danger of easily losing the semi part of that. "Too sore for this, too, I take it?"

I bit my lip. I really wanted *that* again, but I *was* sore. I nodded regretfully, watching him handle himself casually and thinking that it was the hottest thing I'd ever seen.

His white teeth flashed at me in a smile that was more sinister than happy. "I've got just the thing."

And he did.

My hands clawed into the sheets as he introduced me to the skill of his wicked tongue. He lapped at my sex, making himself at home down there, soft and gentle in a way I hadn't thought he had in him.

Something occurred to me as he made me come, yet again.

If he was as complicated of a man as he was a lover, I was in trouble.

He moved up my body, kissing my lips, his sex nudging between my legs.

All soreness was forgotten, by both of us, apparently, as he pushed himself into me.

He did recall it briefly, though, when he was buried nearly to the root. "Too sore?" he murmured.

I bit his lower lip in answer, whimpering into his mouth as I didn't feel coherent enough to talk. He took it for the answer he wanted.

With a rough groan, he shoved himself home.

And then he was gone, as sudden as he'd come.

He never said goodbye.

I passed out and he left.

That was it.

He didn't even leave his number, or ask for mine.

There was no way whatsoever for me to misinterpret what that meant.

I honestly didn't think I'd see him again. I was resigned to that. Not happy about it, but not bitter either.

Not bitter, because he'd given me something. Something I hadn't thought to feel again.

Hope.

Sad as it was, for better or worse, my life had fallen apart soon after I'd turned forty, and I hadn't imagined, couldn't even conceive of the idea that my best years of my life lay still ahead of me.

And now, because of Heath, anything seemed possible.

The revelation was liberating.

A heavy weight had left my body; the dead weight of a marriage that I was *finished* letting deprive me. Of anything. *Just finished.*

I didn't want to be deprived of *anything* anymore, or ever again.

CHAPTER
SIX

I t was a few days later, and I wanted to blame the wine, but I wound up telling my girlfriends all about him. *Way* too many salacious details. I hadn't meant to so much as mention him, but was hard to hold anything back from the girls. They were *those* kind of friends.

We had a running bi-weekly girls' night that I hardly ever missed. The group had been going on and off for several years, and though I'd only joined up with them about a year prior, it felt longer. Like I'd known some of them forever.

It was an impressive group of women. Over a dozen of us. Successful women. Beautiful women. Funny, entertaining. Some single, some married. A bit of anything you could want, really.

It was a large group, but it didn't feel large. We came in all ages, and no one broke off into cliques. We all mixed well together.

Well, I should explain more. It was more than a girls' night. It was more of a weekly, impromptu therapy session with friends. And alcohol.

"How old is he, *exactly*?" Frankie asked, sounding zero percent judgmental, and one hundred percent fascinated.

I'd met Frankie first. She had her own reality show, and I'd been shooting her for a spread in a magazine that featured said show.

We'd hit it off right away, but that was just how Frankie was. I'd been going through a rough time, and we'd bonded, fast and deep. She'd quickly invited me to a girls' night and introduced me to the others.

I'd been impressed with her right away. She was uniquely beautiful and wildly unconventional, in her looks and lifestyle, and the way she handled it never stopped impressing me. She had so much acceptance for herself and who she was, but also of her friends. It was hard not to adore someone who was that loving of both herself and others.

I had a serious girl crush on her, but it was purely platonic. A. Because I wasn't gay. And B. Because I was pretty sure her wife, Estella, would claw anyone's eyes out that tried to come between them.

I grimaced. "Twenty-five."

Her smoking hot wife, Estella, whooped, high-fiving the air. "You go, hot mama! It's about time."

"Hell yeah," Danika said succinctly. She was one of my favorites. A sarcastic soul after my own heart. She was extravagantly gorgeous, a striking, exotic woman of some mixed Eurasian heritage. Her face and body were flawless, aside from a slight limp when she walked, but I didn't think that detracted from any of it.

I'd started attending these get-togethers just after she'd gotten married to a great heaping hunk of a man that put on one of the most successful magic acts on the strip.

"He's not much older than my children," I said, eyes swinging to Lucy, the therapist and voice of reason of the group.

"Don't do that to yourself," said Danika. "He's twenty-five. Hardly a *child.*"

Easy for her to say, I thought, as she was sitting somewhere in her late twenties.

"I don't honestly think I'd have done it," I said, words still aimed at Lucy, "if I'd had a clue he was *that young* before we hooked up. Unfortunately, I only asked him his age *after.*" I knew that was likely bullshit. My lust had been too overwhelming to be stopped at the word *twenty-five.* I was trying to save face, though I didn't actually need to, not in front of this group.

"Stop that," Lucy said gently. "Don't beat yourself up. You didn't commit a crime."

"What's the lowdown on a cougar relationship happening, doc?" another one of the ladies, Candy, spoke up, asking a question I didn't have the balls to.

Lucy held up her hands in a sort of c'est la vie gesture. "It just depends on the individuals involved. I don't hand out verdicts for relationships. You know this."

"But what is the usual pattern for a thing like this playing out?" I asked her. I knew better than to accept her pat answer. She had all the likely scenarios, all the usual dysfunctional relationship patterns memorized.

Ugh, I'd thought the word relationship about a guy I'd only met twice. I was *so* old school.

I've been out of the dating pool too long, I thought.

Lucy looked amused. "What, you want me to cite off the statistics for you?"

"I wouldn't mind hearing them," I mused.

"I'm not going to do that. You are a responsible woman. A good woman. As long as no one is being exploited, and no one is feeling used, I say do as you like. How's that for a lowdown?"

Less than satisfactory, I thought. But I'd take it. At least she wasn't outright cautioning me against it.

"I'm encouraged, frankly," she continued. "I see it as a good sign that you're finally willing to enter the dating world again."

"Don't sound like dating to me," Candy muttered, but there was nothing catty in the way she grinned at me.

I couldn't argue with her. "It *definitely* wasn't a date."

"You should never give it up that fast, sweetie," Sarah, another lady in the group, one well into her sixties, told me. "I'm not judging you. It's just, well, men never come back when you give it up that fast. Any chance at a relationship flew out the window when it resorted to sex that quickly."

She wasn't wrong. I opened my mouth, mostly to say, rather defensively, something like, oh I don't know, 'Who said I was looking for a relationship?' but I never got the chance.

Bianca, one of the quieter members of the group, shocked us all by butting in. "That's just not true."

Every single one of us looked at her. She was a woman that stood out in a crowd, no matter how exceptional her company. She was beautiful, tall, with pale blonde hair and abundant curves. She had just the sort of eye-catching beauty that one expected to see in the wife of a famous billionaire, and it just so happened that she was one.

Her expression was calm, her face angelic, both in its beauty and peacefulness. There was something so suppressed about her manner, as though she'd learned to avoid making much noise in a very profound way. She participated in the group, but she rarely added in her two cents like this. That role was usually reserved for the louder voices. And when she did pipe in, I noticed that everyone usually took it to heart.

"James and I," she continued, a becoming blush breaking out across her cheeks. "We . . . didn't wait to have sex. *Not at all.*"

"But I'd bet money you weren't hooking up that soon after you met him," Candy pointed out.

Bianca's blonde brows shot straight up. "You'd be losing money on that bet. He was going down on me in an airplane galley, it had to be, God, like only the third time I ever ran into him."

That was met with a pregnant moment of shocked silence, then a brief burst of awkward laughter as everyone came to the conclusion that she was putting us on.

She was not, her expression told us.

"Him getting *you* off is a far cry from *you* getting him off, in terms of keeping him on a string," Candy shot back.

"That is fucking hot, though," someone put in. I glanced at the source. It was Sandra. She was a bit older than I was and worked in the Cavendish art gallery with Danika. It was a well-known fact that she was semi-obsessed with Bianca's husband. She was always a little too fascinated with the subject when he came up.

Bianca's blush got a few shades darker, her eyes darting around the room. "I'd already gone down on *him*, by then. Technically, I think that was the *second* time we ran into each other. Still turned into a relationship. A marriage."

Danika let out a low, appreciative whistle. "Wasn't he your *first?*" she asked her, sounding impressed.

We were getting a rare gem if even Danika hadn't known about that, as the two women were close friends.

Bianca nodded.

"That brazen fucker," someone muttered. Frankie, I think.

We were all just staring at Bianca. I, personally, wanted to hear the rest of the story. I'd read some of the tabloids about them, but this was different. This was the *real* story, the most I'd ever heard from Bianca about her much talked about relationship with one of the hottest men on the planet.

"What about *actual* intercourse?" Sarah asked, like it was a perfectly reasonable question.

"That same night, after the galley incident," Bianca answered matter-of-factly.

"Brazen fucker," Frankie repeated.

"He's so fucking hot," Sandra muttered.

"How's it going, in general, and also with your ex-husband?" Jackie asked me, bringing the subject back around since it'd clearly gotten out of hand. Bianca had started to look uncomfortable. "Is he still being antagonistic?"

"He is, but it's tapering off, I think. And things in general have been good. It took some time. The divorce was a big readjustment for me, but now I'm . . . content with having him gone. I have more free time now. Free time that I value. I find that I enjoy a good book over a bad husband. No contest."

That was met with a round of elaborate toasting. We had some enthusiastic readers in the group.

"What about your kids? Has there been any communication between your ex and the kids lately?" Lucy asked.

I shook my head. "He alienated his children when he mistreated their mother, and rather than take responsibility for that, he's decided to blame me. It's baffling, to be honest. I knew how my boys would react. I don't understand how he's surprised by it. They're overprotective and loyal to a fault. Frankly, I'm a little worried that they'll never forgive him."

"It's not your job to mediate their relationship with their dad," Lucy told me in her no nonsense voice. "That is *their* business."

I nodded that I understood her. I tried to take her words to heart. It was a burden I'd be happy to set down for good.

CHAPTER
SEVEN

When the gathering wound down at an early hour, I was still wired. I did not want to go home to an empty house. I told Danika so.

She grinned. "Me neither. Tristan's working tonight, and he has a good hour left of his show. We should take a taxi to the casino and enjoy another round."

"No need to take a taxi," Bianca added, having overheard us. "I have a car and driver right outside."

We all smiled. Sometimes it was very cool to have filthy rich friends.

But still, I mulled it over. My oldest son, Rafael, worked at our friends' bar there, and I didn't think he needed to see his mother tipsy.

"Rafael . . ." I began.

Danika waved her hand in air. "Your boys adore you, we all know that. He'll be happy to see you. Stephan and Javier both work tonight, too, so it's the perfect time to do it."

Stephan was Bianca's best friend, and Javier was his husband. They owned the best bar on the Cavendish property, and soon after meeting and hitting it off with them, they'd offered Rafael a job there when they'd heard he was looking for a bartending gig.

They were delightful, and Danika was right, it was perfect timing as I was always looking for an excuse to see them.

"Sold," I said easily, as it had not been a hard sell.

We tried to talk Frankie and Estella into joining us, but they had plans that involved not waiting an extra hour or two to get home to their St. Andrew's cross. They were heavy into kink, to put it simply.

We said goodnight to them with hugs and airy cheek kisses.

"Hey, Blake," I said as I got into the dark SUV idling at the curb in front of Bev's house.

"Hey, girl," Blake said, smiling at me in the rearview mirror. She was Bianca's longtime bodyguard/driver/friend.

"How come you didn't come into girls' night this time?" Danika asked as she slid in beside me.

Blake was usually a participant. She went where Bianca went, with few exceptions.

"I had to make some phone calls for work, so I stayed out here."

"Hey," Bianca said to Blake, patting her on the shoulder as she got in last. Another security guard, a male I wasn't familiar with, closed the door behind her, then climbed into the front passenger's seat.

"Hey," Blake said back. "How was the therapy session?"

Danika shot me a teasing smile. "Pretty awesome. You missed out with this one. Lourdes had some bombshells to impart."

I found myself blushing as I thought of all the things I'd let slip out of my mouth with just a few glasses of wine as lubricant. "She's exaggerating. You didn't miss anything important."

"You might as well just tell me," Blake said as she put the car into drive. "Bianca will spill the beans later, if you don't. We all know it."

I waved my hand in the air. "That works for me. Let *her* tell you. I can't seem to open my big mouth without oversharing. Some details no one needs to know."

Blake laughed. "Oh no. Will someone at least clue me into what kind of details she's talking about?"

Without a word, Danika met her eyes in the rearview mirror and held her hands out with a good ten-inch gap between them.

We all started giggling.

"Well, hell," Blake said when she caught a breath. "I missed a doozy, huh?"

I glanced at the one male in the car, but he was sitting in the passenger's seat, eyes aimed forward, acting like he couldn't hear us. I appreciated that.

"Where's James?" I asked Bianca. I just assumed he was out of town, because when he wasn't, he usually showed up in person to pick her up, sometimes even coming early to sit in on girls' night.

He was famously possessive of her time and person.

"New York. It was only a two-day trip, and I'd have missed girls' night, so I stayed in Vegas."

Danika snorted. "I bet he loved that."

Bianca bit her lip, but it didn't hide her smile. "He did not. I'm expecting him home anytime now, though he's scheduled to come back in the morning. You know how he is."

"I can confirm that Mr. Cavendish boarded a flight about four hours ago, Mrs. Cavendish," the man in the front seat said.

Bianca grinned. "See. I know my man."

Danika nodded that she did. "Whenever I catch myself thinking that Tristan is a possessive nut-job, I just remember that he's mellow compared to James."

"Just keep telling yourself that," Blake muttered, eyes on the road.

That got another round of laughs.

Going anywhere with Bianca Cavendish was an experience.

The two, yes *two*, bodyguards we had with us that night were what they considered a *light* detail. There was no current known threat to the soft-spoken woman, but due to past dangers to her person, and how high profile she was, (She and her husband were in the tabloids on a weekly basis. Just a few days ago, I'd seen media coverage of her shopping for shoes. Seriously.) she required at least two bodyguards when she went out in public.

I'd once asked her why two, and James had answered for her with, "One to cover her, the other to shoot back."

In this instance, since we were in her husband's resort, and at her best friend's bar, it was fairly effortless to set up. A section was roped off for us, the male bodyguard manning the ropes, with Blake sticking close to Bianca.

We sat on low, cushy sofas in the swanky bar and got beyond the normal VIP service. Both owners greeted us with the drinks they knew we wanted before we could even order, and sat down for several minutes to chat with us.

I took a sip of the spectacular cabernet Stephan had handed to me and waved at my son, who was manning the bar.

He grinned and waved back.

Rafael had a great personality for bartending. He liked people, liked to chat them up, liked to listen to their stories, enjoyed bantering with the tipsy and the outright drunk.

Currently, he was deep in discussion with one of the customers, a middle-aged man that looked three sheets to the wind.

Raf was good at humoring drunk people, though, and looked genuinely interested in whatever the other man was saying.

I decided to leave him be until he was unoccupied, because even though I was friends with the owners, this was a job for Raf, and I'd taught him from a young age that all jobs should be taken seriously, even the fun, part-time ones.

"James is on his way here now from the airport," Stephan told Bianca as he pulled back from kissing her cheek.

Danika snorted inelegantly. "That didn't take long."

"Psh," Stephan returned, his eyes twinkling at Danika. "You're one to talk. Tristan will be on his way here the second his show finishes, I guarantee it."

"He doesn't even know I'm here," she pointed out.

Javier, Stephan's husband, rolled his eyes. "Pu-lease. We all know he will track you down in under five minutes."

She couldn't exactly argue with that. We all knew it was the truth.

Tristan and Danika's story was an epic one. Tragic in its way, but somehow all the more beautiful for it.

I'd joined the girls' night just after they'd gotten married, and Danika had shared a bit with the group about their past and how it affected the present, how every time she woke and he was there beside her, it still hit her like a punch to the gut, because the two had been to hell and back together.

I was a hopeless romantic and so I'd gobbled their story up. After all they'd gone through, that they'd somehow ended up back together after *years* estranged. It was amazing how they'd been able to put the painful past behind them and remarry. It pulled on my heartstrings in the best possible way.

Sure enough, not thirty minutes later, I heard a muttered, "Here comes Trouble," come out of Danika, her eyes across the large bar aimed at the entrance.

She was smiling with what could only be called a besotted look on her face, but it turned mischievous as her eyes swung back to Bianca and I.

"Watch this," she told us. "It's the funniest thing. I can get him to go full caveman in under thirty seconds, I shit you not."

Danika made her way to the bar, taking an empty stool between two men. One of them turned immediately and said something to her, leaning forward as he did so.

She said something back, smiling blandly at the man.

Going by her expression, and his, they weren't talking about anything particularly racy, but it was clear pretty quickly that it didn't matter.

Tristan had arrived. He was a great, massive hunk of a man, several inches over six feet, and built broad and muscular, his fitted shirt hugging every inch of his rock hard frame. It was a white shirt, and you could see under the white that his chest was as covered in ink as his arms.

Tristan spotted and converged on them like a force of nature. He was across the bar, wedging his huge self in the narrow space between the two stools before you could say *caveman*.

We could have counted it down, it was that fast and inevitable.

Five. Four. Three. Two. One.

"You know this is my *wife*, right?" Tristan's voice boomed loud enough to be heard by all.

I covered my mouth, trying hard to stifle my laugh.

Bianca was doing the same a few feet to my left.

"And she calls *him* Trouble," Stephan laughed.

When the smiling couple moved across the room to join us, Tristan's arm wrapped around her small waist, anchoring her to his side.

They made a striking pair. Both with pitch black hair and turn your head stunning looks. They complemented each other in the best way. She highlighted his massive size, and his virile presence emphasized her extravagant femininity. Danika wasn't short, but he towered over her, making her look tiny, like he could pick her up with one hand.

They were walking, but his whole self was focused on her, head bent down, body turned in. He was whispering something into her ear that had her giggling uncontrollably.

What I'd give to have a man love me like that.

Tristan's dimples flashed as he greeted our group.

I wondered who was bigger, Heath or Tristan. It was hard to say. They were of a size. They'd have to be side by side to tell for sure.

The next big entrance was made about twenty minutes later by a fresh from the airport James.

It was apparent, as he made his way to our group, that he only had eyes for one person in the room. And the way he looked at her, God, like he wanted to swallow her whole.

By the way Bianca's gaze stayed glued to him, it was apparent that the feeling was very much mutual.

He went straight to her side. She rose to greet him, and he kissed her lightly on the forehead, then waved her to sit back down, taking the space that had opened up next to her.

His eyes left her only to alight on what she'd been drinking. He touched her wine glass pointedly, licking his lips. "How many have you had, love?"

"This is my second," Bianca answered, looking a bit exasperated with him, "but the first was hours ago."

He swallowed and nodded, tearing his attention from her to greet the rest of us, politely and warmly.

I knew what that strange interaction was all about. It had come up in our group therapy before. James hated alcohol with a passion. He felt it impaired a person, and for a long time Bianca hadn't had so much as a sip in an effort to cater to his strong opinion on the matter.

But Bianca didn't share his opinion, and though she wasn't much of a drinker, (I'd never seen her have more than two drinks, and even that was only over a four hour or more stretch) she did enjoy a drink from time to time.

She never drank enough to impair her judgement, something she slowly, over time, had made James understand, and so the couple had eased into the understanding that, though James would never touch alcohol, and that was fine, Bianca would enjoy the occasional drink with her girlfriends, and James had learned not freak out about it.

Their love story was one that touched me, as well. Both had suffered through dreadful childhoods. Bianca's father was such a monster that she still celebrated every year at the anniversary of his death. She was not a hateful woman, so it wasn't lost on me how awful he must have been for her to do that.

James had suffered through some rough stuff of his own, but I wasn't privy to the details of it, and I'd never be boorish enough to ask.

But I *had* seen his sex tape (before I knew either of them, mind you), and I knew he was into some seriously kinky shit.

From what I'd gathered, he'd introduced Bianca to said kinkiness, and it seemed to be a lifestyle that worked for both of them.

Even as I had the thought, I saw him fingering her collar, his eyes on hers, the two of them so immersed in each other I doubted they even remembered where they were.

What I'd give to have a man look at me like that, with his whole heart in his eyes.

When I lay down to sleep that night, in my big empty bed, in my big empty house, my mind lingered on my marriage.

Why had I not expected more from my husband? How had I settled for such a sterile marriage and not held out for something like what I'd witnessed tonight?

The only answer I could come up with was that I'd never seen it, hadn't known that love like that was out there to look for in anything aside from fiction.

My parents were good people, but they'd had a sterile marriage themselves, and though their parting had been more amicable than mine with my ex, it had been just as inevitable.

I'd always known their lack of love for each other was why I'd been obsessed with romance novels since I was fourteen. It only just occurred to me then, though, that their loveless marriage had perhaps inspired my own.

The twenty-year-old me that had settled for Eduard had never seen anything like the way Tristan smiled at Danika, the way James looked at Bianca, the way Stephan doted on Javier. I'd always been attracted to the idea of a love like that, but that's all it had been to me—an idea.

The realization made me sad, but I could hardly regret my marriage. My children were my everything.

Still, I felt a small change in me that night, a slight shifting, as the resolve in me stiffened. I'd be alone the rest of my life before I'd settle for less than a man that flat out adored me.

CHAPTER
EIGHT

A FEW WEEKS LATER

I ran into Dair at the market, and we wound up going for coffee again. We chatted easily, and I marveled that I could know someone for so long, be interested in them, and have things stop dead at friendship with every encounter.

It was the polar opposite of what had happened with Heath.

I knew that wasn't good. I should *want* to pursue something further with Dair. That would be the healthy urge, because clearly Dair was a good guy, and there was a potential for a future between us.

Instead, I was relieved when we parted ways with just a brief hug a few blocks shy of my house.

I should have felt disappointed that he didn't mention going out sometime, or calling me sometime, or doing something, anything, that could be considered a date somewhere down the road.

Instead, I was stuck firmly at just being disappointed that I wasn't disappointed.

I was almost to my house when I felt someone move in close behind me.

I nearly jumped out of my skin when a gravelly voice said close to my ear, "Who was that guy?"

I swung around, hand flying to my chest, wide eyes on an agitated looking Heath.

"You scared me," was the first thing I said. But the first thing I felt upon seeing him was much more embarrassing.

I was so relieved. Whatever had happened between us, that crazy, passion fueled lunacy from weeks ago, I didn't want it to be a one-time deal.

What I *did* want I wasn't focusing on. It was way too soon for that. I'd settle for relief that the thing I *didn't* want hadn't come to fruition.

"Are you *dating* that guy you were just with?" he asked, eyes moving over my face like he was looking for something, like he could read me like a book.

Could he?

God, I hoped not.

"Um, no. He's a friend. I ran into him at the grocery store, and we went out for a coffee. What are you doing here?"

"I was heading to your house."

"Oh." I smiled. So it wasn't a chance encounter. He *wanted* to see me again.

It was pathetic how relieved and downright happy I was about that.

I licked my lips and watched his eyes move to my mouth. "I could make us a late lunch."

His jaw clenched like he was bracing himself for something. "I don't think I have time for lunch."

My breath stuttered out of my chest. I blinked once, and that one blink was like a light switch. I went from being me to this sexual creature that just couldn't get enough. "What do you have time for?"

He didn't even bother to answer, just took my hand and started pulling me.

And I let him.

Dammit, once I again, I was going to make this way too easy for him.

But one look at his agitated face had left me with an agitated body. The man could make me wet with one look. It wasn't lost on me how twisted it was that that look was a scowl.

Heath angry = Me turned on.

I really hoped that wouldn't turn into a thing for me.

We barely made it into my house before he was on me.

He pinned me to the door, pushing my arms above my head, holding them there with one hand, mouth crashing into mine, and started working my pants down my legs.

He was in a hurry.

I was right there with him, desire pooling heavy in my belly, my entire body throbbing for him.

My trembling, erect nipples were pointing straight at him. They were begging him. I didn't have to utter a word. I doubted I'd keep them in for long, but they were unnecessary. My body was doing the talking here.

I wanted skin on skin, but we never got that far.

He stripped me bare from the waist down, shoved his jeans down just far enough to free his big eager cock, crammed a condom on, and started working me onto his bucking shaft.

I got loud right away. Even when his mouth covered mine, I couldn't keep quiet.

I heard the dog somewhere in the house, moving around with his big clumsy paws, getting close enough to us for Heath to pause and bark, "Tato, out!"

As if the dog understood him, as though Heath ran the place, my huge Great Dane went scrambling loudly through the house, out his doggy door, and into the backyard.

I circled my hips, moaning into Heath's mouth. He was still pushing in, but not fast enough.

His free hand gripped my hip hard and thrusting his tongue in my mouth, he shoved home.

I had one leg hooked high over his hip, but it wasn't enough. He pulled out, ignoring my loud protests.

I didn't protest for long. He turned me, pressing my palms against the door. He spread my legs, grabbed my hips in both hands, lifted me to just the right angle, and started drilling me from behind.

His rough breaths panted into my ear with every thrust.

Neither of us lasted long.

He hit every perfect nerve going in and out, in and out.

My orgasm built like it had its own pulsing life, beating into me with each rough thrust, growing with each hard slam of his dick into my pussy.

My nails scraped against the door as I came.

He shoved home, to the root, and held himself there. After a few beats, still twitching inside me, his hands went from my hips to the front buttons of my shirt, tugging it open, sending buttons flying with a few impatient tugs. He unclasped my bra, not breaking *it*, at least, and palmed my tits.

He kept thrusting, in smaller movements, still milking himself into me, still coming in perceivable spurts.

I wanted to sob in pleasure, it felt so good, barely stifled the sob-like noises that were coming out of me.

He kneaded my breasts, leaning close at my back to speak into my ear. "I need to go," he rasped, nuzzling into my neck. "Now."

What the fuck? I thought. He was the one that came to *my* house. He couldn't spend more than a few minutes here before he ran off?

And on the tail of that . . . *Was I so spoiled from the last time that I just assumed he'd stay for more than one round?*

"Okay," I responded with what little breath I had. What else could I say? I wasn't going to beg him to stay.

And still, he didn't pull out, still making those delicious little movements inside of me, still breathing on my neck, his body against my back, my sensitive breasts still in his hands.

At least I was sure he didn't want to leave. It was something.

With a curse, he pulled away.

I went immediately for my discarded pants, not looking at him as he went into my nearby half-bath and started straightening his clothes. He was fast, I noted, listening to his every move.

He didn't even say goodbye, the *asshole.*

While I was turned around, still fumbling to re-clasp my bra, he walked out the door.

I didn't move to the front window to watch him go, though it was tempting.

Instead, I moved into the half-bath, eyes on the discarded condom in the wastebasket that I'd need to take out right away, like *right away.* I'd be mortified if either of my boys stopped by out of the blue and caught sight of *that.*

Geez, I thought, staring at it. It was just so sordid, one big used condom in my spotless, feminine half bath. The room was painted apricot, and there were flowers on the rug, for Christ's sake.

I gave myself a good talking to, eyes on the condom. I nearly had myself convinced, body still thrumming in a strange combo of desire, disgust, and a delicious sort of soreness that made me think of Heath every time I shifted my body.

This wasn't me.

I couldn't change myself, the things I wanted, what I thought was right and wrong, just for one man. One *too young* man who apparently couldn't spare more than a few minutes out of his too busy schedule to fuck my brains out.

The pep talk/self-lecture was good for me, or so I thought. This sort of thing wasn't my cup of tea. It was too casual. The man hadn't even asked me how my day was going before he shoved his cock into me.

And I hadn't gotten to look at his eyes as he came, when they did that extraordinary thing I loved.

It occurred to me then that this made a *huge* difference to me. Physical relief, no matter how powerful, was not enough for me. Watching what I did to him, how I made his eyes change from cold to that elusive *something else* was required, as well, for me to feel that this passing fling was worth my peace of mind.

All of the productive work I had planned for the afternoon seemed to fly out the window. There was nothing to do for it but open a bottle of wine and call one of my girlfriends to talk it out. It was one of the biggest perks of being self-employed.

"He didn't even say goodbye after? Just walked out?" Danika's voice over the phone was clearly appalled.

"Just walked out," I affirmed.

"What an *asshole*," she muttered. "I'm coming over. Tristan is working, and I'm only a few minutes away from you. Should I bring more wine?"

"I'm well stocked," I said wryly. I liked my wine.

She showed up not five minutes later, still dressed for work. I must have caught her just as she got home. I knew she was like me, and changed into something comfortable the second she got into her own home.

I poured her a glass, and we went out onto my back porch to sip wine and talk it out.

"What an asshole," she repeated, for maybe the third time.

I nodded, taking another drink.

"Is he an asshole in bed, too?"

I wasn't sure how to answer that. He was bossy, sure, but he ate pussy like a champ.

"No," I finally settled on. "He's very aggressive, very forceful, but he's definitely adamant about getting me off first."

"Well, that's something. I'm convinced that men who are assholes in bed are basically hopeless.

I laughed because it was true.

"Asshole in bed—impossible to rehabilitate. Asshole in general, hell, who knows—there's probably some hope."

I laughed harder. This is why I'd called her. Girl always told it like it was.

Danika was fluent in sarcasm. It was one of my favorite languages. I found I always trusted a person more once I discovered they had the sarcasm gene.

She was the perfect balance of practical levity that I'd known was needed to improve my mood.

CHAPTER
NINE

He showed up at my door about a week later. It was a Tuesday and eleven o'clock at night.

When the doorbell rang, I didn't know who it could be, but I still didn't even suspect that it was *him*.

I had the brief urge, after looking through the peephole, not to even answer the door, but other, stronger urges won out.

At least I kept the chain on, talking through the small opening that left.

And the first thing I said when I did open it was, "I don't think I should let you in."

His brows shot up like he had no notion where this was coming from. "What?" he clipped out.

As I gathered my reply, my eyes ran over him. He wore jeans and a tight gray T-shirt. He looked edible, and I still wasn't accustomed to my reaction to him.

"You didn't even bother to say goodbye the last time," I told him, making my voice as cold as it would go, which was still about ten times warmer than his normal tone. "Hell, I don't think you even said hello."

He just looked at me like he had no clue what I was going on about. Infuriating man.

"No woman has ever made you work for it, huh?" I asked wryly.

I didn't even want to think about that. But, of course, I did.

God, the girls his age. I knew what was up. I had two sons that weren't much younger than he was. I'd talked to their girlfriends over the years, talked to them, to the parents of other people in their generation. Girls his age were down for just about any damn thing, and guys did not have to work hard to get it.

Who the hell could compete with that? Who the hell wanted to?

Me, apparently.

"I'm not sure what you're asking," he said carefully.

Me neither, though mostly because I already had my answer. This man was not housebroken. Had never even considered the idea. Why would he? If he wanted sex, he clearly did not have a hard time getting it.

"Look, I don't think this is working for me."

He still looked fantastically confused, like he just had no notion what my problem was. "What isn't working about it?"

I stared at him, not sure if he was mocking me.

"What I mean is, what do I need to change to make this work for you?" he added.

It was downright polite, for him.

And just that easy, I was ready to play again.

Dammit.

I unchained the door and let him in.

"Some manners," I said grudgingly, though not grudgingly enough. "You need to learn some manners. The basics. Hellos, goodbyes, a little bit of small talk. Something that tells me this isn't *just* casual sex. This may surprise you, but I don't do casual very well."

"Who said this was casual?"

Again, I couldn't tell if he was mocking me. But then, I was getting the distinct impression that he wasn't much of a jokester.

I didn't know what to say to that, didn't know how he meant it, so I moved on. "More *manners*," I stressed again. "That's what I need. Can you do that for me?"

My hair was pinned up, the heavy masses secured with several clips I'd thrown in carelessly throughout the day. Heath started taking it down, clip by clip, his clever fingers finding each one unerringly, until the black strands were loose and wavy around my shoulders.

He gripped both hands into it, his arms bunching distractingly as he pulled my face close to his, bending down to meet me halfway.

"Manners. Hellos. Goodbyes. Small talk." He repeated it all back like he really didn't know what I was talking about, but not in an asshole way. More like he was trying to follow along, whether he understood it or not.

I thought that, just maybe, I could work with that.

A big maybe, but not so big that I didn't let him take me to bed almost immediately.

He stripped me down, sat me on the edge of the bed, and knelt between my thighs.

He was leaning down, just a breath away from my sex, and said softly, "Hello."

I smiled, then gasped as he promptly and enthusiastically started eating me out.

He did this for so long (three orgasms and counting) that I finally had to scramble away to get him to stop.

"What are you doing?" I asked him. He'd shown no sign of letting up, like he was just going to go down on me indefinitely, with no signs of stopping for the foreseeable future.

He smiled. Yes, it was a cold smile, but I was starting to like that just fine. "Showing manners."

Dammit. He was really starting to grow on me.

I liked him way too much for someone I had no clue if I'd ever see again.

He climbed onto the bed, pinned me down. He held my wrists with one hand, the other gripping into my hair. He pushed his hips between my thighs and started fucking me.

He started talking while he did it. A lot. And not just dirty talk. Random talk.

"What the fuck?" I asked, after he slipped some inane comment about the weather in.

"Small talk," he explained.

Dammit.

He was a weirdo, for sure, but I *definitely* liked him.

He pulled out of me suddenly, cursing.

I squirmed a bit and tried not to curse myself. Why had he stopped?

"I forgot to put on a condom," he growled, going for his pants.

Shit. We both forgot. How the hell had that happened?

At least he hadn't come inside of me bare.

Still, I couldn't believe I'd missed that. It was a bit sobering.

He wrapped up and mounted me again.

He stayed for hours, but not for the night.

At least he said goodbye this time, though perversely, I wished he hadn't.

Big hands shaking my hip and shoulder woke me up.

I blinked groggily awake to an intimidating Heath looming over me.

"I have to go," he said gruffly.

I sighed out a breath, shifting restlessly under his hands. "Okay."

"You said I should say goodbye when I leave. This is goodbye."

I just shut my eyes and nodded. He was apparently a literal guy.

Still, he didn't move, just staring down at me for a long time.

"I wasn't even supposed to come here," he finally said, each word sounding like it was fighting to come out of his throat. "I'm in the middle of a job, something . . . something I can't be distracted from."

Whatever the hell that meant.

"You're distracting me," he continued.

Unaccountably, I liked that. A lot.

"I'm not leaving because I want to. I need to go. Legitimately. I hate having to explain myself. To anyone. But believe this: If I could stick around longer, I would. Okay?"

He'd told me almost nothing, given me no answers, not that he owed me any, all things considered, but what little he'd said, I appreciated. Whether it was bullshit or not, I liked how he'd taken the time to reassure me, to let me know that he'd have spent more time with me if he could have.

"Okay," I whispered to him in the dark.

He started to pull away. I stopped him with a hand on his retreating wrist. "Will I see you again?" I asked, the words torn out of me.

He cursed and bent down, taking my mouth roughly, his hands pulling my soft sheets up, wrapping them around my body. Tucking me in. I wasn't sure what to make of the tender action, but I liked it. A lot.

Loved it.

"You will if I have anything to say about it," he said cryptically and was gone faster than he'd come.

God, he was rough around the edges.

Why the hell did I like him so much?

He was uncivilized.

Churlish.

Uncouth.

And strangely, kind of sweet.

CHAPTER
TEN

I was soaking in the bath, glass of red wine cupped loosely in my hand and balanced haphazardly on the rim of the tub.

It was eight p.m., and I'd gotten back from a work trip in L.A. about thirty minutes prior.

I couldn't even have said why, but the trip had been stressful to me, and it was sort of a belated shock to realize how relieved I was to be home. I mean, it's not like I wasn't accustomed to traveling, and I'd only been gone a few days. I almost *always* went to L.A. multiple times a month for work. It was typical for me.

I'd gone for an editorial spread for a fashion magazine that had involved dealing with a temperamental supermodel. Maybe that was where all of my pent up tension was coming from?

I didn't think so. I'd dealt with many a prima donna.

That sort of thing never fazed me.

What was it then?

My body was coiled so tight, jaw held hard, lips pursed, shoulders drawn up too stiffly. Before the wine today, I'd looked down at my hands several times, always surprised when I found them made into nervous little fists.

The fists were gone, and the rest I was working on decompressing the best way I knew how.

I was reading on my phone, since it was easier to hold in one hand, the perfect arrangement for doing two of my favorite things simultaneously.

Drinking wine and devouring a book.

I was an avid, lifelong reader. I didn't stick to any one genre. In fact, I read everything, though not all mixed together. I went through phases. My last phase, which had lasted maybe four months, had been a True Crime phase. That one had started when I read my friend Dair's novels and turned into me finding and reading every non-fiction book that covered the crimes his novels were loosely based on.

That phase had ended a few weeks prior, and I was back to my favorite genre of all. Old faithful, guaranteed to get me out of a funk.

Romance.

Who didn't enjoy a good love story? I'd been devouring them lately, one after another, sleep being sacrificed, work being neglected, but somehow it always felt worth it for a good book.

I was just getting to a good part, mid-sip of wine, when I heard a noise somewhere in the house, around the kitchen, I thought. Something very commonplace, like a door creaking open.

My brows drew together. One of my boys, maybe, or Tato being just too big to move around quietly.

I had a brief regret about leaving both my bedroom and bathroom doors open. I'd done it because otherwise, Tato whined at the closed door, no matter which side I put him on.

If he was closed in with me, he invariably needed to go out and do his doggy business. If he was locked out, he felt deprived of my company. With the door open, he usually just parked himself somewhere close by, happy as a clam.

I was pretty sure both my boys knew better than to charge into my bedroom or bathroom unannounced, but I decided that it would be a good idea for me to still make my dripping way across the big bathroom to close the door, just to be safe.

My tub had a big ledge around it, perfect for candles and decorative items. I had a dry hand towel folded in a corner of it for my phone, and I set it there. My wine glass was going next, but as a big, quiet body filled my bathroom doorway, I miscalculated, and crashed it just perfectly wrong into the edge of the bath.

It shattered on contact, raining big chunks of glass and a healthy serving of deep red liquid, right onto my chest.

Even so, I was still more distracted by the familiar figure in the door than I was by the mess I'd just made.

How the hell had he gotten in?

"How the *hell* did you get into my house?" I asked Heath, not sure if I was more alarmed at the sight of him invading my privacy, or relieved that he'd come back, yet again.

Relieved, I thought, eyes running over his body. He looked amazing, as always, in his usual jeans/T-shirt combo.

His eyes were on my hand with the now broken glass.

Dammit, I thought, looking down at myself. I really needed to invest in some of those non-shatter wine glasses I'd heard about. My friend Bev, the one who hosted the girls' night, had some, and they seemed to do the trick. I'd been meaning to get some myself, but this definitely tipped me over the edge from a side-note into action.

"I tried ringing the doorbell, but you didn't answer, so I checked the back door. It was unlocked."

That I couldn't credit. I'd left the back door *unlocked?* I lived in Vegas. I knew better. What a silly, out of character thing that was for me to do.

My naive self just believed it because he'd said it.

"Don't move," he added, voice rough, not his normal rough, but like he was *pissed.*

His authoritative tone brooked no argument, and so I just sat there and watched him approach, holding perfectly still.

He crouched by the tub, reaching over me to take the stem, which was still intact, out of my hand. He set it on the ledge next to my phone.

That same hand moved to my chest where wine and a few large chunks of the jagged glass were clinging to my skin.

Very gently, he plucked the glass away.

"Fuck," he growled.

I glanced down. It was the tiniest cut, but one of the sharp pieces had drawn blood.

Without warning, he suddenly grabbed me under the arms, lifting me clean out of the bath.

My eyes flew to his face as he sat me down on the plush rug just in front of my vanity.

I was dripping a small flood onto the floor, some of it red wine, and I glanced to where I'd had my towel hung on a rack, reachable from the tub. But it wasn't reachable now.

"Could you hand me a towel?" I asked him, pointing.

It was like he didn't hear, eyes trained on my chest. It was wet and red, both with wine and a touch of blood.

He didn't hand me a towel. Instead, he leaned down and started sucking on a wine covered nipple.

"Oh," escaped my lips. It was a high pitched, needy utterance.

My hands went to his head, fingers running through his hair to grip him to me.

He didn't let that go for one second, covering my knuckles with his, pushing my hands away and behind me, turning my wrists until I was holding the counter in my palms.

He just kept sucking, lapping the wine away, the sound of it driving me wild, the way it told of his hunger for the simple act of licking me clean.

And he was thorough. Even after no trace of the wine remained, he just kept going, feasting at my breasts like they were the main course, instead of the appetizer.

His hands stayed on mine while he worked, keeping them were they were. I squirmed, needing more, needing his hands, and my hands, and just more.

Finally, he let me tug them free, and I used them to cup my breasts together, holding them for him, pushing them into his face.

He groaned, hands going to my hips, though he held his body away.

"I think there's still some wine on my belly," I told him breathlessly.

He got down on his knees, eyes aimed up at mine.

He put his mouth to my navel, lapping there for a time.

I watched him, still fondling myself. I wanted to throw a leg over his shoulder, but I restrained the urge, barely.

He lifted his head, looking up at me. "Did I get it?"

I nodded, but said, "I think it dripped lower."

That earned me a wicked smile. His eyes darted to my breasts, which were still held in my kneading hands.

"Keep your hands there," he said, and went back to work, licking lower and being thorough about it.

When he delved between my thighs, he seemed to still be on his mission to ferret out every last drop of spilled wine.

I was pretty certain he'd gotten it all, but I wasn't going to hold him back.

The thought never even crossed my mind.

His scruff scraped against my inner thighs, his nose pushing insistently against my clit as his tongue curled into my sex, lapping in slow, deliberate scrapes like he was still on that determined hunt for any errant wine.

I had to lean back on the counter, than perch there, throwing my hands back to brace as he just kept going.

He pulled my legs over his shoulders and went to work, my heels digging hard into his back.

I came twice before he pulled back and looked up at me.

I bit my lip, trying not to blush at how wet the lower half of his face was.

"Did I get it all?" he asked.

I nodded, still catching my breath.

I only noticed that the tiny cut on my chest was still bleeding when he stood up and started tending to it. It was really quite sweet, the way he took care of that minor cut like it was utterly important, holding a tissue to it until the bleeding stopped.

"I'm going to clean that glass out of your tub," he told me. "Why don't you go fix yourself another helping of wine."

On trembling legs, I grabbed my robe and headed for the kitchen. "Would you like a glass?" I asked, an afterthought, glancing back at him.

"Um, no. Do I look like a man that drinks *wine*?" he asked.

I laughed and he smiled.

I was sitting in my little dining room just off the kitchen when he joined me, though he didn't sit.

"Anything I need to do to make this work for you?" he asked suddenly.

I just stared at him. He was constantly unexpected. Nearly everything that came out of him was a surprise to me.

"Anything that I'm not doing . . . correctly," he clarified.

I smiled at him, my chest warming in a very cozy way, almost like this thing between us was something normal—something romantic, even.

"Say something sweet to me," I told him, feeling playful.

He studied me very seriously, like it hadn't even occurred to him that I wasn't being entirely serious just then.

Flirting was a foreign concept to him.

"You're a peaceful woman," he said, each word uttered very carefully. Like they had some special meaning.

I blinked, long and slow, lashes peeling apart liked they'd been coated with honey.

I was trying to decide what to make of that pronouncement.

Peaceful sounded just a touch too close to boring, I was thinking.

"What I mean is, you make me want peace . . . you bring me peace. Believe it or not, this is a very mellow version of me.

I eyed him. "Are you serious?" I sincerely did not think he was.

"Yeah. Scary, huh?"

To be honest, it was a bit scary, because I'd never seen him approaching anything close to mellow. Never seen him at anything less than intense.

I'd hate to see him at full speed.

Yikes.

And then my mind wandered back to what he'd just said and how it pertained to me.

Wow. He really had come up with something sweet.

He with the deeply cold eyes, always so intensely frigid had somehow found the words to warm me, head to toe.

I thought he might have stayed the night that time when he was finished with me in the wee hours of the morning, but I wasn't sure, because I was certain that he didn't sleep in my bed with me. I'd have noticed a thing like that.

Instead, I suspected he camped out in another room, on my couch maybe. I couldn't have said why I suspected that, looking at the thing. Not a cushion was out of place, but that was no matter. He was the type to leave things just how he'd found them.

I'd never seen him relax, not for a second. Even when I was sitting, drinking my wine, he had remained standing, pacing, waiting. Never just holding still, and only lying down for activities that did not involve anything remotely close to sleeping or resting.

Either way, he was gone in the morning when I woke up.

It should be noted that casual sex might have suited me just fine. I'll never know. Heath was simply not the man to try it with. He hit every single one of my hot buttons.

CHAPTER
ELEVEN

I shut and locked the door, lingering there for a moment.

What a strange night that had been. What a strange kiss.

It was the oddest thing.

I'd just been on a date with my friend Dair. We'd been flirting for quite some time, but we were both so busy, and hesitant, that it never went anywhere. And then he'd called me out of the blue, wanting to go out on an actual date. I couldn't think of one good reason to turn him down, and so I went.

I really liked Dair, knew he was the kind of man I should want, but my heart just wasn't in it.

Perhaps I wasn't ready to move on yet. The divorce had happened over a year ago, but it had been a long, ugly marriage.

Oh, and there was the small matter of my sometimes lover. But that situation was less about moving on, and more about getting off, or so I told myself.

"What was *that*?" a deep, biting voice barked at me from the darkness of my living room.

Of course I knew who it was instantly, but still, I jumped about a foot.

Think of the devil.

"You," I said, breathless now, heart rate accelerated with more than fear with those three rough words.

"Me," he agreed. "Come here."

I shouldn't have listened.

I should have turned on a light and demanded to know why he'd broken into my home. I should have asked him *'Was the door unlocked this time?'* Because of course it hadn't been.

But all I could remember when I heard that rough, bar brawler voice was pleasure that remained so acute in my mind it made my whole body tingle just with the memory.

I moved toward the chair he sat in slowly, just making out his shadowy figure by the dim light cast from the street lamps out front.

I let out an embarrassing yelp when he snatched me by the hips and set me astride him, both of my arms held behind my back by the wrists.

God, he was fast.

All my traitorous body could seem to remember about that speed of his was how fast his hips moved as he hammered into me.

"You're *kissing* him now?" he asked me, voice low and mean.

I swallowed, then licked my lips nervously.

I was stuck somewhere between fear and desire. I knew he was dangerous, every cell in my body knew it, but it didn't seem to be any kind of a deterrent to my damned libido.

"I haven't heard from you in weeks," I said steadily, tone matter of fact rather than plaintive. "You come and go as you please, fuck my brains out, and leave while I'm still sleeping it off. Why shouldn't I be seeing other people?"

"Don't go out with him anymore. And if I catch you kissing some guy on your porch again, I'm warning you now, you aren't going to like his face much when I'm finished with him."

"You have no right to tell me what to do," I told him firmly, even as my body quaked. "I don't even know you, and I certainly don't know where you disappear to."

"I've been out of town," he said, tone surly. "I'm back. And you know me well enough. Certainly enough to know how this night will end."

I struggled against him briefly because he was pissing me off with every word, but that only seemed to add to my problem, as every shift of my body had me rubbing against his obvious hard-on.

"Missed you, too, sugar," he rasped, pulling my face closer to his.

I gritted my teeth, pissed off by his attitude, and more pissed off by my body's increasing reaction to it. "Really?" I asked archly, a sarcastic bite in my tone.

"Really. It's going to be a rough night for you. That little kiss out on your porch has gone and pissed me off, so I've got some frustration to fuck out of my system. But first, I need you to wash your mouth out.

Who did he think he was, telling me what to do? If anything, it should be the reverse.

I was pretty much old enough to be his mother.

He set me on my feet, and I backed away on unsteady legs.

I went to my bathroom, bending over the sink to brush my teeth, but only because I thought it was fair. I'd want him to do the same if he'd just been kissing some other woman.

My eyes shot up as he gripped my long hair, wrapping it around his wrist once, twice, slamming his hard-on against my ass.

"You can't even begin to know how screwed up it was for you to kiss Dair like that."

I blinked at his reflection in the mirror, spitting out my toothpaste. A chill ran through me. Fear.

"How-how do you know his name?" I gasped.

He gave me one of his cold smiles, his eyes scary, even while he kept rubbing against me from behind.

"I know a great many things about you and your life, Lourdes. And there's a thing you should know about me."

I didn't want to ask, didn't want to know. He was really freaking me out now. But it seemed called for. "What?"

"It's unwise to rile me." He reached his free hand around me, cupping my sex crudely. "This is *mine*. It will go much better for all parties involved if you stop questioning that."

My body was throbbing, but it was a distraction I *didn't want* right then. I wanted to focus. He didn't get to say a thing like that and not explain himself.

"How?" My voice was a hoarse whisper, but I got the word out.

"How is it unwise?" he asked.

"No," I answered, voice gaining strength. "How do you know 'a great many things about my life'? How'd you know his name?"

"I told you I work in security." He paused. His fingers never stopped moving, rubbing, stroking. "It's part of my job to," longer pause, "vet anyone I might be," longest pause of all, "seeing. And also, anyone *they* might be seeing."

I mulled that over, or tried to. He shoved a finger inside of me, but I still managed to tell him, voice as firm as it could be with a quaver in it. "I'm *not* okay with that. Don't do it again. It's an invasion of my privacy."

He pulled his finger out, both of his big hands going to my hips.

He gave me a pretty scary look for that.

I knew it should have made me more scared. All of this should have. So why didn't it?

It was becoming clear to me that infatuation could trump caution. Lust like this overrode my instincts, making them hazy, distant. I couldn't focus on them, let alone heed them.

Heath was just too distracting to me. Even now, when I was angry and more than a touch frightened of him, all I could focus on was how *he* was reacting to *me*.

He had all of these little tells I was starting to notice, ones that told just what level of pissed off he was.

Nostrils flaring. Teeth clenching, followed by his jaw flexing were pretty typical. But tonight, with him more pissed than I'd ever seen, he was doing all of that and added into the mix was him biting his lower lip like he just couldn't help himself.

Perverse as it was, and in spite of myself, a part of me kind of loved it. It was hot.

"I'll tell you what," he said in a soft growl that somehow almost managed to be a croon. "You heed what I said. You keep away from Dair, and I won't pry into your business anymore."

"Him *specifically*?" I asked, baffled by it. Did he have a problem with Dair in particular? Or was this jealousy a more generalized thing?

It would have been much better for my ego if it were the latter.

"Him specifically. Stay the fuck away from *him*, okay?"

Apparently it was not.

"It was not okay to—were you—were you actually *spying on me*?" I barely got the question out.

Barely kept the line of thought in my head. One of his hands had gone to grip into my hair, pulling, while the other snaked back down to my sex. He pushed two big fingers into me, working them in and out at a rough rhythm.

He was distracting me, deliberately, blatantly.

And, damn it all, it was working.

What I'd just learned should have been the brakes.

I was old enough to know the difference between an intriguing man and one that was fucked in the head.

"You're upset," he noted. The way he said it, something about his tone, told me that he hadn't expected that, like me being upset about being spied on was totally out of left field.

"You're crazy, you know that?" I spat at his reflection.

He didn't disagree, instead bent down and put his lips to the nape of my neck. "To say the least," he murmured into my skin.

"Listen," his voice rumbled into me. "I didn't know what this was when I first came after you. I still don't know what this is . . . but I care about you. I'm messed up. Majorly. I've got some problems, mental problems, serious problems acclimating back into society, and I'm very well aware of it. There are things I do, habitually, that are not socially acceptable. Yes, I stalked you. I know more about you than I should. I had my reasons, but I understand how it looks. It looks *bad*. And, hell, if I could tell you the full truth, it would probably look even worse than whatever you're thinking.

But I want you to know something, and it is the truth. I'd *never* hurt you. If it was within my power, I'd do anything to prevent you being hurt."

"I don't know what to do with you," I gasped. In spite of myself, I was losing this battle. It was embarrassing how fast he could get me to come with just his fingers.

His hand had wandered down my body to grip at one aching breast. He thumbed my nipple, kneading and pinching at the tender flesh around it.

"I won't keep you guessing," his voice rumbled into my skin, right before he bit the flesh between my neck and shoulder.

My breath punched out of me and back bowing, I came.

What the hell? I thought to myself, eyes on my hands where they gripped into the edge of the counter.

I was still catching my breath when he shoved into me. I glanced up at our reflection, watching the top of his bent head as he started to move in short, rough thrusts, inching in deeper with every shove.

Finally, he slammed home, pulled out, then slammed right back in again.

He pulled my head back by the hair and started fucking me in earnest.

And that was when he looked up, met my eyes, and I realized that he was still pissed the hell off.

Seething as he took me.

He was growling. Literally. Growling.

I just about came right then.

I knew it was perverse, knew it made me fucked in the head right along with him.

But I loved it. Fucking loved that I did that to him, that he was as out of his mind into this as I was.

A series of rough thrusts later, and I was losing my mind. I could barely keep my knees from buckling as I came again. Hard.

It was scary how hard. An utter loss of self, where I forgot what I'd even been upset about. Forgot everything but the man behind me, inside of me, the man owning every inch of my trembling body.

And his eyes when he came captured mine in the mirror and made it all so much worse.

Oh no. No way.

There was no way I was falling for this psycho.

Was there?

Or the real question, *How* had I fallen for him?

I didn't even know him. He was a virtual stranger. An unpredictable one. A complete mystery.

And none of that seemed to matter. I couldn't lie to myself about this. More than my body was involved here.

It was the small glimpses I got of his sweet side, I thought. *The side of him that looked at me in wonder every time he got off.*

"Mine," he said gruffly to my reflection just before he bent to kiss the side of my cheek. "You're fucking mine, you understand?"

I whimpered. That's what he did to me. Took my words away and turned me into a quivering mess.

He took that as a yes, pulling out of me slowly, his mouth moving from my cheek, down across my neck, along my shoulder, caressing down my spine.

And then I was up in his arms, cradled to his chest as he carried me to bed.

CHAPTER TWELVE

"**D**id we just have our first fight?" I asked him, much, much later.

I was lying in bed, naked, well-rested, and he'd stuck around for the night, for once, though he wasn't in bed with me.

He was prowling around my room, fully dressed, like he'd just been waiting for me, instead of sleeping himself.

"If we did, I think I won." His tone was sardonic.

That irked me. Arrogant bastard. But it was true.

If we were going to fight in the bedroom, I was going to *lose*.

"You know, you can be a real pain in the ass?" My tone was not as scathing as it should have been.

He got a kick out of that. I could tell by the unholy light in his eyes, and the tone of his voice when he said, "I think that's understating things. Honey, I'm your worst nightmare."

Ha. Wasn't that the truth.

I got up, got dressed, and cooked us breakfast.

Heath paced around my dining room while he waited for the food.

I was trying to think back and recall if I'd ever seen him sit before. Nothing came to mind.

"Did you sleep last night?" I called out to him.

He stopped pacing, coming to stand a few feet into the kitchen. "Yes. Everyone needs sleep, Lourdes."

I shot him a look. "Well, I slept for eight hours last night. How long did *you* sleep?" It was a pointed question. I was pretty sure I had a clue about the answer.

"I didn't keep track."

"Guess," I prodded.

"Maybe two hours."

I wanted to scold him, but I was well aware that I was not his mother. "That's not enough sleep for anyone, Heath."

"It's enough for me."

I mulled that over. "Where did you sleep?"

"On your sofa. In the living room."

"Why didn't you just sleep in the bed with me?"

"I was being considerate. Trust me, I did you a favor."

It was pretty obvious that this was a touchy subject for him, so I just said, "Let me know if you ever want to talk about it," and then dropped it.

But while he seemed to be in a talkative mood (for him) I decided to pry further.

"Tell me about your family," I tried.

He started pacing again. "There's not much to tell. Not many of us left. How about you?"

THE OTHER MAN

I sighed resignedly, though I'd fully expected him to turn the question on me. Just not quite so quickly. "I'm an only child, and my parents divorced when I was in my early twenties. I have a big extended family, but most of them still live in Europe."

"Where do your parents live?"

"My father lives in Lyon, France. He'll die there, too, I guarantee. He runs a restaurant. He's a world-renowned chef, actually. If you gave a damn about haute cuisine, you'd be impressed. My mother lives in the states. In Florida. That's a fairly recent development, though. She grew up in Spain, and they both raised me in France."

"How was that?"

"Growing up in Lyon?"

He nodded.

I thought about it. "It was pretty amazing, actually. There's little I can complain about. And I'm still close with both of them. I take the boys to visit each of them at least twice a year. What about your parents? Where do they live?"

"They died when I was younger."

"Any siblings?"

He didn't answer for so long that I thought he wasn't going to, but then, "One left."

That sounded ominous. "Brother or sister? And are you close?"

He completely ignored the first question. "We have a complex relationship."

"Too complex to elaborate on?"

"Unfortunately, yes."

I took the hint, and let yet another subject close.

I was plating up the eggs, sausage, and bacon before I tried another. "Why don't you ever let me touch you?" I asked him, tone neutral, almost off-hand. I'd wanted to broach this topic with him from the beginning.

"Do you really want to know? It's fucked up. It will probably just make you more scared of me."

That did the opposite of what he thought it would. Now I was *more* intrigued, with only the slightest touch of trepidation.

I put the plates down on the table, then headed back into the kitchen for drinks.

I grabbed two glasses and a pitcher of orange juice on the return trip, but he still hadn't taken a seat.

I wondered if he'd eat standing up.

I took my own seat, poured us each a glass of juice, and looked up at him.

Finally, he sat, though he looked ill at ease, like he thought it was a mistake the second he did it.

"Tell me," I urged softly.

Without a word he started eating.

I began to eat as well, resigned to the fact that this was yet another subject he wouldn't be opening up about.

I was quickly distracted by the way he ate, as though this was his last meal on earth. It was strange. His manners were fine. He used his utensils and closed his mouth when he chewed. But his every movement was so economical and mechanical.

I had a thought. "You're military, aren't you?"

He pretended not to hear that one, finishing his food before I'd even salted my eggs.

"The not touching me thing. Is that going to be a deal breaker for you?" he finally asked, shooting his eyes at me.

His face was set in stone. So much so, that if he smiled right then, I thought it might crack.

"I would like to touch you," I said carefully. "Is that going to be permanently off-limits?"

He took a deep breath. "It was a long time ago, but you see this scar?" He pulled his shirt up, baring his mutilated torso. He dragged his thumb along the worst of his marks, the long jagged one that went up his side that had to have come from something awful.

I set down my fork and reached out, tried to touch it, but he grabbed my hand, holding it firmly in his.

"I see it," I finally answered, because he seemed to be waiting for that.

"A woman did that to me."

I blinked at him. That I had not expected.

"We were fucking at the time," he added.

Holy shit. "Why—why would she do that?"

He grimaced. "She was hired to kill me. I guess she figured her best shot was to catch me when I was distracted, and it almost worked."

Holy shit.

"Why would someone be hired to kill you? Tell me what you're involved in, Heath. I have a right to know."

His mouth twisted. "For your own protection, I can't tell you much. But . . . I used to be a spy for the government."

That did add up. "Are you still?"

"It's complicated."

"What happened to that woman that tried to kill you?"

"I snapped her neck."

He saw my face, took a deep breath, and added, "It fucked me up, but I was still inside of her when I did it."

He was watching me closely, like he needed to see my reaction.

I was shaking, and it was an effort, but I kept my eyes on his.

"I had to," he continued. "I knew I'd bleed out if I didn't get help soon, and if I'd passed out with her still alive, she'd have finished me."

I nodded, still trembling. I got it. It sounded like a clear case of self-defense, but it was completely awful and like nothing I'd ever been exposed to.

This was heavy shit. Even heavier than I'd suspected.

"And she wasn't the only one," he added quietly. "I've killed a lot of people."

I was outright shaking now. I didn't know how to react to this. It was beyond my realm of experience. So beyond it, I'm ashamed to admit that some small, pathetic noise escaped my throat. It was quiet and involuntary, but Heath still heard it.

And addressed it. Quite perfectly, I thought.

"Shh shh," he uttered quietly, one hand reaching up to stroke my hair away from my face. "Here's why you shouldn't be scared of me. Yes, I am a killer. I will never be a normal guy. I do *not* blend in. There are men out there like me, and God willing, you will never run into one, that blend in, that play normal, that would *not* trigger your instincts, or make you think they have the least thing wrong with them. Those are the ones that you need to worry about. I'm a killer, but I'm not a sociopath."

Either I was completely naive, or he was completely masterful at manipulating me, but his alarming speech helped.

Still, it felt like something huge was stuck in my throat. I swallowed with effort. "But you're only a killer because of your job? You killed, like, bad guys, right?"

Jesus, I sounded like a kid that needed reassurance, I realized.

But I did. I wanted badly to hear that he was one of the good guys.

"I followed orders, and when you've killed as many people as I have, it's impossible to assume that they were all justified."

This actually did make me feel better. At least what he did had been controlled and had been done at someone else's orders, not some compulsion of his own.

"I'm trying to be upfront with you," he told me earnestly. "But, and I know I've said this before, *you* do not need to be afraid of me. I swear I'll never hurt you."

My heart did a slow turn in my chest. The more vulnerable I realized he was, the harder I fell. I knew it was naive of me, but I believed him. Completely.

"I know you won't," I returned.

He took a very deep breath, sitting back, and as I watched him I witnessed some of the tension leaving him.

"Thank you for that," he told me solemnly. "Even my own sister is afraid of me, and while I understand it, it messes me up."

A sister. I tucked that bit of information away.

I was content to learn about him slowly, if that was what he needed, just so long as we were making some kind of progress.

"I'll tell you what," he began in a gruff tone. "I'll let you touch me when we aren't having sex. You let me tie you up when we are."

Oh God.

With just a few words, he had me turned-on and alarmed in equal measures.

But then . . . as much as I knew I was jumping in head first, I did trust him, at least with something like this.

"Will there be exceptions to this rule?" I prodded. "Or is this an every time deal for you?"

He ran a hand over his face, looking tired. "I'll work on it, okay? I'll try my best to be accommodating, but it might take some time. My wiring is off. Has been for a long time."

"I understand," I said. I didn't, not really, but we both knew what I really meant, which was, *I'm trying* to understand.

We were sitting a few feet apart, our chairs aimed at each other. I moved mine, scooting in closer to him, until I was in easy arm's reach.

He sat stiffly, posture rigid, arms folded across his chest. He looked uncomfortable and mean, not the most inviting combination, but I pressed on.

I placed my hands on him for the first time, one on his pectoral, the other on his neck.

He twitched once, like a nervous animal, but let me do it.

Progress.

He was trying, undergoing something that clearly went against his nature, and he was doing it for me.

My heart softened for him all the more.

I'd always had a tender spot in my heart for wild things.

When I was young, I couldn't count the times I'd taken in stray dogs and cats that weren't close to being tame.

I had a patient nature, even as a child. I recalled how I'd handle those feral creatures, caring for them, feeding them, waiting endlessly until they came to crave the touch of my hand.

My lover was not so very different. An untamed challenge, to say the least.

But I could be very tenacious. If anyone was up to the task of housebreaking a man like Heath, I figured it was me.

His flesh felt amazing under my hands, his neck corded and strong, his chest hard and soft in all the right ways.

I rubbed my hands over him in small circles, staying focused on his chest and neck, massaging, soothing. I knew to take it slow.

"Is this okay?" I asked, tone soothing, almost a croon.

He let out the breath he'd been holding, then sucked it in, out, in, out, finally saying, "It's okay."

I kept going, stroking his body with a light touch. I tried to chat him up while I did it, but as usual, he was not too chatty.

"It was nice waking up with you still here, for once," I said.

His only response was a less than encouraging grunt.

"Do you have to leave soon? Or can you stay for a bit?"

"I need to make a few phone calls tonight, but aside from that, I should have some time."

I leaned into him, hanging my arm over his nape so I could put my cheek to his chest. My free hand slipped down to his stomach, rubbing.

"So we have the day together?"

"If you're free, yes."

"I can take the day off. I'll need to make a few phone calls this morning, but nothing important."

"Perfect," he said succinctly.

We stayed like that for a long time, with me straddling his lap while I ran my hands over him tenderly, getting him used to my touch.

At some point (something sneaky on Heath's part) my top and bra disappeared.

He was still fully dressed, and I was decent from the waist down, but it was one of the most erotic experiences of my life.

I stroked his hair as he fondled me with both hands, his face buried between my soft, sensitive breasts, nuzzling endlessly.

I cupped his head to my bosom. I was rubbing my sensitized nipple back and forth, back and forth, dragging it along his rough cheek until he moaned, snapped his head to the side, and took it in his mouth.

I'd tried to prolong for as long as I could before it turned purely sexual, but our chemistry was an explosive with a very short fuse.

I was kind of impressed we'd lasted as long as we had.

CHAPTER
THIRTEEN

I t was a strange day, but not strange in a bad way. For the most part, it was just the opposite.

And surprisingly, we didn't spend it all in bed.

I worked a bit, and then we went for a long walk.

Heath held Tato's leash, and my dog walked just behind him, clearly showing deference to Heath's dominant personality. I swear all Heath had to do was look at him and he dropped to his back in submission.

In his other hand he held one of mine.

Unfortunately, before we'd gone far, we happened to pass by one of my neighbors, Deborah Dillon, and I could tell by the way her squinting eyes latched onto our clasped hands that we'd just made ourselves the hot topic of the day.

Dammit. I knew it was too much to hope that she wouldn't notice how young he was.

It was bound to happen with us walking around my neighborhood like this. I just hadn't given it a thought until I saw my least favorite neighbor hanging out in her front yard, which was surely an odd thing for her to be doing, since most days her kids were outside, roaming the neighborhood. I couldn't remember the last time she'd actually been caught out with them.

Here's why I (and the entire neighborhood) didn't have much tolerance left for the Dillon family, otherwise known as The Dickhead Dillons. (I swear I wasn't the one that came up with that.)

No one blamed their children, who were nine, seven, and five, and boys, but that didn't mean we had any patience left for them, either.

The nine year old had recently slapped the neighborhood sweetheart, a precocious little eight-year-girl named, Gilley, who wouldn't hurt a flea. I'd actually been witness to this (it was a hard slap and shocking to see), as I was walking 'Tato when it happened. His parents hadn't reprimanded him. They'd blown the whole thing off with the disclaimer: 'That's a nine-year-old boy for you.'

I'd had two nine-year-old boys of my own once, so I knew very well that was not the case.

This wasn't even the nine year old's most grievous offense, just the most recent one I'd seen firsthand.

The seven-year-old could be found on any given afternoon pounding his five-year-old brother senseless. Everyone, and I mean everyone, that saw this, tried to interfere and stop it, but the parents were adamant that the youngest brother needed said poundings, to 'toughen him up.'

And the five year old, who I pitied the most out of all three feral boys, was best known for digging beach ball sized craters in other people's nicely tended yards, or in general just destroying property, as all three kids were left unsupervised most hours of the day.

They were all bullies or headed that way, but you didn't blame kids that young for things like that.

Everyone blamed the parents. Because the parents were dickheads.

Messy dickheads. The kind of messy that literally fell onto everyone around them.

Literally because of the unruly dog they let loose to roam for hours, day and night, pooping in everyone's yard and going after any dogs that crossed his path.

My dog, Tato, left a mess in my backyard, but I knew said mess was my responsibility to clean up.

Their dog, in typical dickhead fashion, left its mess everywhere *except* their backyard, i.e. every front yard on the block.

When it was mentioned to them by Virginia Gant, a sweet old lady of sixty-four that lived three houses down from me, that this was perhaps a rude thing to do, their response was to send their three boys door to door, with custom made business cards, offering to clean up the dog poop around the neighborhood . . . for a fee.

They'd turned being irresponsible parents and pet owners into a business. I almost admired their nerve for that one. And of course, the story made for a good laugh.

The dad (when he was around) was the type you had to keep out of arm's reach as he tended to find any excuse to get touchy feely with women who were not his wife.

And the mom, who was always perplexed when anyone confronted her for her many, many messes, had backed her car into the side of the back bumper of mine just a few months back.

My car was in drive, hers in reverse as she'd been zipping like a speed demon out of her driveway, music blasting, right as I'd been pulling away.

I'd honked three times, loudly, but she'd slammed into me nonetheless, and later claimed I'd never honked.

And then she'd claimed we were equally at fault, that we'd backed into *each other*, even though I hadn't even been backing up.

And then she'd claimed that, *no, wait, she took it all back,* because she was pretty sure suddenly that it had been *me that backed into her.*

The entire incident had been wildly frustrating for someone like me, who tended to stick to the truth, because her story had changed about three times before we'd settled the issue, but eventually the insurance company had ruled her at fault, and I'd just been avoiding her crazy ass since then.

The best way to describe the Dickhead Dillons would be to say they got off on conflict. They *enjoyed* negative attention, of any kind, as far as I could tell.

They were the worst neighbors ever, but that being said they only rarely had the opportunity to bother me personally.

For the most part, they were more amusing than anything else, hell, they gave the rest of the neighbors something funny to talk about on a regular basis, but add to that the fact that I knew Deborah had sided with my ex in the divorce, and would tell him what she'd seen before the day was out, and, well, all amusement quickly turned into annoyance.

"Why don't you like that woman?" Heath asked me when we'd passed out of her earshot.

Of course he would notice something like that. I hadn't said a word, hadn't even made an unpleasant face, but I was sure my hand had tightened on his.

Where to start with that question? I stuck to the pertinent issue at hand. "She's friends with my ex-husband. She'll be calling him to tell him all about seeing us holding hands by the end of the day, I guarantee it."

"Will that bother him? Is he still jealous over you?"

I looked for the right words, knowing it would be easy to put my foot in my mouth on this subject. "Not likely. It's more that he'll enjoy . . . rubbing your age in my face. He'll use it to say nasty things to me, I expect."

"Want me to rearrange *his* face for you?"

I smiled, assuming he was joking. I studied him for a moment, and the smile died. "No, no, of course not. My ex is a nuisance, nothing else. He doesn't even bother me anymore. There's certainly no need for violence."

That seemed to settle the subject, or at least he let me drop it after that.

"Would you ever let me photograph you?" I asked him idly sometime later as I studied his stern face in the sunlight. It made me long for my camera.

I shot a look at him as I waited for his answer.

His expression told me clearly that this would never happen. "Not likely," he said, and we both knew it was an understatement.

We were still walking hand in hand, had been for quite some time, sort of like a normal couple. It was nice.

"I'd keep the pictures for myself."

"No can do. Sorry."

He actually did sound sorry, so I dropped it.

"You know, if we wanted to be normal, we'd do something crazy tonight like leave my house and go out on a date."

He stopped walking so abruptly that it jerked on my arm.

"You want that?" he asked. I couldn't read what he thought about the idea, not from his tone or expression.

My mouth twisted wryly. "Most women like to be taken out on dates sometimes, Heath. It's pretty normal."

He looked thoughtful more than anything, like he was taking it all in. "What would this date consist of?"

Impossible man.

"Dinner. Drinks. Maybe dancing."

He looked a little horrified by the last suggestion.

It was exasperating. "Jesus, it was just an idea. Hell, just take me out to dinner and a movie. What is the big fucking deal?"

"You pick the movie."

"I'd be happy to, just so long as you don't complain when I pick a romantic comedy. You probably only like action flicks, I bet."

His face was caught somewhere between bewildered and stiff.

I found it endearing that something this mundane was stressing him out.

"I don't like action flicks," he finally said. "I hate them. Whatever *you* like. A romantic comedy is as good as anything."

I thought that was promising.

"And where would you like to eat?" he asked.

"Surprise me. No fast food, though. I do expect a sit down meal."

He took in a deep breath, let it out. "I'm just going to pick wrong. If you could tell me where you want to go, we'd both have a better evening."

I studied him. This was a foreign process to him, I could see that. And so I made it easier on him.

"Okay. I'll find the right show time, and I'll pick the restaurant. But you're driving, mister."

He flashed his teeth at me in what could only be called a sinister grin. "Of course I am. That was never a question."

I'd suggested it, but the way he said it was a bit infuriating. I wasn't the least bit surprised by his statement, though. He would be the type that always had to drive.

He hadn't even let me hold my own dog's leash on this walk.

CHAPTER
FOURTEEN

I'd taken my cell phone with me on the walk as there were a few clients I was expecting calls from. When it started buzzing, though, and I saw who was actually calling, I cursed.

My fucking ex.

He *would* call today. Talk about the worst luck in the world.

Or worse, had Deborah already called and told him she'd seen me and Heath?

Dammit.

"What's the matter?" Heath asked tonelessly. His eyes were on my phone, and I had this strange thought that he knew who was calling.

The lock screen had lit up with *EDUARD CALLING*, and it was likely he could have read it from where he was standing.

Instead of answering, I was studying him.

He was fascinating to me. Expressionless, toneless, but all of it somehow telling me that he was agitated.

I tried to shake off the suspicion, but it just wasn't working.

"So how much do you know about me?" I asked him slowly. "How much did you uncover in your . . . background check?"

"I know that's your ex-husband calling. I know you divorced him because he's a cheating piece of shit."

Wow. He'd apparently done his research. I was torn on how freaked out I should be about that.

"Why's he bugging you?" he asked, through his teeth. "I know you don't have anything to do with him anymore. What does he want?"

I grimaced. I really hated to talk about this. "He does this every so often, calls to chew me out. He thinks it's my fault that his sons don't want anything to do with him anymore. But if I had to guess why he's calling *right now*, I'd say it's because of Deborah, that neighbor you noticed I don't like. Remember how I said she'd tell my ex about seeing you and me together? I didn't think she'd work this fast, but here it is."

My phone started buzzing again. Irritated, I answered with, "What do you want, Eduard?" My tone was biting.

My ex-husband took immediate exception to my tone. "Is that any way to greet the father of your children?" he shot back.

"What do you want?" I repeated.

He cut right to the chase. "How old is he?"

Ugh. He was so predictably unpleasant about *everything*. Divorce brought out the worst in everyone, but Eduard had sunk to new levels of low over the past year. "Have you been talking to your good friend Deborah?"

"At least older than our sons, I hope?" He was in a mood. Usually he didn't escalate this quickly into straight asshole when he called. Generally he tried cajoling first.

"Not doing this," I bit out, already thoroughly annoyed.

"I had no idea you were such a cougar, Lourdes."

"Not doing this," I repeated, about a second away from hanging up on him.

"Maybe that's why we didn't work out. I was too *old* for you."

That was too much. "It's not a mystery why we didn't work out. You were sleeping with my ex-best friend." I caught myself, just barely, from resorting to name-calling.

"You never even let me explain about that!" His voice was close to a shout in my ear.

Oh. Ugh. This man. How had I been fooled by him for so long?

"None of this matters," I said, voice going very blank and cold. I wouldn't give him the satisfaction.

I was starting to suspect that he enjoyed our hostile interactions. Why else would he go out of his way to make them happen?

"Tell me why you're calling," I said slowly. "And it had better be productive, or I'm hanging up in exactly five seconds."

"You're lucky, you know. I could have pressed assault charges against both you and Rafael for what you did to me."

Ugh. This man. Grrr.

He rendered me incapable of coherent thoughts he was so frustrating to deal with.

"Are you threatening to press charges against your own child right now?" I shot back, astounded that Eduard was even capable of disgusting me more than he usually did. "Is this a joke?"

"If I had known, if I'd had any clue, that you were vindictive enough to turn my children against me—"

I hung up in the middle of his tirade.

"Assault?" Heath's tone was sardonic.

I looked up at him, smiling ruefully. "It's a long story."

"I'm here all day."

I sighed, and let it spill.

"For the record, I'm normally a pacifist."

"Noted," Heath drawled.

"But, and I guess you know this, or at least part of it, I caught him cheating on me. He butt dialed me while he was having sex with my ex-best friend. I heard enough to be certain that it was them and what they were doing."

I paused, trying to read his expression. "My reaction, more than anything, was fury. I became so furious that I *did* assault him."

"How?"

I always felt like a psycho retelling this story, especially now that I was so completely free of my ex. But I told him. If you wanted someone to open up to you, of course you had to reciprocate.

"I waited until he got home, honestly not knowing what to say to him, and he acted like everything was normal when he greeted me. He went right away to take a shower, and that was when I lost my temper. You see, he'd done that a lot, come in from wherever and gone immediately to shower. He must have been stepping out on me for ages, and I hadn't a clue."

I studying him a while, trying and failing to gauge his reaction, and finally continued, "I grabbed the Fabuloso and his belt."

"I like where this is headed," Heath noted, and it made me smile. At least he didn't think I was a complete nutcase. Yet.

"I sprayed the ground right in front of the shower. It's very smooth marble. The second he stepped out, he slipped, cracked his head hard on the counter, and landed on his ass."

"Good," Heath said succinctly.

I smiled. I should have known this wouldn't remotely shock him. "That's when I took a belt to him, buckle first."

"Good," he repeated.

"I beat the shit out of him, beat him until he ran out of the house, naked, just to get away from me. Then I locked him out. Filed for divorce as soon as humanly possible."

"That doesn't explain why he's threatening your son with assault charges."

"Rafael, my oldest, beat him up rather severely when he found out what his father had done. Still, I can't believe Eduard would threaten his own child like that."

"He's a scumbag. Want me to take care of him for you?"

I felt my eyes growing wide. If it were anyone else, I'd have assumed they were joking. "Do you mean . . . ?"

"I'm not talking about killing him. I guarantee I can get him to leave you alone without resorting to that."

Now *that* was half tempting. But I restrained myself.

"He's nothing I can't handle. To be perfectly honest, he just annoys me at this point. And the assault charges are bogus. If he was going to do that, he'd have done it ages ago, when he could've proven it."

"Why do you think he's still harassing you? And why is he so concerned about who you're seeing? Do you think he's trying to get you back?"

"God, no. But, you know, it's started to occur to me that there's a motivation behind it, and it's not that he wants to see more of our sons."

"What then?"

"I . . . " God, I hated talking about this. "Well, you see, I've always had I guess what you could call a trust fund, for lack of a better word. From my father. And I've had a few successful careers over the years.

Long story short, I've got a bit of money saved up." Several hundred thousand, to be exact. "And my ex knows it. He thinks he can use this to somehow get more money from me."

"Motherfucker." Heath's voice was low, and his tone managed to achieve a rather intriguing combination of being both blank and succinct. "You let me know if you change your mind, okay? I'd have no problem whatsoever putting that guy in his place."

I nodded, wondering what to do with him.

We started walking again.

"You should show me your house. Didn't you say it was around here?"

He took a deep breath, and I just knew he was about to lie to me. "It's a mess," he hedged. "I'll take you there on another day, after I've straightened up."

"Are you telling me that you're a slob?"

"Yeah," he said, no hesitation.

I didn't believe that for one second, not any of it. He either didn't live around here, or there was another reason he wasn't bringing me back to his place.

Dammit. And we'd been doing okay, making progress. But at this simple lie, some seeds of suspicion were planted.

What if he had a live-in girlfriend?

Fuck. What if he had a wife?

"Do you have a girlfriend . . . or a wife?" I asked him point blank, watching his face carefully.

A look of very pure annoyance crossed his face, and I breathed out a sigh of relief. He was genuinely offended at the question, and I found that boundlessly reassuring.

"No. Of course not. I wouldn't be with you now if I did. Is that what you think of me?"

Now *I* was on the defense. Oh, he was good. "No," I said carefully. "It's just never bad to be clear, I figure."

He grunted (this one was annoyed, I thought), and we started walking again.

CHAPTER
FIFTEEN

Next, I took him to my gym, because he asked what I liked to do on my day off, and my first and favorite choice, spending time with my boys, seemed inappropriate. I didn't even want to guess what my sons would think of Heath and our age difference.

My next few choices were shot down emphatically. Shopping was not his thing, and I had a good feeling that I wouldn't be changing his mind about that.

And no, he hadn't changed his opinion about me photographing him.

So we settled on a plan. We'd hit the gym, then I'd head back to my place to shower, and he'd go grab a few things from his place, make a few phone calls (for work), then come to pick me up for our date.

We actually went over all of this, every detail. Heath seemed to think the day needed to be handled with a well thought out strategy. I figured this was just another one of his quirks.

"I'm guessing you'll head straight to the free weights," I said, after I'd checked us both in. I got a few guest passes every month, so Heath had been able to accompany me without a hitch.

"I'm guessing you'll start out with cardio," he returned.

We smiled at each other. So we did have a few things in common that didn't involve a bed.

I found a treadmill with the best view of the free weight area, tossed my hand towel across the top, and started stretching, my eyes on Heath. I figured that watching him workout would be a treat.

And he did not disappoint.

When we'd been going over the day's plans, he'd mentioned to me that he didn't have a gym membership anywhere, or even a home gym, and I'd had a hard time believing it. He was in perfect shape. Beyond perfect into mind-blowing, to be precise. No one got that way without work.

But, watching him work out, I quickly caught on why it made sense.

I'd clocked him as military, and his workout was surely proof of it. It was grueling, but called for little beyond some room on the floor and a pull-up bar that took a lot of weight.

I didn't even realize I was counting his pushups in my head until a voice from the machine next to me started counting off the numbers in a mutter. They were that impressive.

I was running by then, but I shot a glance to my right, taking in the other woman who was shamelessly watching Heath go through his routine.

She was pretty. And at least ten years younger than I was. And clearly into Heath.

I started looking around the room, noticing *all* of the female attention he was getting.

I could certainly see why.

He didn't pace himself at all, going through his routine at full speed, and in a way that could only be described as punishing. Even in a large building full of people in excellent shape, his body and methods caught the eye.

When he got to the pull-up bar, I even heard one of the fawning women gasp, and I couldn't really blame her.

His pace was astounding. If this was the end of the world, and the only way you could save humanity was to do as many pull-ups as possible, Heath was definitely going to save us all. And it wasn't just the pull-ups. This was how he approached every new maneuver.

I had to squint and do a double take when I saw the size of the weights he used for a long round of surrenders.

At one point, a very hot young brunette approached him, smiling, flirting from across the room.

Oh wow. I was jealous, and it was *awful*.

I was not the jealous type. I'd always been very confident in myself, had felt secure even with my cheating husband, until of course I found out he was a cheat and my best friend was a home-wrecking whore.

But even then, rather than getting jealous, I'd gotten rid of the dead weight that was my loser of a husband. I'd known it was he that was flawed, not me, and I'd moved the hell on with my life.

I was not a jealous soul.

Or so I had thought.

But then Heath did something that I found made me feel kind of wonderful.

He blew the girl off rather aggressively, with a less than friendly go away motion of his hand, and a sharp, short shake of his head.

She went away, looking baffled.

It was hard not to smile about that.

I wrapped up my cardio at the fifty-minute mark, and he was still going strong, so I hit some of the lighter weight machines, doing lower body reps and mourning the loss of my perfect view of him.

I only had two machines left in my rotation when he showed up at my side, looking oiled up with sweat and good enough to eat.

"You finished?" I asked him on an exhale.

He jerked his shoulder up in a half shrug. "Whenever you are." He was studying me intently. "We've been at this for hours. How do you never sweat?" As he spoke, his eyes raked over me.

I did sweat, it was just minimal, and what was there was hard to see, but there were a few spots: Into my hair, but the dark color hid it well. And strangely, the outsides of my elbows.

I showed him said elbows. He traced a finger over the slight bit of moisture there.

"That's it?" he asked.

I nodded.

He opened his mouth to say something, I'll never know what, because he was interrupted by another hot young thing brushing up beside him.

"I saw you working out," she told him, smacking her gum. She had one of those Kardashian accents that made me cringe, and she was acting like I wasn't even there or like she assumed he wasn't with me. It was infuriating, and I felt another hot stab of awful jealousy.

But his focus was so sharply on me that the feeling went as quickly as it came. He didn't even notice, let alone care about all of the attention and admiration being sent blatantly his way.

"Do you mind backing up?" he said tersely, not so much as glancing at her. "You're in my personal space, and I don't even fucking know you."

She sent him a dirty look and stalked away.

I covered my mouth to stifle a laugh. He was brutal.

"I hate your gym," he told me. "It's a fucking meat market. I don't know how you can stand it."

I bit my lip, again to stifle a laugh. I couldn't really blame him. I got more than my fair share of male attention on a pretty regular basis, but it was never anywhere approaching what he'd been put through in a few short hours.

"Let's get out of here," I responded.

We went for coffee next door to my gym.

"What kind of music do you like?" I asked him.

Of course he turned it on me. How very Heath. "What kind do you like? I bet I can guess."

It struck me at that moment how we were looking at each other, with near twin expressions, if you could discount his broken, lifeless eyes. We were smiling at each other like old friends, neither of us hiding our obvious affection for the other.

What strange things we brought out in each other. Strange, wonderful things.

"Go ahead," I told him. "Guess."

"You like *everything*. You're a moody listener. Whatever strikes your fancy."

Dammit. "It's like you know me."

One of his big, rough fingers stroked feather light over my cheekbone. "I want that. To know you. I really want that."

Sweet, strange man. "My turn."

His smile widened, and it nearly took my breath away. I'd never seen him do anything quite like it, all of his inherent meanness gone from his face, the ever present tough guy gone for one brief moment.

He looked happy. God, he was gorgeous. And so young. It was easy to forget.

"Go for it," he prompted. "I can't wait to hear what you'll come up with."

"Death metal. You're a metal head."

He laughed, threw back his head and laughed.

I can't deny, just seeing it had me falling just a little bit harder for him.

I knew this was precious, a rare showing for Heath, and all I wanted to do was devote my time and energy into bringing this out of him, to cultivating his softer side.

I was a chronic fixer. Hopeless, really.

"No," he said finally. "Not even a little. That sort of music gets on my nerves. Too loud and disorderly."

"Rock?"

"No."

"Rap."

Another laugh, and I fell a little deeper, damn him.

"No."

"Country?"

"No."

"Um . . . pop?" I was running out of options.

He leaned forward and kissed me on the forehead. "Not likely."

"Okay, I give up."

"Classical music is the only stuff I listen to by choice. It's . . . peaceful. The rest is just chaos to me."

I never would have guessed.

He was so complicated, and God was I a sucker for a complicated man.

I had kind of assumed (and hoped) that we'd mess around before getting ready to go out, but no such luck. Heath left me at my front door with an obligatory goodbye and a warning that he'd be back in an hour.

Eek, I thought. I wanted more than an hour. I was pretty sure I *needed* more.

This was, after all, our very first date.

I'd never even gotten a chance to dress up for him. He'd seen me sans makeup/sans clothes more than anything else.

I hopped in the shower in a rush, washing my hair, though I knew it took nearly an hour just to get the thick masses dry.

I had my wet hair wrapped in a towel as I perused my closet. Dinner and a movie was the strangest kind of date to dress for, but this was Vegas. Just a few days ago, I'd seen someone in a full out ball gown at the grocery store. *Anything* went here. It was one of my favorite things about this town.

I loved clothes. Shopping was an enduring obsession of mine, but I was dressing for a man who I knew would not appreciate anything about the latest trends.

So I went for sexy and flirty with my favorite little black dress. I hadn't worn the thing in ages, but nothing flattered my figure more. It showed off my legs and just enough cleavage to turn some heads.

The stretchy jersey material hugged my chest and waist, dipping in to accentuate my curves, then flowed out in a short, A-line skirt.

I left my hair wavy, which saved time, but went all out with the makeup, going for a smoky eye and red lips, so I was still pushing it to the very last minute.

I slipped into my favorite black Lady Peep Louboutins. They were sky high, but Heath was tall enough that I could get away with it.

I grabbed a light jacket since I always got cold at the show.

I was ready almost to the second, which was a good thing, because Heath was at my door exactly on time.

CHAPTER
SIXTEEN

His reaction to my efforts was gratifying. His eyes were indecent as they took me in head to toe.

He was wearing a dark polo and dark wash jeans, and he looked good enough to eat in tiny, savoring bites.

"You sure you want to go anywhere tonight?" he asked.

In answer, I shut and locked my door.

He cursed under his breath.

He led me to his car, a Jaguar F-type that I knew had to cost upwards of a hundred grand.

"Is this your car?" I asked him as I slid into the passenger's seat. I was back to wondering again if he was a criminal.

"I'm borrowing it," he said after he got behind the wheel. And of course he didn't elaborate.

I picked a gourmet burger place for dinner. I didn't imagine Heath would appreciate gourmet French cuisine the way I did, so I settled on my second favorite—a perfect burger.

"So if they leave out the e, it makes it gourmet?" Heath asked as we approached the restaurant *Burgr*.

I sent him a sideways smile. He did have a sense of humor, I was finding out. It was just very dry. "Do you like burgers?"

"Yeah. I have to say, I was worried you'd pick someplace with frog legs or something."

"I found a compromise."

The restaurant was crowded, and I wasn't imagining it, people were definitely staring at me, then him, then back at me as we were shown to our table.

"People are staring at us," I said quietly.

Heath glanced around and stared at some people until they looked away. "So?"

"They're staring at us because I'm sixteen years older than you."

He leaned in close, his eyes all over me. "You're right that people are staring. But not at us. At you. But this I guarantee, no one is staring at you because of that."

I felt instantly better. He really did have a sweet side.

I ordered a martini, and he ordered a water.

"You don't drink alcohol?" I asked him when the waiter had left.

"I do, occasionally, but most of the time I like to keep my senses sharp."

I gave him my best imploring smile. "This is a date. You don't need to stay sharp. This is when you *relax*."

After staring me down for a brief moment, he called the waiter back and ordered a beer.

"Anything look good to you?" I asked him after he'd perused the menu for a bit.

He just shrugged.

"I can tell you what's good."

He shrugged again. "I'll just have whatever you're having."

"Do you mind having an egg on your burger?"

"Sounds fine."

I ordered the truffle fries and two farm burgers. It was simple, but the best burger: duck breast bacon, English sharp cheddar, and a fried egg. Perfection.

"So good, right?" I asked him after the first bite. I was one and a half martinis deep, and he'd downed nearly his entire pint of beer. I was feeling great and it might have been my imagination, but I thought he was starting to relax.

"It's good," he agreed, then proceeded to finish the burger off in under two minutes.

I was about a third of the way through mine. "Should we order you another one?" I teased him.

His answer was to finish off the fries. Then my fries. Then his beer. He ordered another and I almost cheered. I wanted him to have a good time tonight, wanted him to unwind and open up, and alcohol seemed like a great way to make that happen.

"Do you like to gamble?" he asked me.

The restaurant was located inside of a casino, as most of the good ones were in this town.

"Very rarely. How about you?"

"Never, if I can help it."

"I don't mind losing the random twenty dollars on a few rounds of blackjack," I shared, just to keep the conversation going.

His brows went up like I'd said something fascinating. "My . . . friend is obsessed with blackjack. She counts cards. Makes a fortune whenever she needs it."

"Really? Isn't that illegal?"

"It's actually not. The casino will blacklist you if they catch you, but she sticks to the smaller establishments, wins little bits at a time, then moves on."

"Wow. She must be smart."

"She's brilliant."

I wondered who this brilliant friend was. She was important to him, I could tell with just a few sentences. And the hesitation before he said the word friend bothered me a bit.

Also, he quickly changed the subject, like he hadn't meant to bring her up at all.

Other than that, though, dinner went well.

The movie, well, that was another story.

Intense was the best word to describe that part.

He was bored as hell walking in the door. This was not his thing. He was humoring me. Proving a point? Or just trying to be nice? I couldn't say.

Once the actual movie started, though, things changed a bit.

I had a loud laugh. I knew this. It's also the kind of laugh I just couldn't hold back.

I loved me some romantic comedy, and this was a good one.

I laughed hard.

Once I started laughing, he stopped being bored. He didn't watch the movie so much as study me for most of it, putting his arm around me and leaning close when I started laughing like he was taking it in, inhaling it. Soaking it up.

I reached over and touched his knuckles lightly. He grasped my hand instantly and firmly, interweaving our fingers, watching himself do it like he couldn't quite believe it was happening, like he'd surprised himself with the action.

We both just stared at our hands for a while, and the whole time I was thinking about how horrible I was at casual sex. An utter failure at the casual part of it.

And then I went back to laughing, and he went back to watching me.

He didn't even smile much, but something about the way he was staring at me, his eyes losing some of their usual shutter, had me feeling things I hadn't thought I'd ever feel again.

When he looked at me like that, it's hard to even describe, but I'd never felt more beautiful, never felt more desirable, never more joyful, or hopeful.

How could the way someone looked at you change the way you saw your life?

And how was I just now finding this?

And—what *was* it?

But I knew. It was different from the first time, *I* was different, but, regardless of how fast it was happening, I knew what it was.

That first sweet blushing bloom of the L word.

I was embarrassed to even *think* it, but we did have a moment in there, where something occurred. Both of us softened toward the other just that little bit more, that profound distance between intense interest and true affection, between adoration and endearment, and suddenly the future looked very bright and exciting.

This new, familiar, *alien* feeling was as scary as it was utterly addictive.

"So that was a date," he stated.

We were driving back to my house.

"Yes, it was," I agreed, tone wry.

"Was it a good one?"

I bit my lip to keep from laughing. "You tell me," I urged him.

"Depends. Do I get to fuck you soon?" He sounded surly.

I tensed. Just when I thought things were going so well that I was giddy with it, he had to open his big mouth.

"It seems likely," I told him slowly. "Though the more you talk, the less likely it is."

"Noted. Shutting my mouth until you're ready to fuck."

I tried not to grit my teeth. He could be such an asshole. The only redeeming part of that was that I didn't think he had any idea how to be any different. For whatever reason, he'd never developed that kind of a filter.

"Do you enjoy spending time with me, doing anything besides fucking?" I asked.

He sighed. "I hated that movie."

My mouth twisted. He hadn't had to tell me. I'd known that.

"Fuckin' *hated* it. But I'd sit through it again. I'd put that thing on repeat just to watch *you* watching it. To see you laugh like that."

And just like that, he turned it all around. Sneaky man.

"I love it when you say sweet things to me," I told him, voice breathless.

"I'm not good at sweet."

"You have your moments. Tell me another sweet thing. Let's see if you can do it again."

He didn't even miss a beat, like it had already been on the tip of his tongue. "You're the best sex I've ever had."

Wow. That shocked me into silence. And made me feel good, *really good*, because I believed him. I didn't think he'd lie about something like that, didn't think he'd waste the energy or the breath.

"You too," I finally managed to respond.

"Good," he growled, his hand going to my knee.

And just that easy, from that one simple touch, hot life flooded inside of me.

I realized that he hadn't had me since this morning. Nearly a full day and it felt like *ages*.

I felt deprived. Needy. Desperate for him.

I leaned toward him, hand going to his chest, touching softly because I knew the area was sensitive. "Drive faster," I breathed into his ear.

He floored it.

When he parked at the curb in front of my house, I pretty much shot out of the car and ran to the front door, fumbling to unlock it fast enough. But I needn't have rushed. He was still at his car fishing a big duffle bag out of his trunk, by the time I got the door open.

I stopped what I was doing to stare at him.

"I'd like to stay a few days, if you don't mind," he said as he approached and saw that my gaze was transfixed on the bag.

"Not at all," I said, voice faux casual and went inside.

"There's not much extra room in my closet," I told him. Which was a huge understatement. Due to my lifelong love of shopping, the thing was stuffed. "But there are other closets, and feel free to put whatever in my bathroom. Just make yourself at home."

I cringed inside. *Did I sound too needy?* I didn't know. I'd never done anything like this. Sleepovers were out of my realm, one of the many quirks of marrying young and staying married for too damn long.

This relationship, for lack of a better word, was unprecedented for me.

He didn't seem interested in unpacking. The second we got into my bedroom, he tossed the duffle in the middle of the floor and started rummaging through it.

I saw why a few seconds later as he straightened, grinning at me, a pair of padded handcuffs hooked on one of his fingers.

Oh yeah. That.

I'd almost forgotten about our little agreement.

"Undress," he told me gruffly.

I did it leisurely, slipping the shoulders off my dress and dragging it sensuously down my body.

I stood straight when I was left in just my bra, panties, and stilettos.

"All of it. Except the shoes. Keep the shoes on."

I smiled at him as I shimmied out of my lacy underthings.

"Get on the bed," he enunciated slowly.

I took a deep breath and obeyed, climbing onto the bed in my platforms, doing it seductively, gazing at him over my shoulder to give him a sultry smile and take in his reaction, which made me feel as beautiful as I knew it would.

"On your back. Arms above your head."

I lay down on my back, throwing my arms up above my head, a willing lamb to the slaughter. An eager one.

I'd never done kink, though I knew a lot about it, thanks to having made some very kinky friends in recent years.

I'd never done it, but I wasn't against it. I thought it was hot, in a vague, *probably not my thing* sort of way.

But right then, I was thinking, *maybe it's* just *my kind of thing.* Or at least, the part that Heath seemed interested in.

"Just handcuffs, right?" I asked to be sure.

Handcuffs I was pretty comfortable with. The idea of him having me helpless the first few times we were together had been too much for me, but I felt like I knew him well enough now. I mean, if he wanted to hurt me, if he was even capable of it, I'd have gotten some sense of it by now.

And I trusted him, in a way. In a few important ways, actually.

"Yes. Just handcuffs. Now spread your legs," he ordered.

I spread them wide, flexing and angling my body to its best advantage.

It seemed to do the trick.

He fell on me, shoving his tongue down my throat as he cuffed me to the bed. He did it so fast, like he'd trained for it, and hell, maybe he had.

His big hands grasped at me, fondling my breasts, then twisting and pinching roughly at my nipples.

He reared back abruptly, grabbing my ass in both hands and pounding into me with a guttural moan.

He didn't take me slow or gentle.

He took me like he had a point to prove, a point that could only be found by hammering so hard into me that he reached the other side.

It was heaven.

I screamed. And came. The most explosive orgasm of my life.

"Are you okay?" he asked a few beats later.

I couldn't really blame him for asking. I'd let out a racket for a good minute back there.

"Yes," I panted back.

"Good," he grunted and seemed to take it as permission for the next round.

He freed my hands, turning me onto my stomach while I was still catching my breath. He forced me up onto my knees, and I felt him at my entrance again, his stiff, thick length pushing at me already, while I still twitched from the last invasion.

He fucked me again, jolting into me roughly from behind, both of us on all fours.

It was a long time later, when we were capable of getting out full sentences again, that he spoke. "I *do* like spending time with you out of bed. But for the record, if it'd been up to me, we'd never have left your bed today."

"Oh." I paused. The day had been nice, very nice, but . . . "I wouldn't have minded that one bit." Vast understatement.

"I didn't want to be an asshole, so I thought it was safest for you to decide how we spent the day."

"Well, you were a good sport, so how about you pick what we do tomorrow?"

"Okay. I have one errand I have to run sometime in the morning, but after that, you're all mine."

I swear I fell asleep still smiling.

CHAPTER
SEVENTEEN

The next morning did not turn out quite how I had expected.

Not even close, actually. It was both better and worse.

I awoke to hearing noises in my house that I couldn't figure out. They just didn't compute in my sleep-dazed mind.

I walked out of my bedroom, wearing nothing but a thin silk robe that hit at mid-thigh, to find Heath, shirtless and just in his boxers, in the kitchen, a cup of coffee in his hand, chatting with my oldest son, Raf.

I might have had a small heart attack.

Thank God it was Raf. My youngest would have taken a swing at a shirtless man in my kitchen, whereas Raf seemed to be chatting him up. He was not one to swing first and ask questions later. That wasn't to say he wasn't every bit as protective of me as his brother. He was just more levelheaded.

He was more likely to ask the questions, and then swing if he didn't like the answers.

I approached the two men tentatively, wondering if it would do more or less damage if I ran back into my room to put on more than a robe.

The opportunity was lost to me as both of them noticed me right away.

Raf grinned at me, and Heath turned back to the coffeepot and began to make me a cup. He prepped it just the way I liked, though I couldn't remember why he should know that.

"Good morning, Mom," Raf said.

"Morning," rumbled Heath, his voice sounding gravelly and unused, as it usually did, no matter how much he used it.

I hugged my son briefly, took the perfectly tailored cup of coffee that Heath handed me, murmured a quiet, "Thank you" to him, and leaned against the counter about two feet from Heath and across from Raf.

My gaze moved back and forth as the two of them continued chatting as though all of this was perfectly normal.

It was not. Inside, I was freaking the hell out.

Did this make me a horrible mother?

And, *how horrible of a mother did this make me?*

But then I remembered how old Raf was, and observed how well he seemed to be taking it all, and I felt worlds better.

But then I remembered how old Heath was (not much older than Raf!) and went back to freaking the hell out.

Oh my God. What was I doing? And why did they both seem to think this was way more normal than it was? And . . .

Were they actually getting along?

Hitting it off?

Never in a million years would I have imagined this could go down the way it did. But it only did for two simple reasons.

Raf.

And Heath.

It was like they wanted to get along even more than *I* wanted it.

I started blinking rapidly as I realized why this was. Heart melting for both of them.

They *did* want it more. And the reason was simple. *Me.* They wanted it more *for me.*

How wonderful was that?

And that was the moment I was sure that Heath cared about me. Not just wanted me. *Cared* about me. About what would trouble me, and what would make me happy. And he knew me well enough, apparently, to know how to handle this specifically awkward situation.

I'm not sure I can describe it, but it was endearing as almost nothing else could have been, and in a way that could only pave its way *straight* to my heart.

The way Heath, this gruff man of few words, bent over backwards to be respectful of me, and to me, to my son.

Sincerity fairly oozed off him as he tried his best to portray to my son that, while it was obvious he had spent the night at my house, he was there, not for some sleazy reason, but because he *cared* about me.

Heath glanced over at me, and his whole hard face softened as he caught what must have been a smitten, dazed look on my face.

He took a deep breath and moved to me.

"Hey," Heath said, cupping the back of my head and giving me some intense eye contact. "I need to get ready to go work for a few hours, but I'll be back in time to go to the grocery store with you."

Whatever that meant, I thought.

He kissed me lightly on the forehead and went back to my bedroom to get dressed.

After he was gone, I faced my son as squarely as I could, tried to make eye contact, but couldn't stop a grimace. "Busted," I said with a sigh.

He laughed, and a weight lifted off my shoulders. I'd been worried that, I don't know, I guess that my dating again would somehow affect my sons badly. Like it would *damage* them somehow. But Raf did not seem at all damaged. I couldn't have been more relieved.

"So . . . you're actually okay with this?" My tone was hopeful.

"To tell you the truth, when he answered your door at that hour of the morning and everything, wearing what he was wearing, my first gut instinct was, well, I was a bit appalled about the whole thing. It's sort of a worst nightmare of mine, you . . . hooking up with one of my old classmates or whatever."

I just stared at him. I had no idea what he was talking about.

"I'm sure you noticed," he continued, "but in high school, and even in college, we've had some friends who were pretty f—", he corrected mid-word, "freaking obsessed with you and things would slip, they'd say stuff about you. Well, we got in some fights."

I had noticed, in a vague kind of way, how weird all of his friends were around me, how awkward, and I wasn't stupid or oblivious, and they were teenage boys, so it was easy to figure out why they were being weird and awkward, but I hadn't known that it bothered my boys so much.

And I did remember the fights. I'd hated it when they got in fights. Seeing cuts and bruises on them was a special kind of torture for me. It literally made me feel faint when I thought of either of my children being physically harmed. My reaction to seeing their blood had always been extreme.

"But anyway," Raf continued, "he's not an old or current classmate, so that's not really the issue. He's just young . . . and a little strange, with all the scars on his chest . . . But who the hell cares? He obviously cares about you. And, well, Dad was a *bastard* to you, and you deserve so much better. You deserve to have *whoever* the hell you want, and *you* get to pick who that is. So if you're happy, we're happy."

It was one of those moments you can only have when you're looking at your own child and thinking, *Well, here it is, this is who my child is, and no matter what happens, how they mess up, or what mistakes they make, as people invariably do, I am looking at a* decent *human being. I raised a* good *person.*

Pride could be as profound a thing as love. In its own way, just as powerful. And God, was I proud of my boys.

It wasn't lost on me how ironic it was, the pride I took specifically in Raf's sensitivity.

When he was young, it had manifested early. As early as three I could remember him just *suffering* when he saw anyone else in pain, even if it was just a scraped knee. If he saw another kid get hurt, he was the one that would set up the second ear piercing scream, and I'd run to him, ask him what was wrong. He'd always say something, in the serious little way he had, something like, "I don't want my friends to get hurt," or, "Do you think they're okay? Will they be all right?" Or when he was a little bit older and protective of his kid brother I'd get random outbursts of, "I don't know what I'd *do* if something ever happened to Gustave."

He was the sweetest boy, but it had worried me endlessly how keenly he felt the suffering of others.

But live and learn. What a beautiful person that too sensitive soul had turned into.

"Will you put in a good word to Gustave for me?" I asked him. Gustave, my youngest, was more stubborn, less accepting than Raf, but Raf had a way winning him over to his point of view. "I know . . . the age difference and the suddenness of it all. It would be totally understandable if it freaked you guys out."

"I'll tell him. He'll be fine with it, Mom. I promise. He—we both just want you to be happy. There's not one single thing in the world I want more."

I turned away from him, busied myself, put my mug in the sink, rinsed it out. I didn't want him to see that he'd made me tear up. He hated, more than anything to see me cry.

But he was silent for so long that I knew he'd seen it.

Without even looking at him, I moved into him, burrowing into his chest to give him a hug.

He'd outgrown me when he was fifteen, but to this day, I marveled at how much taller he was than I was. I was not by any means short, but he could still fit my head under his chin.

He squeezed me back.

"I love you, bud," I said into his shirt. "Oceans deep. Rivers wide."

"I know it. I love you back. Just as much. And Gustave is going to take this better than you think."

"I hope so."

"I know so. And it's a good thing, too, since I invited Heath to have dinner with us here."

"You invited him to dinner? Here? With the family?

"Yeah. I like him. I think he's good for you."

Did my son have terrible instincts, and I'd just never noticed it before? Poor judgement on a scale that was until now, unknown to me?

Certainly, where Heath was concerned, I knew I was operating at less than full capacity, as far as brain cells went, but that had everything to do with the fact that I couldn't be in a room with him and form more than a few coherent thoughts in a row.

What was Raf's excuse? What did he see in Heath that made him trust the guy and want him in his beloved mother's life?

I didn't think Heath would ever hurt me. Wrong or right, I *felt* he wouldn't. Felt it deep in my womb, the place where my deepest instincts were grounded. But that didn't mean I thought he was a nice guy or even a normal one. I knew something was up with him. I knew he was dangerous in a very fundamental and literal sense. He'd told me so himself, and I knew there was plenty he hadn't told.

And Raf wanted him to attend a family dinner? Even the thought was ridiculous, for so many reasons.

"I don't think he'd be up for that," I told him, because it was the easiest, shortest way to end the conversation. Because it was true.

"He said yes."

Or not.

"What?" I asked, thinking I'd misunderstood.

"Tonight. I volunteered to help you cook, but he called dibs as your sous chef."

I honestly thought at first that he was messing with me.

Heath came out from the back of the house right then, fully dressed now and called out, "See you tonight, Raf," as he walked out the front door.

Unless they were both messing with me, it looked like this was happening. Tonight.

So much for spending the day in bed.

CHAPTER
EIGHTEEN

Raf left a while later, promising to be back for dinner at six. I'm not sure if I was just being paranoid, but the way he said it sounded ominous.

I *am* being paranoid, I quickly decided.

I found myself in my closet, wondering what the hell a woman wore for a day like this. I'd never introduced my boys to anyone I was dating, for obvious reasons. Most of their lives, I'd been married to their father, and after that I'd been on only a few casual dates with no one special.

And now this. What *was* this? Boys, meet the man I'm sleeping with who, though I'm borderline obsessed with him, may or may not still be around a week from now.

Ideally, I could have avoided this altogether. Well, maybe that wasn't ideal because that would mean Heath was gone for good. But certainly, if I had any luck at all, I wouldn't be dealing with this quite so early on in a budding relationship with a volatile, unpredictable man.

I gave myself a pep talk. At least the age difference thing hadn't freaked Raf out *too much*. At least Heath had been on his best behavior. Both of them had, so there was that. And it was a lot.

And so, what to wear. Casual? Feminine? Flirty? Definitely nothing too sexy, certainly not for the first time my boys were meeting my—whatever Heath was.

I settled on a short, patterned tank dress in a soft nude and gray that set off the warm glow to my skin tone. The sweetheart neckline hugged my collarbone in an appealing way, but didn't reveal too much cleavage, and the pleated wrap bodice was fitted and showed off all of my curves, but could in no way be considered tight.

It was a touch sexy, but in a romantic, feminine way, which I thought (hoped) was the appropriate balance for the occasion.

I picked out some pale pink sandals to wear when we went to run errands, but stayed barefoot around the house, as I was always barefoot around my house.

I left my hair wavy and loose and wore minimal makeup—a soft pink lip, a touch of blush, mascara.

And then I set to work, planning in detail a meal to impress.

I had an extensive list made out when Heath returned in time to hit the market with me, just like he'd said.

"You don't have to come to the store with me," I told him.

He just shrugged and ignored the statement.

We took my car, but he drove. He was not content to be a passenger, it was clear. His car wasn't around at all, and while I couldn't figure out why or how he'd gotten back to my place,(aside from walking) I just went with it.

"Are you sure you're okay with this?" I asked him, studying his granite profile while he drove.

"Having dinner with you and your kids?"

"Yeah. That."

"I'm sure. We need to face this head on. It might feel a bit sudden to them, but there's nothing to do for it but meet them now with the way Rafael found me at that hour and in your kitchen."

And half naked, I thought, still mentally wincing over that.

"Otherwise," he continued, "your kids are going to think this is some casual hookup situation."

Which clearly implied that . . . ?

"And it's not that, and I don't want your boys thinking that of me and you."

Wow. I had not a clue what to say to that. But he was absolutely right. We did need to face this. If he'd met Rafael like that, and then looked to be avoiding my boys, they could well become hostile.

"You're very sweet," I told him finally.

He shot me a level look when he'd stopped at a red light.

"I'm not sweet, so if I said something that was, you should take it to heart."

I did. In spite of all of my reservations, I absolutely did.

Like all normal, mundane, everyday things I found myself doing with Heath, grocery shopping turned out to be much more interesting and strange than normal.

First of all, it was a Saturday morning, and our first stop was the best organic market in town, so it was a madhouse. Eventually, we split up to get through the list faster. The line for the meat counter alone was a good thirty minute wait, so Heath (sweetly, I thought) volunteered to wait for me.

I knew he was willing to do it because he said so, but he looked like he wanted to be anywhere else. He was too restless and edgy to ever take waiting in stride.

Having this in mind, I tried to go through the rest of my list quickly, hoping to relieve or at least keep him company before he lost his patience, and oh, I don't know, stormed the meat counter.

I caught glimpses of him as I perused the produce. He had women on either side of him in line, and the redheaded one behind him seemed to be trying to get his attention.

Of course this had me peeking between shopping, watching in small glimpses as she inched closer to him.

She was young. No surprise there. And hot. Again, no surprise. Sin City was teeming with young hot things, all here to pursue a career in the seedier side of the entertainment business.

She struck me as a performer on an off day, her face scrubbed free of makeup, her clothes casual but revealing a shapely, lithe figure. She had the body and looks that fit anything from an acrobat to a showgirl, or perhaps a cocktail waitress if she was really new to town.

And she just kept inching closer to Heath. Every time I looked, she was a step further into his space.

Oh my God. I was jealous. Again. Viciously so. And I hated it.

Jealousy was more powerful of a thing than I'd ever given it credit for, I realized.

The idea of it was so much less volatile than the *feeling* of it.

The actuality of it, where before it had always been in my mind some sort of abstract concept, was quietly blowing my mind with how *awful* it was.

No wonder it was so destructive.

I wanted to do something *violent* and *mean* to that nitwit for so much as trying to get his attention.

It was insane. I hated that woman. She was my enemy the second she made a move on him.

Which was so out of character for me.

I was a girl's girl. It was kind of ridiculous how easily I made female friends on a regular basis.

I was a woman that bonded with other women, fast and easy.

I was close with every girl my boys had ever dated for any length of time. Hell, I made new girlfriends nearly every time I went shoe shopping.

I racked my mind and couldn't come up with a time in recent memory that I'd met a woman and had it even cross my mind to look at them as competition.

And here I was, hating on some woman at the grocery store.

I tried to shake it off.

The funny thing was, Heath did nothing on his end to provoke my jealousy.

His arms were folded across his chest in a standoffish manner. His feet were planted far apart, and the closer forward she would edge, speaking to him now, the more he'd turn his body away from her.

He was not encouraging the woman.

He was not flirtatious. Just the opposite. Like at the gym, he was hostile to the woman for so much as speaking to him. Brutally so.

But I remembered clearly how fast, how aggressively, he'd gotten me into bed.

And he hadn't had to *flirt* to do it.

On the other hand, though, he had definitely been the one to approach me, so there was that.

He turned and said something to her briefly, then faced forward again. The girl looked properly put in her place.

I didn't have to hear a word to know what had happened.

She came knocking, and he slammed the door shut in her face.

I fucking loved it.

Biting back a smile, I continued my shopping.

It made me feel all warm and fuzzy as I realized that I'd never seen him show even a remote interest in another woman within my presence.

He made me feel good about myself, and the feeling seemed to be very mutual.

I approached him with a full cart when he was nearly to the front of the line.

I was just in time, it seemed.

The girl was still talking to him, still trying. She must have been one of those pretty girls who'd never been told no before and didn't know how to take it gracefully.

Heath pointed his chin at me as I moved closer. "That's a good question," he was saying, his biting voice intimating clearly that it was *not* a good question. "Why don't you ask my *wife?*"

My eyes went wide, mouth drawing open into a surprised O.

"Your . . ." the girl's voice trailed off as she got a look at me.

"Ask me what?" I spoke to him, playing along, because I thought it was adorable and kind of fascinating that he'd gone with *wife* instead of *girlfriend* in order to get this random girl off his back.

"What do I like to do for fun, honey?" he asked me, deadpan.

I bit my lip to keep in a laugh. The wicked part of me wanted to say *Me*. He likes to do *me* for fun.

Instead I said, "He *loves* movies. Romantic comedies are his favorite."

The silly girl didn't say another word.

And Heath gave me a smile that was downright fond for that.

"Waiting forty minutes for some meat," he muttered to me as I moved to stand next to him. "Never seen anything like it."

I grimaced. "Yeah. Sorry about that. Saturdays at this place are a bitch."

"You have nothing to be sorry for. This whole plan was hatched by Rafael and me. I'm the one that volunteered us to cook tonight."

Well.

That was something. Nothing he did or said was ever what I expected. I was constantly caught off-guard, mostly in a good way, and I wondered if this man would ever stop surprising me.

CHAPTER
NINETEEN

B y the time we finished shopping, Heath was fairly twitching with impatience. Standing around or even moving leisurely made him very antsy.

As soon as we got into my car, I saw at least part of the reason for it.

He was all over me in a flash, mouth on mine, one hand diving into the bottom of my dress, the other into the top.

In the store, he hadn't so much as touched me, and I hadn't minded or been surprised. He didn't strike me as the type who liked PDA.

But here, with the most superficial veneer of privacy around us, he didn't, or couldn't, hide his ravenous hunger.

"We're just a few minutes from my house," I gasped into his mouth.

He groaned and wrenched himself away. With impatient movements, he put the car in gear and started to drive.

He seemed to have himself in hand by the time we made it to the house.

It took two trips between the both of us to get all of the groceries into the kitchen.

I was unloading the first bag when he pressed in behind me, mouth going to my neck, his big hands palming my breasts.

I leaned back against him, my eyes rolling up in pleasure.

"I have a lot of prep to do before dinner," I told him, trying (and failing) to use a firm tone.

"At some point today," he breathed into my ear, "I'm going to snap and take you. I can't spend this many hours with you in a row and not have you. That's a fact. You want it to be now or right around the time your sons show up to have dinner with us?"

He made a very good point. A very good, panty dropping point.

"Better we do this now than later," he continued. "Trust me on this."

My hands covered his, just one of many signs of my acquiescence.

I didn't let him take me in the kitchen, but it was a close thing.

We made it to the bedroom, but only just. The bed was far too ambitious. We ended up on the floor, on hands and knees with mad abandon, a few feet shy of our goal.

He gripped handfuls of my hair and rode me, hard and fast.

We were showered and re-dressed, a good hour later, before we got to the task of tackling dinner.

I could cook to impress. It was a fact that I took pride in. My gourmet chef father had taught me from the time I was a small child. But I didn't want to overdo it for this meal.

I wasn't planning to make anything too highfalutin. My boys were used to that sort of thing, but I didn't want to be inconsiderate to Heath. I was certain from what I'd gathered about him that he liked simpler food. And that was fine. I could do simple and give it a nice gourmet edge. Sometimes that was the best food of all—the simple and superb.

I'd decided to go with a chestnut soup with bacon and chives for an appetizer, green beans with shallots, hazelnuts, and tarragon accompanying a comfort style beef bourguignon pot pie for the main course. And, after briefly and frustratingly trying to grill Heath about his preferences (the man would never tell me what kind of food he liked), I decided to go with a classic chocolate mousse for dessert, because who didn't like chocolate mousse?

It was a bit alarming how good Heath was at being a sous chef. Alarming because he knew his way unerringly around every inch of my kitchen.

When I needed bay leaves, he knew which shelf in my extensive spice collection to search. When I asked for a star anise pod, he didn't have to ask where or what it was.

Some part of my brain kept picking at that, but I was having too nice of a day, so I brushed it off.

He was so efficient, in fact that I wound up giving him a break from the position about an hour before my boys were set to arrive.

He didn't seem to mind at all, just grabbed an apple, set himself away from me on the far side of my large kitchen leaning back against the counter and ate his apple while he watched me work.

I was fine with that. I had grown to love the way he watched me. It was amazing how fast I'd become accustomed to being studied like prey, how much I'd come to crave it, when I knew precisely what was at the end of that intent stare.

That wasn't to say that I wasn't distracted by his idle self. He could distract me by doing absolutely nothing.

Hell, he was legitimately distracting me right then just by eating a freaking apple. I loved, seriously *loved*, how he consumed it with purpose and intensity as he did everything, it seemed.

It was a treat to watch him devour it in big succinct bites, going to the very last bit of fruity flesh until you wondered if he would devour the core or not.

"You aren't going to like how your pot pie crust turns out if you keep looking at me like that," he told me.

Biting back a happy smile, I turned my back on him and went back to cooking.

God, I loved all of his little quirks.

My boys, Rafael and Gustave, arrived at the same time though they came in their own cars.

Raf came with a bouquet of white daisies, and Gustave brought pink carnations.

My father had taught them this when they were very young. *Always get flowers for beautiful women,* he'd told them more times than I could count. And, as I was the only daughter to my doting father, he'd been sure to point out to them, *and there is no woman on this earth more beautiful than your mother, so she can never have too many flowers.*

They'd both taken it to heart. More often than not, even on the most casual, quick of visits, they came bearing flowers.

I flushed in pleasure. "You shouldn't have," I said. I always said this, but never meant it.

I adored this ritual.

"Nonsense," Raf said.

"Mother," Gus chided.

They both sounded so much like their grandfather that it filled my heart with joy.

I embraced them, giving Gus and then Raf a light kiss on the cheek.

They both favored me. My ex and I had similar coloring—dark eyes, black hair, dusky skin, and so did the boys, but their actual features, sharp straight noses, almond eyes, lush lips that stayed a natural dark rose in color, even their square white teeth, it all came straight from me, and I couldn't have been happier about it.

Raf was taller, leaner than Gus. And Gus, while still over six feet, had a shorter, more bulked up build than his older brother. Small physical differences aside, though, anyone could tell at a glance that they were brothers and that I was their mother.

There weren't many men out there as good looking as my boys. They were outrageously attractive. I'd seen it early on, made a point of keeping them humble, while still knowing their own worth.

Me being their mom helped as they adored me and didn't disrespect the women in their lives because of it.

While my sons had a striking physical resemblance, personality-wise they were opposites in many respects.

Raf was so sensitive. Not to himself. Rarely for his own pain did he suffer. He suffered for others. It both broke my heart and overfilled me with pride to see the way he was moved.

Gustave, on the other hand, was insensitive to almost an extreme. He was a fighter. He could both take and land blows with precision. He fought for everything he thought was worth his concern. Causes. People. He'd always been a tank of a boy, designed to defend.

For being so dissimilar, I thought their personalities complemented each other quite brilliantly.

But when they fought. Oh, Lord. It was agony for all three of us. Just the worst. They hated being at odds with each other. Went to great, careful, tedious steps to avoid it, so when it happened, it was usually unavoidable and *terrible*.

Terrible for me because my boys were hurting, and your children in pain is at least ten times worse than literal pain to yourself.

At least.

Terrible for Raf because he was sensitive, all criticism focused inward, and he kept it bottled up tight, rarely letting it lash outward. But when it did go outward, and he said things that were usually true but that he knew were hurtful, he suffered double the impact.

Terrible for Gustave because, though he was the insensitive ying to Raf's empathetic yang, he treasured his brother's vulnerability, felt it was something he should protect, and so when it was not protected, he knew he had failed, and in his own resilient way, he was every bit as self-critical as his brother.

They had a row back in high school (over a girl) that I swear was more painful to go through than my divorce. That bad. Eyes were blackened, young hearts broken. They hadn't spoken to each other for nearly a month.

When they'd at last reconciled, we'd all been unutterably relieved.

They worked well as a team, and suffice it to say, anything else was unthinkable.

There were a tense few minutes, when I initially introduced Gustave, the younger, more volatile of my boys, to Heath, but all things considered, it was to be expected.

Me even having a love life was going to be an adjustment for them, and the reality of it in the form of a man like Heath, well, I just assumed that would not go smoothly right away. I knew it would take time.

That being said, I could tell Raf had spoken to him, convinced him to behave, even if it was just with cool civility.

I'd take it.

I put the flowers in vases and set them as centerpieces along the middle of my large dining room table.

Without having to be asked, Raf began to set out plates and napkins, while Gus put out the silverware.

I hadn't raised my boys to be idle little princes. They always pitched in. They'd moved out of my house knowing how to take care of themselves, and while Raf liked to tease his brother by announcing to me that Gus had girls doing his laundry for him at his dorm, I'd made sure he knew how to do it himself from the time he was thirteen.

Like tonight, for instance. Since Heath and I had cooked, it was no question that the boys would be in charge of cleanup. This was how I was raised and a system I'd passed on to them, because it worked perfectly.

My father would perhaps have cringed, but for convenience sake, we ate buffet style, filling up our plates in the kitchen and carrying them back to the dining room.

Clearly thinking the same thing, Raf smirked and muttered, "Grand-pere would have a fit," as he carried his loaded plate out of the kitchen.

I entered the dining room last, but all of the men were still standing behind their chairs, politely waiting for me to sit first.

I felt near to bursting as I took them all in. I couldn't help feeling more than a twinge of pride at being surrounded by such magnificent men.

I said a quick prayer that they all wouldn't kill each other and took my seat.

CHAPTER
TWENTY

No fists flew. No dishes were thrown. No profanity was
spewed.

All in all, I counted the evening a victory.

Of course it wasn't perfect. Gustave and Heath did not meet and hit
it off. They didn't bump fists, talk about sports and become best friends,
but I'd known they wouldn't.

For the most part, Rafael and I kept the conversation going, light
and easy. Heath and Gustave were largely silent, answering questions
when asked, but in general just eating in silence. This, also, was how
I'd known it would go.

Heath loved the pot pie; going by the way he cleared his plate and
went back for seconds.

Gustave was not far behind him.

I was fairly preening, knowing that at least with my cooking I'd done well tonight.

We hit a slight bump in the road when Raf asked Heath in a friendly way, "What was it that you do for a living again?"

"I work in security," was Heath's typical vague answer.

Gustave took exception, instantly and obviously.

He set down his fork, eyes boring into Heath. "What does that even mean? What do you do *in security?*"

Heath was unfazed. "Lots of things, most of them confidential for the sake of my clients."

Raf, ever the peacemaker, promptly changed the subject to something else.

Another little bump occurred some time later when Gustave burst out with another question, delivered with a frustrated tone. "How old are you, anyway? And how did you meet my mother?"

Heath finished chewing his mouthful of food. "I'm twenty-five, and I met her at the grocery store."

"Are you *usually* into older women?"

"Gus! Rude!" Raf's voice barked, uncharacteristically sharp. His brother had managed to offend him.

"Sorry," Gustave muttered, and I could tell by the dark flush to his cheeks and the way his eyes darted to me that he was instantly remorseful of the rude remark. I even knew why.

He'd only just realized that it was insulting to more than just Heath.

"No," Heath drawled, his amused eyes swinging to mine. "To be honest, I didn't realize our age difference was quite so dramatic when we met, but I didn't care when I did find out. Have you *seen* your mom?"

It was my turn to bark out sharply, "Heath!"

The last thing he needed to do was egg them on, but thank God my sons just seemed to find his remark amusing.

"Do you live around here?" Raf asked, again trying to turn the conversation to something innocuous and friendly.

It was like my children had decided to approach the dinner with a good cop/bad cop dynamic.

"Not far," Heath replied easily. "I rent a place a short walk from here. I'm in town on a job that's turned out to be longer term than I'd expected."

This, if it was true, was all news to me. Apparently Raf was better at getting information out of Heath than I was.

"How long do think you'll be sticking around?" Gus asked, a hint of belligerence in his tone.

"It's impossible to say," Heath returned, eyes staying on his food.

Raf and I made eye contact, and I swear I could read his mind we were so much alike.

We've pushed it enough tonight, I thought at him. Best to wrap it up shortly after dinner before any blood was drawn.

We finished eating and made short work of dessert. The boys cleared the table and did the dishes, while Heath and I put away the extra food.

When he finished his chores, Gus declared that he had to go, and I walked him out to his car.

"You're having a hard time with this," I observed. "The age difference is understandably shocking."

"It's not his age, Mom. I honestly don't care how old he is. He just, he strikes me as *off.* There's something *wrong* about him. Like he's, I don't know, he's playing nice enough, but there's something wrong with his eyes."

That was another thing about Gustave. His instincts had always been very sharp.

I gave him the shortest, most to the point answer I could think of. "He's ex-military. He's lived through some rough stuff. I believe he's still acclimating to normal society, to be honest."

"That adds up," Gustave admitted grudgingly. "But, really, Mom, I don't care what he's been through. I want you to be with someone normal, someone that's good for *you*."

I sighed. "I'm the only one that can decide what's good for me, sweetie. And, frankly, I've never in my life given a damn about what's *normal*."

"Is it serious? Are you guys, like, boyfriend and girlfriend?"

How to answer that one? I thought a non-answer was best. "This whole thing is new to me, too, and I'm just taking it a day at a time. I've been seeing him for a few months, and I like him. That's all I know for sure, so far."

"Does Dad know about him?"

I frowned at him. Why would he even ask that? "It's not his business," I hedged.

"I agree, but just so you know, if he ever finds out, he's going to freak."

I frowned harder. "What's it got to do with him? Or are you just referring to the age difference?"

"I'm sure he won't be happy about that, but I'm referring to everything. You seeing somebody. *Anybody*. You may have moved on, but I doubt he ever will."

"I don't know why you say that. He moved on while we were still married."

"He knows he blew things with you forever, but that doesn't mean he's okay with it."

"I think you're wrong about that, but honestly, it just doesn't matter to me what he thinks. Seeing as you and Raf are grown, I don't even have to worry about co-parenting with him. He's just not in my life anymore, and he never will be."

"I know. Doesn't mean he's accepted it yet. And believe me, I don't want him in my life, either."

"I'm sorry about that."

"Don't apologize for him. It's not your fault. It's all him. He's a liar, a hypocrite, and an asshole. I can't stand anything about him, and I know you think we'll change our minds, but we *won't*. We're just done with him."

"I'm sorry," I whispered. I felt guilty about their disdain for him, though I'd never done anything to actively court it. It just was. They'd seen too many things in their father that they couldn't make peace with. I thought perhaps in time that might change, but I was starting to accept that it was out of my hands, either way. I thanked God every day that my boys were in my life and remained close to me, and I'd do anything in my power to keep it that way. What my ex-husband did or didn't do to re-establish or maintain a relationship with his boys was his duty and his business, at this point.

"I promise to try to play nice with your new boyfriend," Gus said, grudgingly.

I thought it counterproductive to correct him on the boyfriend thing at this stage in the game. "Thank you," was what I said instead.

"Sorry if I was a jerk tonight. It's just, I don't know, it's hard. You seeing some guy I don't know is going to be an adjustment."

"I know. I understand. And you did *fine* tonight. You tried your best. That's all I've ever asked."

He swallowed hard, his throat working with the motion. "Love you, Mom."

I hugged him briefly and kissed his cheek.

"Love you, sweetie."

I came back inside just in time to see Raf out.

"I think it went well," I said.

"It could have gone much worse. Gus'll just need time. You know how he is."

I did. I knew him well enough to be encouraged by the fact that he'd shown up at all and been as well-behaved as he had.

"He said something odd to me," I added, "that if your father found out I was seeing somebody, he'd freak."

Raf grimaced, and it was like watching my own expression on someone else's face. "He's not wrong. Every time Dad calls either of us, the first thing he asks is if you're seeing anybody. I honestly think he's more interested in learning about that than he is in actually talking to us."

I found it encouraging that either of them even took his calls, and I told him so, "At least you're speaking to him. That's something."

He gave me a look, a *seriously, Mom?* look. "I only answer his calls to reiterate to him that he better not be bothering you."

"Oh."

"And if that's why I'm picking up the phone, you can just imagine what Gus has to say to him."

Nothing good, I knew.

"It's not your burden, worrying about what we think of our father, but yeah, I think he'd freak if he knew you were seeing somebody."

"And somebody like Heath."

He sighed. "Yeah. The age thing . . . and Heath himself. He wouldn't react well to any of it, but you can bet he won't hear it from either of us."

I hugged him, kissed his cheek, and said good night.

Heath was waiting for me, right at the front door, when I came back in.

"It went okay, right?" he asked. He said it like he was worried and that made my heart soften for him all the more. He might be rough around the edges, but I was starting to feel some genuine affection for those edges.

"I think it went brilliantly," I reassured him.

"I learned something important tonight," Heath said.

"That my boys are overprotective?"

"That's true, but not what I was talking about. They're attached to you, and who can blame them?"

I swear I was blushing. I wasn't even sure why that one got to me. Likely it was the look on his face, and the affection in his normally affection-less voice.

"Flowers," Heath continued. "I need to bring flowers when I come to see you."

"You don't have to. They learned that from my father who dotes on me to a ridiculous degree."

"Not ridiculous. You should be doted on. By all of us. He sounds like a wise man."

"To be honest, I'm not sure you two would like each other."

"We'll see. I'm hard to get used to, but I promise to be on my best behavior if I ever do meet him."

That sounded promising, and I didn't press the issue about him meeting my father or a future for us in general. Everything was moving fast enough as it was.

Heath had been a perfect gentleman for the duration of my sons' visit.

He was sure to balance that out, however, by promptly tying me facedown to my bed and pulling my hair while he fucked my brains out.

It was a balance that I thought I could get used to.

CHAPTER
TWENTY-ONE

I woke up the next morning to another rather alarming development.

It was becoming a pattern.

A commotion in my house.

What the hell was it today?

Someone was at my front door. Someone loud. They were yelling.

Ah hell.

I knew that yell.

Fuck.

What the ever-loving *fuck?* Could I not get a break?

And what the hell was *he* doing at my house?

Once again I came out of my bedroom in only a thin robe having not a clue what to do with the sight in front of me.

The first thing I took in was an agitated Heath at my open front door wearing nothing but a pair of boxers and a scowl.

And just outside, looking harried, outraged, like he was trying, and had tried, to charge into the house, was my ex-husband.

Eduard had always been a handsome man, and still was—dark eyes and black curly hair that set off his olive skin. He was tall and lean, but next to the bulky mountain that was Heath, he suddenly looked thin to me. Skinny. Had he lost weight, or was it just that the comparison left him lacking? I really didn't know.

Eduard saw me and stilled. "What the fuck is this, Lourdes?" he called out, sounding outraged, like he'd caught me at something.

He'd always had a nerve. When we'd been young I'd called it pluck and found it charming.

That was a very long time ago.

I almost laughed.

Instead I shook my head at him. "What in the world are you doing here, Eduard?"

"What's *he* doing here?" he shot back as though he had some right to question who should be at *my* house.

"What are *you* doing here?" I repeated.

"He *spent the night?*" Eduard cried out like he was honestly shocked.

"What gave it away?" Heath asked him dryly.

"What do you want, Eduard?" I asked him. "This is not a good time. If you have something to say to me, you need to call, not just show up at my house."

"I can't believe you! How long has this been going on?"

It was strange. The divorce had had opposite effects on us. The longer we were apart, the more indifferent I became to him and the more bitter he grew toward me.

It was a refreshing change from our marriage where I'd cared too much and he too little.

I looked at Heath, who was calm as could be, just watching me while he kept my ex easily out of the house. "Just shut the door on him," I told him. "If he has something important to tell me, he can call and leave a message that I may or may not listen to."

"I'm telling the boys about this!" Eduard shouted as the door started to close on him.

"They already know!" I shouted back.

"We all had dinner together last night," Heath added and shut the door in his face.

"Does he show up here often?" Heath asked me, the doorbell ringing enthusiastically to punctuate his words.

"No. Hardly ever. Did he say what he wanted?"

"No. I think the sight of me changed his focus, but I'm pretty sure I can guess what he came here for."

"What?"

"You. He wants you back."

I couldn't help it. I made a face. "God, I hope not. That's never happening. Not in a *million* years."

"Good. I'll have a word with him sometime; make sure he gets the message loud and clear."

"You don't have to do that. I can handle him. He's harmless. Just an annoyance these days. Honestly."

He didn't say another word about it, which should have worried me more, but I was distracted just then, as he took me back to bed.

We didn't get a day in bed, but we did get a morning, so I couldn't exactly complain.

Heath left for a few hours in the afternoon, for work, he said, but told me he'd be back in time for dinner.

I thought it was him at the door sometime later, and so was doubly surprised when I opened it to find a young blonde girl standing there.

"Is Heath here?" she asked me.

I was caught off guard, for obvious reasons. "Um, no, no he's not. He stepped out for a bit. Can I help you?"

"Could I wait inside for him? I'm supposed to meet him here."

I let her in. What else could I do?

I went back into the kitchen. I'd just been about to open a bottle of wine, so I offered her a glass.

"Oh, no, thank you. I'm pretty sure I'm pregnant, so I definitely shouldn't."

"Excuse me?" I asked her. I just didn't know how to place her in my mind. Who was she, and why had she come here to find Heath?

"Also, I'm not actually old enough to drink," she added.

That had me studying her. She *was* a young thing. She had white-blonde hair and was drop dead gorgeous. She looked like something you'd see in a Victoria's Secret catalogue come to life wearing sweats and nerdy glasses.

She studied me right back.

"I'm Iris," she said, breaking a long silence. "And you must be Lourdes. So nice to finally meet you."

"Nice to meet you," I mumbled back.

Iris beamed at me. "So you and Heath, huh?"

She sounded so happy about it that I found myself studying her face some more. And then it hit me. Of course. Aside from their different, striking eye colors, they even looked alike. "You're his sister."

She laughed. And laughed. I didn't get the joke, but her laughter was contagious and so I found myself smiling.

"Oh my God," she gasped. "You are so much more observant than Dair. It took him *forever* to figure that out."

I blinked at her. "Dair . . . Alasdair Masters? You know him?"

For that, she started studying me again, her eyes intense in a way that made me think I'd underestimated her. Greatly.

"Yes, I know him," she said quietly. "He's a friend of yours, right?"

"Well, yes, we've worked together a few times, and we're friendly. How do *you* know him?"

She shook her head sharply. "Long, long story. How are things going with you and Heath?"

I didn't know how to answer that.

And she didn't seem to need an answer.

"I didn't really come here to find Heath," she said. "In fact, he'll be upset when he finds me here, but I actually wanted to talk to *you*."

Saying unexpected things clearly ran in the family. "Oh?" was the only response I could come up with for her.

"I just wanted to give you some background on him, on why he doesn't let anyone get close. It's not because he doesn't care. He—he'd do anything for me, I know this, he's proven it, but even *me* he won't open up to. He can't. It breaks my heart the things he's been through. I can see the burdens he carries . . . I carry some of my own, but his, I'm sure you've noticed some of his issues, if you've spent any time with him."

I just nodded that I had.

"He's been hurt bad. Tortured. Well, I don't have to tell you. You've undoubtedly seen all of the scarring. And he's had to do some things that people just don't come all the way back from. But his stint with the CIA is just one piece of the puzzle. The dysfunction runs deep in our family. We were raised as feral things. We come from a family of pathological liars. We're packaged to sell, though. We learned to hide it. Learned to hide everything. We were taught to lie so consistently that it still comes more natural than the truth. It's not malicious, the way we lie. It's protective, if that makes any sense."

"Protective of what?"

Her pretty mouth twisted. "I can't say. I'm sorry for being so vague. And I'm telling you all of this because I know he'll be just as vague. More so. I think he cares about you, and I just hope that, in spite of all of that and all of his other issues, you'll give him a shot."

I opened my mouth, to say what, I haven't a clue, when the doorbell rang.

Iris cursed. "He figured it out faster than I thought he would."

"Figured out what?"

"That I came here. You see, he left you earlier to look for me."

"He told me he left for work."

"That's actually not a lie."

I was more confused than ever. I moved to answer the door.

"Don't tell Heath about the pregnancy thing I mentioned earlier," she said quietly behind me. "He'd *freak*."

No way would I ever be telling the volatile Heath that his too young to drink sister might be pregnant.

Not a chance in *hell*.

When I opened the door, Heath didn't even address me, instead headed straight for his sister, who was hovering in the doorway to the kitchen.

"I've been out looking for you," he barked at her. "I can't believe you pulled this again, and for *what*?"

"I wanted to meet Lourdes."

His hand went up to pinch the bridge of his nose, as though relieving pressure.

His other hand was clutching a bouquet of roses.

He'd brought me flowers.

"Do you know what you've done?" he asked, addressing Iris.

"No, Heath," she said, clearly distressed. "No. Please. I'm sorry. *No.* No one followed me, I swear. Nothing's been compromised here."

He looked back and forth between the two of us. "She's scared of me," he told me. "My own sister is frightened of me."

"Not of you," she said, voice thick with tears. "*For* you. And I'm worried more than scared."

"Mason is coming to pick you up now."

"Okay, fine. I'll go back and I won't do this again, but promise me this didn't ruin things for you."

"How can I promise that?" His tone was biting. "It was bad enough that I couldn't stop coming here. Now, well, you know what happens now."

Iris was openly crying at this point. She gave me an imploring look. "I'm sorry. I swear I wasn't followed. I *swear.* I was so careful."

I was baffled by it all, but I could tell something bad had just happened.

"What's going on, Heath?" I asked him.

He shut his eyes tight, taking a deep breath. "I wish I could tell you. Iris needs to go."

"She could stay for dinner," I offered. I didn't know her well at all, but it was distressing to me to see her crying like that. To watch her go from so joyful to so genuinely despairing. I wanted to help.

"She can't," he said dully. "I can't now, either."

"I'm sorry," Iris said again, but I couldn't tell which one of us she was talking to.

"Oh," I said, wanting to do something batty like wring my hands I was so damned confused. "You aren't staying for dinner, either?" I asked him. I thought for certain he was planning to come back for the night.

"Not now, I can't. Excuse me. Mason's here. I'm just going to walk Iris out."

That's when he handed me the flowers he'd brought me. I murmured a thank you.

I didn't ask who Mason was or even walk them out. I just stared at the door, my mind racing, trying to make sense of their interaction. It was clear I was in the dark about whatever was going on.

I was still staring at the door when Heath came striding back in. He slammed it shut and came directly to me.

He set the flowers I was clutching on a table, pulled me into his chest, his arms like steel around me, offering hard comfort. For a moment, I felt like everything was going to be okay. He lulled me into thinking that, his lips tender at my temple.

And still comforting me, still giving me false hope with his strong body, he murmured, "I have to leave. Not for a little while, but for a very long time. We have only minutes left together."

"How long is a very long time?" I murmured into his chest.

"I wish I knew."

"I don't suppose you're going to explain that scene back there with your sister to me."

"I wish I could. If I had a choice, if it were up to me, I wouldn't be leaving, I promise you that."

For what it was worth, I believed him.

CHAPTER
TWENTY-TWO

Ａnd then he was gone, and I had no idea if I'd ever see him again.

The first day after he left time passed like it was rolling through tar.

The second day was worse.

The third the same.

There was no word. Not a note. Not a phone call. Nothing.

He was gone, had been gone for days, then weeks, but he'd left his mark in every single inch he'd occupied.

But even with that mark of his ever present, the man himself—gone.

I longed. For his touch. For just the sight of him. For the sound of his voice.

It was such a strange thing, longing. It felt so *necessary*. Like the very urge created the problem. Because somehow it felt so right.

All because you needed a thing you didn't have.

Such a vicious cycle, longing.

And then, all because of him there was my reawakened sex drive.

It was the sweetest agony.

I found myself suddenly *fixated* on sex. So aware of my own body that I couldn't concentrate on much else.

I was showing more skin, enjoying the attention. I worked hard to keep my figure, and I was proud to show it off and add thinking constantly about sex to that equation—I was like walking man catnip.

During that three-week stretch, I kid you not, I even had a bank teller hit on me mid-transaction.

It was out of hand.

And while I was obsessed with sex, I was not remotely interested in having it with anyone but the one man I couldn't have. Because he was gone.

It's the funniest thing, how the woman who couldn't be less interested in dating gets asked out the most. I was suddenly that woman. I swear, I couldn't beat them off with a stick if I tried.

I said no, categorically.

But every night I went home and masturbated repeatedly, nothing I'd ever done before, because something about getting myself off all alone had always felt singularly unsatisfying.

And it still did.

I did it anyway. Over and over. Because I suddenly had a hard time going to sleep without it.

I got myself off, fantasizing about a rough voice in my ear and a big, scarred body on top of me, and would eventually fall into a fitful sleep.

I tossed and turned every night, and then I woke up every morning with my covers on the floor, and my fingers on my clit.

Nearly three weeks to the day he'd left, he showed up again, right at my bedtime.

I knew it was him when the doorbell rang at such an odd hour. I'd just been performing my nightly try to sleep method, naked in my own bed, vibrator in hand.

I wondered briefly if I should answer the door like that.

No, I decided, shoving my toy under a pillow and throwing on a thin silk robe.

I checked the peephole, undid the chain, but only opened the door a tiny crack.

I met his wintry eyes and felt a jolt of something powerful move through me.

He looked fatigued. Just dead tired. Had he been going through the same thing I had? Did he miss me?

"I shouldn't even be here," he began, sounding like he didn't *want* to be.

I stiffened, my stomach turning over in dread. *What the hell did that mean? Was he just here to break things off more officially? Was this even the type of thing that needed an official breaking off?*

My voice was hard when I shot back with, "So why are you?"

He took a deep breath, then another. He was trying to communicate something to me with his eyes, but he was just *too damn good* at hiding everything there.

His eyes would never be the window to his soul. It was hidden somewhere else.

I wanted to strip him down, climb on top of him, and study every inch of him with squinted eyes and thorough fingers until I found it.

But I knew where it wasn't. His eyes were too everlasting frozen *to death* to house his true self.

I tried to read them anyway, tried to decipher that broken gaze of his. It was nearly useless, but only nearly. I didn't know what *exactly* they were trying to tell me, but I swore I caught a glimpse of something approaching contrition.

"I can't stay away." It was a tortured utterance.

It was everything I craved to hear in that exact moment. Because if I'd known where to find him, there's no way I could have stayed away.

Just like that, I was his for the taking.

I barely got the door open before he had me across the entryway, pinning me to the wall.

I trembled under the touch of his big, rough hands. No soft touches for me. I was beyond them. I only wanted what Heath wanted to give me, which was a thing that could never in any way be mistaken for soft.

He didn't kiss me at first, just took me in his big hands, running them over me like he was committing every curve to memory.

He pushed my robe off my shoulders, unwrapping me like a present, making a noise low in his throat when he found me completely bare underneath.

"It's like you knew I was coming," he groaned out hoarsely.

I squirmed under his scrutiny, wanting to touch him, wanting to touch myself, anything for relief. But I held back. I wanted too badly to see what he would do.

"Were you waiting for me, honey?" he asked softly, dropping down to his knees.

He shoved his beautiful face between my thighs, tongue stabbing at me without further ado.

"Were you?" he breathed into my sex.

I gasped out a yes. Then his name. I put my hands slowly, gingerly into his hair, never forgetting for a second, even in my near hysterical wanting of him, how hard it was for him to be touched.

He threw one of my legs over his shoulder and set to work on me, fingers delving inside, tongue exploring slowly, thoroughly, laving at my sex, inch by inch, scraping his tongue against me, fold by fold.

I loved it, but I needed more almost instantly. I wanted to come with his cock inside of me, not his fingers.

"Heath," I pleaded, wanting him to stop, *needing* to come with *him* inside of me, but I quickly lost the train of thought. He had me finishing before I saw it coming.

He nuzzled into me, fingers still inside of me as I trembled out my release.

"Heath," I said again.

"What do you need?" he asked, then proceeded to lave my clit generously with his tongue.

When I found my voice again, I rasped out, "I need your cock. Please." I was panting as I begged. "Please. Please. Please."

He moaned and surged to his feet. He got his dick out of his pants like he'd been trained to do it, like those military guys you see in movies, dismantling guns, every small motion keyed to the utmost efficiency.

He pushed into me bare. Even in my lust haze, I caught that right away.

"I'm not on the pill," I gasped.

He knew that, dammit, and I couldn't stand the thought of him pulling out long enough to wrap up.

"I know," he groaned out, already moving inside of me, rutting mindlessly like he just didn't care. "God, Lourdes. I missed you."

That, and the big erection banging me against the wall had me distracted enough to almost let it go. Almost.

Insanity.

I pushed against his scarred shoulders in a last ditch effort, and that got his attention, as I knew it would.

"What . . . ?" he asked, hips still surging at me, the part of him that just couldn't stop was not stopping for even a second.

"Don't you have any condoms?"

His face screwed up in what could only be called agony. "Fuck me, I don't. I'm not even supposed to be here."

I wanted to cry. And he kept moving all the while.

"I'll pull out, okay?" he rasped into my ear, still rocking into me.

I did some very bad math in my head, expedient math that's sole purpose was to get us both off in a hurry.

Pure idiocy.

Believe me, I know.

"We should be fine," I gasped. "I don't think it's the right time of month, so we should be fine." As if I said *we should be fine* enough we would be?

And the rational me knew damn well that I had never been regular enough to rely on math like that.

Rational me was gone while hedonist me was getting her world rocked.

Pure idiocy. I know, I know.

"Thank God," he growled, ramming into me faster, harder. "Fucking miracle, that."

I really thought the timing worked in our favor. I really, really did but that being said, when I'd told him that, I'd still been thinking he'd pull out. Just to be safe, that extra bit of insurance that was by no means a guarantee, but still better than *not* pulling out.

I came first. Of course I did. He'd pound me all night before he let himself go before me.

He gripped both of my wrists and started kissing me on the mouth like he wanted to eat me alive as he let himself go.

He was buried to the fucking hilt when his cock started jerking out its release inside of me.

Even with my brain still lust fuzzy from orgasm, I felt jolted back to alertness when I realized what was happening inside of me.

"Pull out," I moaned into his mouth.

He started to, genuinely gave it a try, I thought, but about halfway out, he shoved back in deep and held himself there, rooting inside of me.

Like he just couldn't help himself.

This was one of many, many reasons why the pull out method was a terrible form of birth control. Oh yeah, that, and the fact that it really didn't work, just felt a lot more safe than him shooting his whole load inside of me, as opposed to say, smaller amounts of pre-cum.

"Heath," I tried to make my tone plaintive, but it came out breathy and pleading. Even I couldn't tell if I sounded more like I wanted him to pull out or stay inside.

"Fuck, I'm sorry," he muttered, but he still didn't pull out, instead jolting inside of me.

And, God, I was just as bad, still clenching around him, milking out every drop, not putting my foot down, not making him stop.

And then he said a thing that thrilled and terrified me, and I couldn't have said which reaction was stronger.

"Do you want to have any more kids, or are you done for good?"

I'd never (not for one *second*) ever even considered this. My boys were grown. That was it. I probably could have more. I was in perfect health. I'd just never thought of it.

And what the hell did it mean that he was asking me this? I was scared to even contemplate it. Scared to hope for any possibility.

"I've never thought about it," I said honestly. "Why do you ask?"

He shook his head, a short jerk of a motion, as though he was making himself stay quiet on the subject.

But it didn't work. Miracle of miracles, he *couldn't* keep himself quiet.

He pressed his forehead to mine, still shamelessly inside of me, still pinning me to the wall. "If somehow you *did* get pregnant, I just want you to know, and I understand and respect that it's *your* choice, but if you were to wonder what I want, just know that I'd want you to keep it. *Us* to keep it. Even if the timing is horrible, and I'm off working. Even if you don't see me for a long time. That's what I would want. No question."

Holy shit. I had no clue what to do with that. Whether to be happy or horrified.

"Good to know," I finally said.

Lame, I know.

I just never thought I'd get pregnant.

When he finally pulled out of me, he didn't go far, sprawling right there on the floor, on his back.

He reached up, grabbed both of my hands, and pulled me to straddle him.

I knew what this was. He was giving me something of himself. Doing something that was uncommon for him. Allowing himself to be vulnerable. For me.

"Can I . . . ?"

He swallowed hard and nodded, putting my hands on his chest. "Yes. Touch me. I need your touch. It's helping. The more you do it, the better I feel. Just . . . go slow. Not too much at a time."

A feeling of pure, unadulterated tenderness shook through me.

It was kind of sick, but I couldn't even decide if this need I felt to soothe him, to mend him was maternal in nature. Maternal, or else maybe that other intangible woman feeling we all have, the, *oh this man is broken, let me fix him* urge, *because when I fix him, he'll be mine.*

Maybe it was an unwholesome combination of the two. I honestly didn't care. He was covered on the outside by scars, but inside were the real wounds, the deep ones, and all that mattered was that I needed to help him heal every part that pained him.

I traced my fingers over the scars on his chest carefully, circling my hips on top of him, rubbing our spent sexes together until he stirred again, grew hard and huge again. I was so slick and ready, so keyed to every inch of him that it took no effort at all, no guiding hand, no careful shifting. I thrust my hips and sucked him back inside of me, where he belonged. It was beautiful.

I stopped touching his chest when I took him in, knowing it would alarm him. Too soon.

Instead, I grabbed both of his hands, cupping them over my aching breasts as I started to move.

He cursed. He praised. My stoic man even begged for it as I rode him hard.

I gave it my best, used every toned muscle in my body to rock his world. This was where all of my hard work at the gym paid off, where I finally got to show him that he wasn't the only one with some spectacular moves in bed.

And then it happened again.

I let him empty himself inside of me. Again.

I guess at that point we were both just kind of thinking, *ah well, damage is done, might as well enjoy the rest of the night like this.*

Because, God, it was beyond divine.

He snaked a hand down between our sweaty bodies, gripping himself at the root, twisting his hand, rubbing against us both where we still joined.

"Jesus," he muttered. "Fucking *bare* inside of you. I can't take it. You don't even know. We're both going to be *raw* before I'm done with you this time."

He wasn't exaggerating. By morning we were both sore and aching.

And the entire night, all the times he came, he never pulled out.

CHAPTER
TWENTY-THREE

He was back two nights later, as desperate and needy as the last time.

"I didn't expect you back so soon," I gasped when we came up for air.

It was strange with how little I still knew of him how much peace I had made with our situation. Somehow, with him being mostly gone, I'd wrapped it all up and tied it with a nice pretty bow of justifications.

So many excuses that made our age difference, his lack of forthrightness, his random coming and going somehow okay in my mind.

I was good at talking myself into the most romantic explanations.

It was a talent, really.

Well, yes, he was young, and yes, of course, he was quite a bit younger than, say, me, but what toll did it take on a person to see the things he'd seen? To withstand the things he'd withstood? To do the things he'd done?

Yes, quite a toll, I could see. In every line of his tense, readied body, every word out of his cold, hard voice, in every thought in his fractured, paranoid mind, laid that toll.

What did years matter when held up to that?

Not a lot, indeed. Tragic as it was, violence had aged him more profoundly than years would ever touch the average human.

And, after all of that, who was I to push him? Of course he'd have secrets, but he could reveal them to me at his own damaged pace.

I'm a patient woman, I reasoned to myself.

I'd laid out all of the justifications for him in a scrumptious little buffet that he hadn't even had to prepare himself.

He was on top of me, spent but still planted deep inside of me, his hips between my thighs, pinning me to the mattress.

He'd tied my hands, but he was already undoing the restraints, his mouth on my neck, tongue on my skin, while he worked at the knots with his agile fingers.

"I shouldn't have come, either time," he murmured, his voice rumbling into my flesh with every word. "What I'm working on right now—it's very sensitive—I don't have the right to be doing any of this, but none of that mattered enough, apparently, because here I am. Again."

"Well, for what it's worth, *I'm* glad you came," I told him just as my hands came loose. I wrapped my arms around his head, cradling him to me.

"This can never be what we want it to."

That sounded ominous, and I felt myself stiffening. "*We?*" I asked him. "We've never talked about what *we* want this to be, so how can you know that? How can you know we even want the same thing at all?"

"I think we do," he said simply.

He was nuzzling his way down my body. He paused when he found one soft nipple. He rubbed his lush lips back and forth, once, twice, until it puckered for him. With a groan, he sucked it into his hot mouth.

My hands stroked over his hair as his rough hands pushed my breasts together, and he let go of one sensitized nipple and kissed his way to the other.

"What is it you think *we* want?" I asked him, a needy quaver in my voice.

With a gasping sigh, he pulled himself out of me, took his lips away, and just lay on me, low on my body, his cheek pillowed on a soft breast. He was so heavy that his flat abs, pushed high between my thighs, were pressed flush against my sex.

I kept stroking his hair. I was struggling to breath under his great weight, but not wanting him to move so much as an inch from this very spot.

His body was trembling on top of me. "I want you and you want me. It's that simple. Every time I get to be with you, I'm better for it. Every *single* time."

For Heath, a man of few words, this was as good as a declaration.

With the way he was laying, ear to my chest, I knew he could hear how my heart rate went wild at those words.

"Just when I think I've given up on you completely, you say something sweet like that," I whispered, kissing the top of his head.

"Like I've said before, I'm *not* sweet, not even close, so if I said something that was, you should take it to heart."

I did. Once again, I took it all to heart.

And then he ruined it.

"This is the last time I'll be here to see you," he told me. "It has to be."

"Why so final?" I kept my voice surprisingly even.

"I *have* to leave. Have to go somewhere far from here, and I can't say when I'll be back. Too long to ask you to wait for me, certainly."

Something in his voice was asking me to anyway. Like he knew it wasn't fair, knew he couldn't ask it, but some part of him couldn't help but try.

"Days, months . . . years? Can you tell me that at least?"

"I can't." At least he sounded like he regretted that.

But still, regret was not enough. I needed more. I deserved more.

Just give me some information, I wanted to say to him.

Give me an excuse, any sort of explanation, and I can work with you, I almost told him.

Tell me you'll be back someday, just make me that paper thin promise, and I'll wait for you, I almost said.

So many things were on the tip of my tongue to say to him, but they never quite came out.

And so we both had regrets.

I wasn't bitter about any of it, I swear.

Not then at least. Later, I'd find my bitter (with some help), but it was not my first inclination.

I went through stages after he left. Which was surely bizarre when I thought about what a short time we'd actually been together.

I mean, what did we have, really? We'd spent mere days together, mere hours. And it was a fact that most of that time we were in bed, and some part of him was inside some part of me.

That did not a love story make.

But no matter what I told myself, he'd made an impact, left an imprint, on every part of me he'd touched. When I took inventory of just what that meant, there was very little he'd left of me unscathed.

Even so, I found myself trying, more than anything, to just make peace with his leaving.

I was good at making peace with things I couldn't control or change. I always had been. It was what made me a great photographer, and hell, even a good dental patient. I could hold still, without complaint, as long as it took until the job was done.

I had a bit of a temper, but it usually burned out fast, and in its wake, I always found peace. Heath had been right. I was an inherently peaceful woman.

The peaceful stage didn't last long, but then, it had help in its exit as it was forcibly removed.

CHAPTER
TWENTY-FOUR

I t was ten p.m. when my doorbell rang.

Of course I assumed it was Heath. I wasn't expecting anyone else, and though he'd said he wouldn't be back, it was a strange hour for a random drop in from someone who was not my mysterious lover.

I guess it was excitement that had me not so much as glancing in the peephole or bothering to put on more than the thin tank and tiny panties I'd been about to wear to bed.

I'd had what felt like endless hours after to regret the things I hadn't said to him, hadn't tried to get him to say to me, and so even if this was just another goodbye from him, I wanted it, if only to get a few things off my chest.

I flung my front door open without a thought toward caution.

I was just so sure it was him.

It was not.

It was a woman, a stranger. She was very young and staring at me with wintry eyes and a bitter twist to her mouth.

I was about to learn that that bitter was contagious.

She had short, dark hair, and a lean muscular build that was apparent under her tight navy shirt and tighter jeans.

She was very pretty, but I doubted she was called that often. There were too many other things about her that stood out. The pretty was far from one of her dominant features.

She looked hard. Not in an unflattering way. Not hard as in brittle, but hard as in carved stone. Soft just wasn't an option for this woman. I knew that at once.

"Hello, Lourdes," she said. She had a husky voice, the kind of raspy tone men talked about.

Sexy. Another word she'd be called long before you ever got to pretty.

"I work with Heath," she added when I just kept staring at her. "May I come in? I'd like to speak to you. It won't take a minute."

The way she spoke had me reassessing her age, because I'd had her pegged as very young, but with a few words I was guessing closer to twenty-five than, say, eighteen.

"Um, sure, okay," I said, stepping back.

She came inside briskly, and I noted with surprise that she was actually shorter than I was when she swept by. She wasn't short, more like average height, but something about her had made me assume, at first impression, that she was tall.

She struck me as a badass, I decided, and in my head badasses were just always tall.

"Let me go put on a robe," I said, feeling awkward in just my minuscule top and lacy panties.

She'd been headed into my living room, but at that she stopped and snapped around. Her eyes raked me, top to bottom. "Whatever you prefer, but don't cover up on my account. I've seen it all."

It felt like a dare, or an insult, an insinuation that if I did cover up, it was because I was self-conscious or maybe even ashamed of my body.

I was not, and by now I could tell this woman was not here for a friendly visit, so I stayed how I was.

Let her see that I was proud of my body. I was forty-one, a mother of two grown men, but my skin was smooth and flawless and not one thing on me sagged. I was toned, but still shapely in all the right places. Due to countless hours of hard work, my body was as killer as it'd ever been, and this seemed like a situation where it suited me to use it.

She pursed her lips and strode into my living room. She didn't sit, but faced me, arms crossed over her chest, eyes level on my face.

There was another quiet spell while we just studied each other.

She was very attractive, in a tough girl kind of way, a way that women perhaps appreciated more than a lot of men. Girl crush material would have been a good way to describe it, if she'd been more pleasant.

"I'm not sure what Heath has shared with you," she began. "But he and I are close. We're partners, but I see he didn't tell you about me. No matter. Doesn't change why I came here. I have some things to share with you, about Heath that I think you need to hear. He and I are very similar, so I can give you some good insight into why he acted the way he did with you. He shouldn't have left you hanging like that, and I'm here to correct it."

I did not like the sound of that. Not at all.

She continued, "Our backgrounds are nearly identical. We were both recruited for a very small unit in the CIA before either of us were old enough to vote."

Wow. And she was *still* young. So young. *God, how did the government recruit these kids so young?* I kept thinking, my mind stuck on that.

It seemed wrong and sad.

"Why?" I asked her.

"Why what?"

"Why did they recruit you so young?"

She smiled unpleasantly. "It wasn't random. There's only one reason for the choices of recruits in our particular program. They found something, a talent, a skill, a *specialization* in each of us that made us valuable to them." The way she spoke was inherently sharp, every word very pointed, shaped to cut, though I didn't understand why.

I thought at first that it was just the way of her and not a personal attack on me.

I was wrong, but I wouldn't realize that until much later.

"What was it?"

"That made them recruit *me?*"

I nodded.

"The same reason they went after Heath." She paused, brows raised, as though waiting for my response.

I just stared back. I wasn't going to ask. I didn't know exactly where this was headed, but I knew I wouldn't like it.

"You know his story, right?" The question was whittled into a very sharp, stabbing point.

I shook my head, hating the way that made her look at me, like I was less significant than she'd assumed.

"Oh," she said, putting worlds of meaning into the word. "Well, to oversimplify it, we were both very good at killing people from an early age. By sixteen I was a hardened criminal, working for the same organization as Heath, one that employed individuals like us to do their dirty work."

Well, hell, part of me had guessed that. Something about him had always struck me as part military/part criminal, so this added up.

"The law caught up with Heath first," she continued, "found him in the middle of a particularly gory killing. Care to hear the details?"

I didn't have time to answer or even figure out the ramifications of what she was asking.

"He was rather vigorously eviscerating this piece of work named Tony G., who was the top goon of a rival crime family. Have you ever seen a human eviscerated? It takes skill not to kill them quickly like that. The poor bastard was still alive, what was left of him, but Heath wasn't done. He was determined to get some information out of the guy before he put him out of his misery. You see, Heath was always quite talented at getting information out of people."

By then I was shaking so hard that I knew she could see it, but she just kept talking.

"But back to the story. Tony G. had a rap sheet a mile long. That's why the feds happened upon the crime Heath was committing. They were actually going after the other guy.

Her eyes were on my shaking hands, clasped in front of me, and I knew I was giving her exactly the reaction she had hoped for.

Her smile turned more vicious as she continued, "Tony didn't live long. He bled out while Heath was arrested. So they had him on murder one and a slew of other awful things. Caught in the act. Life in prison, easy."

I felt faint. I'd known, absolutely *known*, that Heath had a violent past, and being that violence had never been a part of my life, I'd known that past was something I could not fully comprehend or relate to, but I'd never imagined anything like *this*.

"Want to know how old Heath was when this happened?"

I nodded.

"Fifteen. He was fifteen and a cold-blooded killer. For a crime like that, with the proof they had that not only was he a killer, but that he had *talent* with a blade, the kind of talent that you only get with *a lot* of practice. It was a given he'd be tried as an adult. The feds that found him were shaken up by what they'd seen. He was always big for his age, but he was still *fucking fifteen*. It freaked them out, seeing a *kid* doing a thing like that. Freaked them out, and got their attention."

"I think it was the control he displayed, the utter calmness of the way he operated, that made them realize he was not just your average mobster psychopath. I heard one of the agent's version of the story later. To hear him tell it, it was like they'd walked in on Heath reading a newspaper. That was how calm he was in the middle of the act.

"Long story short, he got a full pardon, well, more like a new life, a new identity, but of course it wasn't free. He just had to serve his time in a different way, though it wasn't all that different for him than what he was used to. Murder and torture for a more honorable cause, I think is what Heath would call it."

"What about you?" I asked her, when I could find my voice again.

"Heath got me in, told them about me, that I was like him, that we worked well together. It was all true, and he knew I wanted out of that life. The way they treat women in there who aren't family, even ones working for them, well, let's just say I was more than happy to defect. I'm sure he saved my life. I wouldn't have lasted long."

"I'm not sure why you're telling me all of this."

Her unpleasant smile came back in full force, and her voice sharpened until each word was a piercing nail. "Heath is the only person in this world that means *anything* to me. Anything at all. He's *more* than my partner."

"You're sleeping with him," I told her, trying and failing not to make it an accusation.

Her mouth twisted until I couldn't tell if she was trying to grin or scowl. "You've met him. You see how he operates. Did you imagine that you were the only one?"

I hadn't imagined that.

I'd hoped for it.

Wished for it, but clearly that had been foolish.

"Would you like to know why he slept with you in the first place? I mean, a woman twice his age? He can take his pick. Haven't you ever wondered why he picked *you?*"

I badly wanted to correct that. The twice his age part. It was an exaggeration when the actual truth was bad enough.

And that entire train of thought was just a distraction for myself and the way that I felt in that moment, which was awful.

"Why are you here? What do you *want?*" I was done, and I wanted her to leave before she told me another awful thing.

"I want you to know what's been going on. How in the dark you've been from the moment you met him."

"Why? Why are you so worried about *me?*" I asked this knowing the answer, but hoping she'd give me another option.

She was involved with him. It was obvious. Sleeping with him. She'd as much as admitted it. The only question was, *how heavily involved? How deep did his betrayal run?*

"Do you know that he's spied on you? Extensively."

My eyes narrowed on her, studying her face as though it would tell me what this new angle of hers was. It did not. "He already told me that he did a background check on me," I explained, begrudgingly. "He said he had to do that with anyone he was seeing because of his job, and I believed him."

She laughed. It was much too bitter for her years. "Do you want to know just how much he's spied on you and the real reason for it?"

I didn't answer, just folded my arms across my chest and watched her. I figured she was going to tell me, regardless of how I responded.

"He swept this place, top to bottom. I guarantee it. Went through everything, from your filing cabinets to your underwear drawer."

My mind shot immediately to the time we'd cooked a meal together, to how he'd known every inch of my kitchen, every ingredient in my spice cupboard.

Then it shot to the first time I'd had him over. He'd known exactly where I kept my vibrator, but I'd been too distracted by him to wonder or care at the time.

Considering all of that, I was certain then that she wasn't lying.

Still, it confused the hell out of me. "*Why?* Why on earth would he do that?"

"It was all for Iris. All of it. The reason he spied on you, approached you, seduced you. It was all done *only* to protect her."

And that confused me even more. "His sister? You're saying he seduced me for *his sister?*"

She laughed, and it gave me the chills. She was a scary woman, and she was clearly enjoying herself at my expense.

"It all goes back to your friend Alasdair Masters."

What the fuck? Why did it keep coming back to Dair?

I was more lost than ever. "Dair?"

"Yes, Dair. Dair and Iris."

"Dair and Iris?" I repeated back dumbly.

"Yes. Iris is obsessed with Dair, and she was worried that he was interested in you. Heath knew she was worried, and Heath would do *anything* for his sister. What his sister wants, Heath makes sure she gets. First, he needed to check you out because that's what he does. And then he needed to eliminate you as a threat to his sister."

"How would I be a threat to his sister?"

"A threat to her not getting what she wanted."

I just stared at her.

"Dair. She wanted Dair, so Heath made sure, firsthand, that you wouldn't be in her way."

"That's ridiculous. I don't believe you."

Only that was a lie. What I meant was, *I don't want to believe you.*

But I did. She had a confidence about her that left so little room for personal insecurity that I just believed her. Why would this woman come here and lie to me about a man that had already declared himself out of my life? I couldn't find a good reason, and so I gave her the benefit of the doubt.

Because it all made sense somehow. With what I'd known, and what she'd told me, things started to connect about the way he was, the way he operated.

I saw it so clearly now. How everything about him was a weapon.

Engineered to get what he wanted.

Calculated to yield the proper results.

And he'd wanted something from me. Pushed all of my buttons to be sure he'd gotten it.

And he had. Above and beyond.

"And where do you fit into this?" I asked her, but again, I knew. She had the scorned lover role down pat.

Only I was wrong. It was worse even than that.

"That night you went out on a date with Dair, and you came home to find Heath waiting for you. I was sent to follow Dair, to track him down with orders to interfere if he so much as touched you.

"This is sick. He had *you* spying on me?" I asked slowly.

"Yes. And even now, he's got me keeping an eye on you, making sure no one traced him to your place."

"He *still* has *you* spying on me?" I was disgusted and appalled. At him, at her.

At myself.

"Yes."

"Let me get this straight," I began, my rare but memorable temper coming to the surface. "Your lover tells you to spy on the other woman he's been sleeping with, and you do it? What the hell is wrong with you?"

I'd scored a hit; it was clear by her flashing eyes and the malevolent twist to her mouth.

I got the distinct impression that her temper was even more memorable than mine, and I had a brief feeling of regret that I'd provoked it on purpose. This was not some normal woman. If I pushed just the wrong button, she'd have no qualms about taking my life. I knew it instinctively.

Luckily, I hadn't pushed her quite that far.

"I'm his partner," she said through gritted teeth. "He and I have a history you couldn't understand. You're *nothing* to him. Part of a job. I just thought you should know that's all you *ever* were. He never broke character with you. Not for a second. I just wanted you to know that."

And then she left, because she'd accomplished what she came for.

CHAPTER
TWENTY-FIVE

And so began the next stage of my Heath withdrawals. This one was much less pretty than the first and lasted quite a bit longer.

I'll confess, I had a few bitter moments there, a few man-hating days, where I cursed him as a bastard, and vented, ad nauseam, about what a deceitful son of a bitch he was to my girlfriends.

A brief moment in time where I swore off men for good.

I felt so foolish. How had I fallen so easily for his act?

How had I made him out to be something that he wasn't?

Had I always been a chronic romanticizer?

It was a serious question I asked myself, and the answer was not long in coming.

Yes, of course I was. How else had I stayed married for so long, in ignorance, to a man whose main characteristic had to be, above all things, narcissism?

I put things, ideas, *people* on pedestals. I made little poems in my mind about my loved ones, and though they didn't rhyme, they were beautiful poetry, poetry that shaped the better things in my life.

So, of course, when I'd met a man like that, who consumed, who dominated, who was stoic to the point of unreadable, I turned him into a romantic figure, his feelings for me far too complicated to be said in words.

Foolish, I know. I felt it keenly.

I'd taken in a wild animal. How could I be surprised I'd been bitten in the process?

I rewrote the story in my mind, this time with Heath in his proper role, as more of a villain than hero.

Even after my divorce, bitter and ugly as it was, I'd never doubted in my life that I was a complete woman, with or without a man. I'd never *needed* another person to complete me. That just wasn't who I was.

I loved myself, and my life, and being single hadn't changed that.

I found joy in the simple things, a perfectly composed picture, one of my children smiling.

But now, unaccountably, there was a void, some hollowed out hole in me that needed filling, so much so, I found myself constantly looking for someone who could.

I didn't need a man, it was true, but if I wanted one, there was nothing wrong with that, either.

Sometimes I felt a bit of clarity about the whole thing. That's what I was calling it: the whole thing. Relationship hardly seemed an accurate description. Affair felt and sounded wrong.

I started looking at it differently. Because that's what you did when you moved on. And I needed to move on.

Right after that woman had confronted me, I'd taken her at her words and swallowed whole the vicious things that she'd said to me.

But, after a time, a bit of reason slipped back in, and it occurred to me, that, like all things, there wasn't only one side to this story, and her bit of venom was just one piece of the equation.

She was bitter. She felt scorned. Of course she'd try to twist things and shove them down my throat.

I didn't know what the full truth was. I figured I probably never would with Heath so definitively out of the picture, but I knew some of it.

Regardless of his motives and his lies, I did believe that on some level he'd cared about me. And I did believe we'd helped each other in some way.

He never could have been a permanent fixture in my life. It was naive of me to think so. But, despite feeling foolish at the end, he'd been good for me.

So I took that and ran with it.

We'd been good for each other. That was a fact. Regardless of what that bitter girl had said to me, something profound had happened between Heath and me.

I helped him heal, and he helped me move on. The end of the thing didn't negate the purpose of it.

His name was Kevin. He was calm as still water and had the second most fascinating pair of eyes I'd ever seen.

They were a deep blue flecked with little bits of green, but that wasn't what made them so unique.

First of all, he was an amiable guy, very go with the flow from our very first encounter, which happened to be a fender bender.

It was his fault. I'd hit a red light in heavy traffic, which in Vegas could easily be mistaken for a yellow (we're all color blind drivers in this town), and I'd had a brief moment of indecision, deciding whether to speed up or halt, when I'd stopped suddenly, and he rammed into my back fender. It wasn't a hard hit, but it was jarring.

It should have been an upsetting occurrence, but the way he handled the whole thing impressed me enough to actually cause me to give him my real number when he asked for it.

He was just so unfazed. I was still catching my breath when I saw a lean figure emerge from the black Camry currently attached to the rear end of my Tesla.

He made a handsome picture, wearing a nice suit and dark shades.

I rolled my window down when he stood in front of it, looking at him, wondering how he'd react to the accident.

Men usually had two reactions when they were at fault. One, which was how my ex-husband would have reacted, was to blame the other party, regardless of the facts. Two was to apologize and talk about how best to proceed.

Kevin chose an extreme version of the latter.

He crouched down at my window, not close enough to be in my personal space, but making a point of not looming over me.

"My God. I can't believe I did that." His voice was soft and cultured and profusely apologetic. "I'm *terribly* sorry. I looked down for a second and didn't realize I was right on top of you. Are you okay?"

His cajoling, sincere tone had me at ease instantly.

I nodded, attempting to smile it off. "I'm just fine. Accidents happen."

He took off his shades, giving me my first glimpse of his compelling eyes.

They were ice cold. The rest of his face moved frantically into a smile meant to put me at ease, but the eyes, they were wrong, broken.

I was caught fast.

That incongruity, with him being so kind, but having those cruel eyes.

I found myself drawn him.

Of course I was. His very expression was at odds with itself.

And needless to say, I'm a sucker for a complicated man.

At the time, particularly that first, bemusing meeting, I didn't connect the dots of just whom he reminded me of that made him so attractive, but it was right there all along.

In many ways, though, he was the opposite of Heath, which was also a draw.

Where Heath struggled to express himself, Kevin *over*-expressed.

He smiled at me, a warm smile, to belie the cold eyes. He was a tall man, but lean with an attractive, angular face. He was dark in the way that I was dark, where you couldn't have placed his race if you tried, a good mix of something Latin, I assumed. With the exception of Heath, I'd always been drawn to the tall, dark, and handsome type.

With every contact, I found myself comparing them. It was hard not to. So much about them was either identical, or opposite.

In spite of myself, I was working up a tally with two columns.

Identical/Opposite.

Heath/Kevin.

One clearly meant for the opposite column: He stated from our first date that what he wanted was a serious relationship.

Another opposite: He didn't want to rush into anything physical.

He was content instead to take things very slow, letting the anticipation build in its proper time, he said.

"I'm an old-fashioned kind of gal," I told him with a smile, "so I'm okay with that." I was more than okay with it. It was, in fact, one of the reasons we got on so well so quickly. It made me feel comfortable with him, knowing he wasn't expecting to get physical right away. I wasn't ready for it. Not by a long shot. Heath had been an anomaly for me in that respect, to be sure.

He was an accountant (one for the opposite of Heath column) and his schedule was as consistent as clockwork (another opposite).

"Tell me something about yourself," he'd say often, his tone imploring and endearing enough that I always obliged.

"Like what?" I asked on our very first date. He'd surprised me by taking me to one of the best French restaurants in town. There was no way he could have known that was my favorite, so I chalked it up to the two of us having preferences in common. How lucky was that?

"Anything, to start. I want to know it all."

I found that sweet. And refreshing. So I gave him something good. "I have slutty feet," I told him playfully. Yes, I was flirting, quite shamelessly.

He looked more than intrigued. He was delighted. "It just so happens, foot rubs are a specialty of mine. See how perfect we are for each other?"

That first date, he didn't try to steal a kiss. I was learning fast that he was a true gentleman in that way (opposite column).

But he did come back to my house, shared a glass of wine with me, and rubbed the hell out of my feet.

He was *good* with his hands *(identical column)*.

I went to bed smiling.

If I was brutally honest with myself, Kevin was, more than anything, a tremendous stroke to my ego. He pursued me relentlessly, not leaving me guessing about *anything*, not his feelings or his intentions. It was just what I thought I needed.

We'd been seeing each other pretty regularly for a few weeks when Kevin said out of the blue, "I'd love to meet your boys."

That made me uncomfortable, but I leveled with him as best as I could. "I'd rather hold off on that. Give it some time. I doubt they're ready to meet someone I'm dating just yet."

Of course I hadn't told him about Heath, but he did know about my messy divorce, and the fact that my boys were overprotective to a fault.

He looked briefly annoyed, but his face smoothed of the expression so fast that I almost thought I'd imagined it. I'd never seen him show so much as a hint of annoyance before, so it threw me for a brief moment, and I stared at him.

"That makes perfect sense, of course," he finally said. "Whenever you're comfortable with it."

This was more the response I'd expected from him, so I took it in stride and didn't give the incongruous expression that he'd first shown another thought.

I found out on our fourth date that he wouldn't even consider letting me photograph him (identical column). Not for any reason. He was adamant about it, which surprised me. It was such an innocent request. What did he have to hide?

But of course he had nothing to hide, I told myself. That was Heath baggage, clearly.

A quality of Kevin's that I was pretty shocked went into the identical column hit me on our fifth date.

He was unreasonably enraged by phone calls from my ex-husband.

Kevin didn't even get a true preview of how unpleasant our actual conversations were, but he reacted nonetheless.

My phone rang, I checked the screen, and shoved it back into my bag.

"Who was that?" Kevin asked, his tone polite.

My nose wrinkled up. "No one I wanted to talk to."

"Oh."

His baffled expression had me explaining further. "It's my ex-husband, but there's no good reason for the call. In general, he just says something unpleasant to me, and I hang up on him, so I just skip the middle part now and don't answer."

He scowled, actually scowled, something I'd never seen him do before. "Want me to have a word with him?"

I almost laughed out loud. What would mellow Kevin say to my volatile, asshole ex? I couldn't even picture him confronting someone, let alone someone that hostile.

"No, there's no need. He doesn't bother me. I just ignore him. Someday he'll get the hint."

"He needs to get the hint sooner rather than later. You should let me handle it."

He was so menacing when he said this that I was taken aback. Clearly there was a side to Kevin that was unknown to me.

"I can handle my ex," I reassured him. "Trust me on this."

"Okay," he begrudgingly agreed.

I didn't write the list down on paper, but I didn't need to.

It was branded into my brain. It was the strangest thing, how the opposites and identicals grew.

And it was tedious, how fixated I was on it, though I tried not to be.

I'd have myself talked out of it, determined not to think of it at all, and then something would come up to trigger it.

Okay. Many things. There were just so many. That was the whole problem.

Kevin spoke five languages. Heath barely spoke.

Kevin called me five times a day. Heath had never called me once.

Kevin could read me like a book. Just like Heath.

Kevin knew his way around my house like he had it memorized. As had Heath, though Heath had spied on me.

I found myself worrying the first time Kevin came to my house and made himself at home. He went right into the kitchen, grabbed my corkscrew, picked out just the perfect bottle of wine, and worked it open.

I told myself firmly it was all a coincidence. The paranoia was Heath baggage, obviously.

Tato hated Kevin with a passion. So much so, that by the second week we were dating, I found an excuse to have Raf take my dog to his place for a few weeks.

Tato had adored Heath.

It was all breakup baggage, I knew. The comparing. The obsessing. Heath shouldn't have made enough of an impact to leave me with baggage, but here it was.

I tried my best to ignore it and move forward with my life.

CHAPTER
TWENTY-SIX

"I'd like to spend the night tonight," Kevin told me over dinner.

My whole body stiffened. I knew this was coming, eventually it had to, of course, but I didn't feel ready for it.

We'd been dating for almost a month. I probably should have felt ready.

I just didn't.

"Kevin," I started to say.

His hand covered mine across the table, and he gave me what I thought was supposed to be a reassuring smile. "Not for that. I wasn't trying to be crass. I'll stay in your guest room or something. I just happen to have a day off tomorrow, and I thought it'd be nice to share breakfast with you. In your home."

It struck me as an odd request, it really did, but I was too relieved at what he wasn't asking for to give it much thought.

"Sure," I said awkwardly and went back to eating.

We were trying a new French restaurant that night, as we did on most of our dates. Kevin was a foodie, and his favorite just happened to be gourmet French cuisine. He even ordered in French.

How lucky was that?

The rest of the night went down basically how he had sold it.

We made out for a bit on my sofa. We'd worked up to making out, but that was about it.

He was a good kisser.

I didn't feel a Heath level of attraction for him, but I knew better than to expect that. It was not normal the way Heath got me going, and I didn't plan to set myself up for disappointment with every future relationship by expecting such a thing.

But kissing Kevin was nice. That was something.

And then we went to bed. Separately.

He's a man of his word, I thought as I drifted off to sleep. He hadn't even *tried* to take it further.

I woke up turned on and to the smell of bacon.

I recalled vaguely the feverish dreams that had my sheets twisted up around my hips.

Stretching, I smiled and wondered if Heath could actually cook.

And then it hit me.

Fuck.

That wasn't Heath cooking for me. It was Kevin, and I felt guilty as hell for the slip-up.

I got dressed and tried my best to forget how I'd woken up.

We had breakfast. Kevin made a killer omelet. There didn't seem to be a thing he was bad at.

"I got us tickets for that romantic comedy you wanted to see. Matinee tickets," Kevin said as we were finishing up.

Kevin *loved* romantic comedies.

I had that tick again. Opposite.

We were leaving the house, headed to the show in Kevin's car, which was parked at my front curb, when the strangest thing happened.

Deborah of the Dickhead Dillons, my least favorite neighbor, crossed the street and approached us. She was a small woman, thin, with a haggard face and eyes that seemed never to blink. Today her dark hair hung lank and oily around her face, clearly in need of a wash.

"Um, hey," I said to her, awkwardly, because I'd stopped trying to greet her ages ago. She was one of those people that didn't wave back. I'd never understood how you could do that, just ignore a wave or a greeting, but it seemed to be a consistent attribute for crazy people. I mean, how hard was it to stop pretending you didn't see anyone around you and just wave? Why wouldn't you want to be friendly in the most casual of waves with the people that lived next door to you?

Because crazy.

She didn't hey me back, just launched into one of the strangest speeches I'd ever heard in my life.

It was so disconnected and hard to make sense of that I didn't catch what she was talking about for a solid two minutes.

And when I did, I raised a hand and stopped her. "Are you telling me that my ex is *suing* me?"

Eyes wide, she nodded.

"For what?"

"For money." She said this part like it was obvious, which I suppose it was.

R.K. LILLEY

"But *how* does he think he's going to sue me for money?" I tried.

"Remember when you beat him up, back when you first separated?"

I sighed and nodded.

"For that. Damages for that."

Kevin had been silent for the duration of our strange exchange, but I felt his hand on my waist tense when she said that.

"Why are you telling me this?" I asked her. She was not the type to do anyone any favors without incentive. "What does any of it have to do with you?"

"Well, he came straight to my house the day you beat him. Did I ever tell you that?" I shook my head. She had not, because we never talked to each other.

Because crazy.

"Well," she continued, "he was bruised and bloody, and I saw him come out of your house that way. I'm part of the lawsuit. A witness, since I saw that it was clearly you that beat him up, since he came out of the house and only you and he were home."

"That's hearsay," Kevin piped in quietly. "You weren't there for the event, so nothing you have to add has any relevance, in court or in life. You have no idea who else was in that house."

She glared at him and shrugged jerkily. "I guess we'll see, won't we?"

"Why are you telling me any of this?" I repeated, my tone very careful, as it usually was when I dealt with crazy people.

Her glare moved to me. "I'm telling you this because if you don't want me to testify, I'll be happy to stay silent . . . for a price."

I barely managed not to roll my eyes. "Not interested, Deborah. You have a nice a day. We were just on our way out."

"You'll be sorry," she said to my departing back. "I won't make this offer to you again."

I didn't say anything snotty back. All she got from me was silence.

I figured Kevin would comment on that exchange, but he didn't say a word, just drove us to the movies, pretending like it hadn't happened.

I was fine with that.

CHAPTER
TWENTY-SEVEN

I was dreaming.

I was in bed on my stomach. My lacy underwear were being pulled down my hips in slow, gentle tugs.

I squirmed a bit as they were freed past my thighs, down my knees, then poof, gone.

Hands started rubbing at my feet, running a big thumb up the soles, then knuckles ran down the arch. Special attention was spent working at the sensitive pad below my toes, knowing just where to target, lulling me with a rough, addictive touch.

I knew those big, skillful hands.

They were Heath's, of course.

Who else would I be dreaming about?

I moaned into my pillow as he massaged his way up to my calves, digging deep into the muscle tissue.

When he reached my thighs, I pushed up on my elbows and knees, rising a few inches from the bed.

This was my dream, after all, and I was in the mood for more than a massage.

I felt his knees wedge between mine from behind, denim abrading against my bare skin, keying me up.

His chest pushed into my back as his hands snaked down under my shirt, fondling my breasts, his lips brushing lightly against my nape.

Desire hit my bloodstream like an opiate, overtaking my senses with one strong pull.

He didn't take my top off, just wrenched it high on my collarbone and out of his way.

He palmed my tits roughly right as I felt his tip nudging my sex.

I arched my back, legs spreading wider, welcoming him, a willing lamb to the slaughter.

He bit down on my nape and shoved into me hard.

And that's when I knew.

Oh God.

This wasn't a dream.

But it was too late. I was too far gone for it to matter, one way or the other.

We rutted mindlessly, quick and savage.

I had my sheets in a death-grip while he surged into me, again and again, hips slamming against my ass with each downswing.

He made jarring direct contact, then pulled out, rubbing, dragging along my walls until only his tip remained, then slamming in again.

It was so good. I couldn't form a coherent word, not in any language, but I didn't need to. The cadence of begging was pretty universal.

He was still pumping into me, his pace relentless, when I lost it coming with loud cries.

He jarred deep, rooted there, and came in big, tangible spurts, my cunt milking each one of out him, our bodies in perfect sync.

The silence was punctuated only by our pounding hearts and gasping breaths for a good long while.

He stayed inside of me, his breath punching against one sensitive shoulder blade, his hands braced in fists on either side of me.

God, I wanted him again. The first time shouldn't have happened, and here I was, ready to submit to a second.

I whimpered when he started to pull out. It was a protest.

He ignored it, dragging himself free even while my slick flesh tried to suck him back in.

"Miss me?" Heath's voice was clear and sharp and right next to my ear. His tone was lethal, like he was delivering a blow.

Some vicious feeling tore through me. Something strange, an incongruous mix of rage and relief, of savage comfort.

"You said you wouldn't be back." My voice came out wrong, not how I'd intended. It was supposed to be accusatory, but instead was imploring and delicate in a way I found intolerable.

He had left. *Left.* I had *nothing* to feel guilty about.

"That's not what I said. I said I didn't know *when* I'd be back." As he spoke he was climbing from the bed.

I dropped flat to my stomach as light flooded the room.

"We need to talk," he growled at me.

I rolled onto my back just in time to watch him stride, still in his jeans, into my attached bathroom.

He peeled the condom off, dropping it into my little bathroom wastebasket.

I didn't look away while he cleaned himself off and tucked his spent member back into his boxers.

At some point he'd taken his shirt off, and he didn't bother to zip his jeans.

I enjoyed the view while he came back into the room and started to prowl.

But more than his spectacular body caught my attention as he moved around my room, shooting looks at me every few steps, like he couldn't help himself.

He was off, more than usual off.

There was a darkness in his eyes, a great black void of it, that called to me, to some integral part of me, deep down inside the marrow of my bones, that I hadn't even realized existed.

It was heady.

I was witnessing some new level of his rage, and it did nothing so much as draw me in further, even when I knew that all I should be doing was sending him away.

"You got rid of Tato," he growled, moving out into the hallway, then back into my room again.

I sat up, drawing the sheets to me, covering my nakedness.

That caught his attention, and he stopped pacing, just in the doorway, his eyes on the sheets.

"He's at Raf's," I said defensively. "He's Raf's dog as much as mine. It was his turn." This was kind of the truth. Part of it, anyway. Raf loved that dog as much as I did, and he'd taken him without a qualm.

But the reason I'd sent him there, of course, I wouldn't be sharing with Heath. *Tato wouldn't stop barking at this new guy I'm seeing*, would not go over well, I knew.

He seemed to catch the hint of deceit instantly, though, going by the way his demeanor suddenly changed.

His lip curled, eyes running over me in a way I didn't like. Like he was only just seeing me then. Like he'd only now noticed something about me that he found unpleasant.

"I know about that other man." His tone was more than accusatory. It was disgusted.

My entire body stiffened. *How dare he?!*

"That was fucking quick," he added quietly and vehemently.

It was a short sentence, not many words, but somehow it was enough to convey something so much worse than accusation or disgust.

It told me he was wounded. Like I'd hurt him badly.

Like I'd done something *wrong*.

Like *I* was the bad one here.

That set me off.

"Excuse me?" I spat at him.

"I do not excuse you."

That had me cursing at him. Loudly and fluently. Losing my cool. Completely.

"He's not the other man," I snarled. "*You* are, and that's all you'll ever be. I don't know what I was to you, but you were *never* my man. That wasn't what we had."

One second he was nearly in the hallway, the next he had me pinned to the bed, moving so fast it made my head spin.

"That's a *lie*," he growled into my face. "And you're not a liar, Lourdes. I think you only tried to pull off that one because you're lying to *yourself*."

I tried to buck him off, but that only had him moving his hips, seating himself more securely against me, our bodies flush. I felt the hard bulge of him growing with every movement, grinding crudely into my pelvis.

And I felt my temper going. Felt myself losing it.

"You left," I spat at him, all of my bitterness, every ounce of my ire in those two words.

He shuddered on top of me. "I didn't want to. Can't you see that *I didn't want to?*"

His voice was pleading, and the tone of it was like balm to my rage, calming it instantly, and though my feelings were every bit as volatile, they were no longer as uncomplicated as the wrath I'd been feeling mere moments before.

"You left," I said again, but the tone had changed completely, so that now I was pleading back at him.

He groaned, a pained noise, and started kissing me.

I let him. No, not let. Welcomed.

I sucked at his tongue and didn't stop him even when I felt his hands between our bodies, freeing his rock hard erection.

It sprang free, slapping into my thigh. He gave me time to stop him as he reached into his pocket, ripped open a condom, and rolled it on.

I didn't stop him. Didn't even consider it.

His hand guided his tip slowly to my entrance.

God, I'd forgotten how impossibly hard he was. How big. How perfect.

That first time, I could have blamed on being on the edge of sleep. On thinking I was dreaming.

I had no such excuse for this round.

As soon as his hand slipped out from between our bodies, my legs snaked firmly around his hips.

He gripped my hair in both hands, still kissing me as he stabbed into me with one heavy thrust.

He didn't hold my wrists captive, for once, didn't bind them.

Left free, my arms curled around his shoulders, clutching him to me.

He slammed our bodies against the bed, over and over, his jeans abrading against my inner thighs as he drilled me deep into the mattress.

At some point his hands left my hair and went down to my hips. He ripped his mouth away to watch me as he rose up onto his knees.

He grabbed my ass in both hands and lifted me into his possessive thrusts.

My hands, which had been forced from his shoulders, moved to my own body, gripping the sensitive mounds of my breasts into my palms, pushing them together, giving him a hell of a view.

It did not go unappreciated.

He tensed and heaved on top of me, getting close.

The lights in the room were bright, and so my view was unimpeded as I saw him start to lose it, the coldness going, the wildness overtaking his beautiful, broken eyes.

His jaw went slack, gaze boring into mine, taking me with him, dragging me under, straight into the heart of this madness we shared.

If it was up to me, and it wasn't, I'd have slept after that.

I knew we needed to talk, but it was the middle of the night, and my body had just been exhausted. Twice.

He wrenched himself out of me, off me, climbing from the bed.

I was already on the edge of sleep when I felt his hands grip my ankles and start to pull.

"Oh no you don't, honey," his gravelly voice was a rough croon. "You don't get to sleep. Not tonight."

He dragged my hips to the edge of the bed, spreading my legs wide.

I listened to the sounds of him putting on another condom.

I still hadn't opened my eyes, but I wasn't in the mood to sleep anymore.

"Look at me," his voice rumbled.

I opened my eyes just in time to watch him push between my thighs. I scrambled up onto my elbows to see as each thick inch of him disappeared inside of me.

"You're insatiable," I told him, voice low and needy.

"Had you forgotten?" he shot back. "And besides that, it's been months . . . for *me*." His tone was so dark and accusing that my eyes shot to his face, raking over it, trying to decipher if he'd meant what I thought he had.

But I couldn't tell from his expression, and he wasn't elaborating.

He was otherwise occupied. And so was I. There was no room in my overtaxed brain to spend on wondering what was in his just then.

He planted his fists on either side of my hips, rocking in and out of me at a jackhammer pace.

I tried to go to sleep again after that round, but he, again, was not having that.

"Get up," he said, hands on my shoulders, pulling me to sit. "There's no time to sleep. We still need to talk."

I propped myself up on my hands, looking down at myself.

He was still wearing his jeans. He'd cleaned up, again, and even zipped them up this time.

But I was still nude, completely, sitting on the edge of my bed, legs splayed wide apart.

It was so undignified, the way I was spread open for him, just letting him stare at every part of the body I'd just let him have *three times*, that it spurred me into action.

"If you want me to stay awake," I informed him, standing and moving to shrug on my favorite silk robe, "I'm going to need coffee."

He left the room without a word to make said coffee, I presumed.

I took the opportunity to clean myself up and finger comb my disheveled hair.

Also, I gave myself a good berating in the mirror.

What's wrong with you? I asked myself. *Why do you just keep going back for more?*

But it was swiftly clear the berating did no good, as, after I'd straightened myself up to a minimal degree, I went out to join him in the kitchen.

Going back for more.

He handed me a cup of coffee right as I got to the kitchen, moving past me, into the dining room, and taking a seat.

That was unusual.

He never just sat down.

It was so strange that I found myself standing over him, right in his personal space.

He just sipped his own cup of coffee and stared at me.

I sipped mine and stared back. I had not one clue what to say to him, where to start.

The truth was, I didn't want to start, because I knew how it would end.

Don't come back here. We're finished.

How was I ever going to manage to make those words come out of my mouth? I had not a clue.

But I knew that they needed to.

CHAPTER
TWENTY-EIGHT

"**I** don't know what to say to you," I finally told him, after we'd both drained our cups.

We'd been silent the whole time, watching each other between long drags of coffee.

Neither of us wanted to have this talk, it seemed.

He took the mug from my hand, set it on the table, then picked me clean off the ground by the hips, setting me astride him.

We were breathing our coffee breath into each other's mouths. "I thought you said we needed to talk," I said softly. "*This* won't solve anything."

He didn't answer, just stared at me while he worked between our bodies, getting us both ready.

"Heath," I chided when I realized he was hell bent on fucking me again.

He stilled, cold eyes intense, then spurred into action, reaching for my hands, setting them, palm down, over the muscled flesh of his pecs.

"Go ahead," he rasped. "Touch me. Do it."

I did, hands moving over his chest, softly tracing at his scarred flesh, and as I watched the way it made him cringe, I knew why he wanted me to.

It was painful to him, and he *wanted* to hurt.

But, regardless of everything that had happened, all the ways I was hurting myself, *I* didn't want that.

I took my hands away, gripping his where they held my hips.

He made a pained noise and kissed me.

So much for talking.

He took me right there in his lap, opening my robe and impaling me.

"Condom," I cried out. Just because we'd had that one night of a slip up, months ago, didn't mean I meant to be so careless again.

"I've got a better idea," he rasped into my mouth. As he spoke, he closed his eyes, dropped his head back, and rocked his hips in and out, fucking me hard, bouncing me on his lap with firm hands and bucking hips.

Perverse as it was, his words, what they might have implied, combined with the way he was working me, had me coming in a flash, gripping around him, wondering what the hell was wrong with me even as I clenched on his thick length and got off.

I was still catching my breath when he pulled me off his dick, setting me down on the ground. On my knees.

He hadn't finished.

He gripped my hair in both hands and dragged my face to his lap.

He was still hard and throbbing. His engorged cock was slick and close enough to lick. When his tip touched me lips, I couldn't seem to help myself. I opened up and started sucking him off like I'd been starving for it.

He didn't last long like that.

He rasped out my name as his seed burned down my throat.

I was still licking his twitching length clean when he spoke.

"I know he spent the night."

I moved away from him like he'd just caught fire.

My robe had been opened, but not removed, and I closed it and retied the belt with shaking hands.

For once it was my turn to pace. I didn't look at him for a long time, and when I finally did, I wished I hadn't.

He was still sitting, his thick, spent length hanging crudely out of his pants, but I don't even think he noticed it.

His arms were folded across his chest, and he was staring at me in a way I couldn't stand.

He looked wounded and vengeful all at once.

It was several pounding heartbeats later that I found my voice. And my indignation. "And just how do you know that? Did your spy *girlfriend* tell you that?"

He went still as stone. "What are you talking about?"

My lip curled. I could feel this getting ugly. "You know."

Something happened to his face, something scary.

He stood, tucking himself back into his jeans and zipping them up, his eyes never leaving me.

A ruthlessness I'd never seen before had overtaken his expression. "I *don't* know," he bit out. "Explain it to me."

"That woman you have spying on me. *She* told you, didn't she?"

His whole face clenched up, and I knew something bad was happening.

He'd gone so still, but something volatile was writhing *in agony* under the surface of that stillness.

"How do you know about the woman spying on you?" he asked me.

I wanted to curse at him in five languages for the question, but I managed to answer civilly enough. At least he knew now that I was aware of her. It was something I'd needed to address, needed to have out in the open. "She came to see me. Didn't you know?"

His face didn't so much as twitch, but his shoulders started shaking.

He looked like he was about to snap, to lose it completely.

I was afraid of him, that's how much he was losing his ever-present composure.

I'd always known he was dangerous. But my instincts, which I'd trusted before Heath, had always told me that, while he was dangerous, he was not at all dangerous to me.

I did not feel that way now.

Something dark and vile had overtaken him. He'd barely moved, but I still knew, deep in my gut, that he was incensed to a degree that I'd never seen before.

To the point of violence.

I was shaking. This was not Heath and his usual combination of mean and magnificent. This was not Heath angry = Me turned on.

This was something unmanageable. I knew it.

"She contacted you *directly?*" His face was fraudulently collected, but his voice hid nothing. He sounded murderous.

"She came to my house. She had all kinds of interesting things she wanted to tell me about you."

I couldn't speak of her without revealing my feelings, though I tried to hide it.

My jealousy was very thinly veiled, but as I studied him I realized that that didn't matter. He'd never notice it, because he simply wasn't looking for it.

He was much too wrapped up in his own volatile emotions then to notice mine.

"She came *here*? To your *house*?"

I didn't answer, didn't bother to repeat myself, just staring at him.

He cursed, fluently and savagely. "Did she lay a hand on you? Hurt you?"

I couldn't manage an answer for several pounding heartbeats, because the way he asked it made me realize something.

This fury, this unadulterated rage he was going through was not directed at me.

It was for her. I was both relieved and as baffled as ever.

"No," I finally got out.

That seemed to take some of the steam out of him, which was good. I could breathe again when he didn't look so close to the brink.

"She just came here . . . to talk?" he finally managed to get out.

"Yes. She told me everything, Heath. I know *everything*."

His brows drew together menacingly. "*She* told you everything? I don't fucking think so. She doesn't *know* everything, and I've worked with her for a long time, so I can guess what she *did* tell you. A convincing combination of lies and truth. But I see it got to you."

"Are you saying you've never lied to me?"

"Not like you seem to think. Have I been completely upfront with you? No. Have I lied? Yes. But not more than I had to."

"I know that you only approached me because of whatever was going on with your sister and Dair."

He cursed, and it was as good as an admission of guilt. "Yes, that's why

I approached you then. But it has fuck all to do with me being here now."

I recoiled. It was an awful thing to hear, because it made me think that— "So you only slept with me because of—"

"No! Fucking no. Stop it. I checked you out for my sister. I searched your house. I got a feel for your patterns, trying to figure out if you were seeing Dair. But, like I said, that had fuck all to do with us having sex."

"Then why—"

"I fucked you because I couldn't fucking help myself, okay? It was never part of the plan. It was always *against* the goddamn plan, okay? I'll admit that I invaded your privacy way more than was fair. I, shit, Lourdes, I started watching you and I liked what I saw. More than liked."

He took a very deep breath. "Listen, to understand why I became so obsessed with you so quickly, you need some background on me. I've done a lot of things. Terrible things. Things a man can't come back from. You never come back. Instead, you end up owning those things, and they just become a part of who you are.

"For better or worse, I own a lot of bloody baggage that I can't ever walk away from. I've survived a lot of things I can't come back from, and hell, I know there are some still to come."

He studied me for a moment, trying to gage my reaction, then continued, "I carry all of my burdens as best I can, but I know better than anyone that I can *never* lead a normal life. Even if all of my problems were solved, and my sister was safe, my life will never be peaceful.

"I wouldn't even know where to begin to be *peaceful.* I am not acclimated to the rules of normal society.

"When you're that fucked in the head, deceit becomes a way of life. Lies become a pattern.

"I don't lie because I like it. I've never enjoyed the burn at the back of my throat when I open my mouth and deadpan endless falsehoods, big ones, small ones, omissive ones, day after day.

"I lie because the bottom line is: the truth is death for me, no matter how I might crave it.

"But God, I do crave the truth.

"Imagine damaged me with all of that inside of me, abhorring deceit, craving elusive honesty.

"Running into a woman like *you*.

"There wasn't a thing about you I couldn't read. Even if it was hidden a bit, no matter. You're a piece of *glass* I could hold in my palm. So what if it clouded a bit, got a bit of sand on it? All I had to do was turn it this way, brush it off, and poof, shiny and transparent as ever.

"But really, I didn't even have to do that. The beauty of you, this gorgeous creature that for some fucking reason let me have her, over and over, was that if I wanted the truth from you, all I had to do was ask, and you'd tell me. You play no games. You're incapable of deceit.

"You're the truth, Lourdes. So what if I couldn't, shouldn't have you? I *craved* you, and so I kept coming back.

"I'm not dead inside. Not all of me. Something remains, something that doesn't only live for vengeance.

"That's what you taught me."

He'd left me speechless, breathless, without a leg to stand on.

He did care about me. I was positive of that now, at least. So many other questions remained, but that was the one that had bothered me the most.

I was such a girl.

I moved to him, laying my cheek against his chest.

He wrapped his arms around me.

We stayed like that for a long time, pressed together as I wondered what the hell I was supposed to do. Had this changed anything? It felt like it had. But feelings and reality were two different things.

"She said she was your lover," I finally broke the silence. I'd tried to keep that in, but I just couldn't.

He sighed and stroked a hand over my hair. "She's a good liar. It's what makes her great at her job. We're *not* sleeping together."

"Since when?" Another thing I couldn't keep in.

"Since I was fifteen, and only then to mark her as mine to keep her safe from the other people we were working with. They were scared of me, and her being mine made her off-limits."

"So why is she so interested in me?"

"Hell if I know. If I had to guess, I'd say it's some leftover jealousy from the past. But I'll tell you one thing—she won't bother you again."

I took a deep breath, trying to hold in yet another question. Tried and failed. "Have you been with . . . anyone else, since you've been with me?"

He stiffened up, but didn't hesitate. "No." Long pause. "I won't be asking you the same question." His voice was pained. "I don't want to know."

I was gearing up to answer him, to set him straight when he continued, "Once I was tortured by a particularly sick motherfucker. He sliced me to ribbons with a rusty, dull knife. When I heard about you and your other man, heard he'd spent the night here, it hurt worse than that. Just so you know."

I started trembling. "Heath," my voice caught on his name. "He didn't—we haven't, err, I didn't have sex with him. He spent the night, but he slept on the couch, okay? I haven't done more than kiss him."

"I don't understand. So why did he spend the night?"

"Hell if I know. He wanted to. But he never even made a move. We were taking it slow."

I barely got the last word out before he was kissing me.

CHAPTER
TWENTY-NINE

I woke alone in my bed.

I sat up.

He'd *left?*

I was instantly angry.

Not angry. Furious at him, for so many complicated reasons, but one of them, the most important one, was terribly simple.

He'd *left.* I'd wanted him to stay, and regardless of why, he had not stayed. He had left. It was that uncomplicated and that devastating.

And I had not a clue where we stood. He'd finally let me sleep after that last round of sex, and I'd passed out cold, but what we'd needed to do was *talk.*

How could he do that?

Back for only half a night, but he'd done his fair share of damage.

Messing up my head.

Messing up my heart.

Then leaving without a goodbye?

I couldn't have it. I *couldn't* do this again. Not for sex or for love.

But what did I think we could've settled?

He couldn't offer me *anything*. I'd gathered enough about the current job he was on to understand that much, at least.

Not even an occasional something, which sadly I'd have taken.

All he could give me was a big fat maybe, just maybe someday, and I needed more than that, plain and simple.

I had myself worked up into a temper when I heard the front door opening.

I threw on my robe and charged through the house.

And there was Heath, locking the door behind him with one hand, a bouquet of pink lilies in the other.

My temper left me in one long, dreamy sigh.

"I forgot last night," he explained, holding up the flowers. "But then I remembered this morning. I noticed that your boys brought you different kinds, so I thought I'd surprise you."

I smiled, moving to take them from him. "It's true, I like variety."

"Hopefully you're only talking about flowers when you say that."

I laughed, shooting him a look over my shoulder. "You tell jokes now? Surely that's a sign of the apocalypse?"

I was rewarded with his version of a fond smile.

I put the lilies in a vase and was just setting them on my entryway table when his voice made my breath catch in my chest.

"If you tell me to stay away, I'll do it. Otherwise . . . I'll never leave you alone, never let you move on.

I shut my eyes tight. "Stay away."

"Do you mean it?"

I stood my ground, barely.

I let out a deep, stuttering breath and gave him a very soft, tremulous, "Yes. I need to move on, and I'll never move on if we keep doing this. Not if you can't give me something real, something lasting."

"I've always given you something real. This is real. And for what it's worth, it'll last as long as I live."

Powerful emotion made my voice thick. I couldn't quite believe what he was saying to me. "Then why have we never so much as talked about the future?"

"I don't have a future, Lourdes. But if I did . . . if I did, it would be yours. I'd give it you in a heartbeat. I wish I could give you everything you deserve."

"Will you explain that to me? Why don't you have a future?"

"They're not my secrets to tell."

"This is our entire problem. If you could just stop being cryptic for one second and tell me what is going on."

His fists clenched. "I'm doing my level-best here," he enunciated slowly.

"Well, I need you to do *better*. If you're asking me to do what I think you are, to wait for you, for some indeterminate amount of time, then I need at least some answers."

His eyes closed, jaw clenched in defeat, and I thought we were dead in the water.

But then he proved me wrong about him, yet again. "Ask me a question, and I'll try my best to answer it, okay?

I didn't know whether I was relieved or appalled. What would I be willing to do for a Heath that was actually upfront with me about his life?

It boggled the mind.

I started with the most important question. "Why don't you have a future?

"I'm on an assignment right now that is very dangerous. I've already taken six bullets for it over two different occasions and lost several men. I'm protecting a witness, a very important one, one that is in a great deal of danger. I can't discuss the details of the case, but it is high stakes, and there is no other option but for me to see it through to the end."

"Can't you just go into hiding for a while?"

"We have, and we do, but this witness has powerful enemies working in the government, and my team's already been compromised twice. And besides that, at some point my witness will be taking the stand in a very public trial. We can't hide for that part."

"I got the impression your sister is right in the middle of this mess. How is she involved?"

His mouth turned down into a frown that made me want to burst into tears, it was so full of pain. "She's the witness."

Oh God. There really was no way out for him.

"I'll fight to the end to protect her, to stay alive myself," he continued. "But our odds are shit poor. Impossible to sugar coat it. And even if somehow we succeed, and I keep Iris alive long enough to do the job she has to do, I still have years of work ahead of me before I can ever sleep easy at night."

"So," I said slowly, "if we're optimistic and things work out in your favor, we're talking *years* you're asking me to wait?"

"It's a very good possibility. I'm sorry. I wish I could give you a better answer."

I wished he could too.

"Tell me something sweet, Heath," I uttered softly.

"I know I'm not being fair to you here. I know I should let you move on. But I can't. I'll do anything to be with you for as much time as I can. Anything you ask."

I soaked that up. I don't know how he did it, but he always managed to say the thing that made it worth me sticking around, no matter how little he had to offer.

"Okay," I finally said, even while my mind still raked over all of the things I'd learned. "I'll wait for you. As long as you're faithful. And as long as you try your damned hardest to get back to me as soon, and as often, as you can."

He closed the few feet of ground that separated us, his hands going into my hair. He leaned down, touching our foreheads.

"Thank you. Now I need you to do something for me."

"Hmm?" I asked, eyes closed, soaking up his tender touch.

"Dump that fucker you've been seeing. Call him right now and tell him it's over. And also, we both know I'm paranoid, but deal with him carefully in the future. Don't be alone with him again. My people couldn't find out much about him, aside from the basics, and they got nothing solid on his history. I don't like that. I've never met a man with no past at all."

"Okay, I'll do it right after you leave." I told him, feeling a little disappointed in myself that it didn't make me more sad to just be letting Kevin go that easy.

Had he meant nothing to me at all? Had I just been using him as a rebound?

The answer made me feel guilty. I'd expected better from myself.

"Just make sure he knows it's fucking final. Hammer every nail into that fucking coffin."

He was jealous, and I didn't blame him. I'd have been just as jealous.

"I will. I won't leave him hanging. It wouldn't be fair."

Somewhere in the house, my cell started ringing.

I tracked it to the bedroom.

Eduard was calling.

What the fuck? Could I not get a break?

Heath was right behind, and he saw the name on the screen when I did.

He plucked the phone from my hand and answered it with an oh so charming, "What the fuck do you want?"

I perched on the edge of my bed and watched him, arms folded across my chest. Hell, maybe he could talk some sense into my idiot ex. I'd sure as hell never been able to.

I couldn't hear what Eduard said on his end, but I could see from Heath's reaction that he didn't like it.

"Her fucking man, that's who," he thundered into the phone. "There's nobody else. Just me from here on out, motherfucker."

I tried and failed to keep from smiling.

"Suing? You have the nerve to talk about *suing* her? Are you fucking crazy? You threaten her again, and I'll make you sorry." Pause. "How? I'll hurt you, slowly, you piece of shit."

Okaaaay, I thought to myself.

That was about enough of that.

I plucked my cell from his hand and hung it up, giving him an exasperated look. "I can handle him. Trust me."

He opened his mouth and I held up my hand. "Trust me," I repeated. "You have enough on your plate. I can deal with my pain in the ass ex all by myself. Okay?"

He nodded, but he sure as hell didn't look like he liked it.

And then, because I couldn't prolong it forever, I asked the question I'd been dreading. "How long can you stay?"

He cursed, and I knew I wouldn't like the answer.

And I didn't.

He was gone within the hour.

I did what any woman would do when she'd just had a night of absolute bliss in the arms of an ex.

I called a girlfriend.

Danika knew the most about my current fucked up dating situation, so she got the honors.

"I had sex with him five times last night."

Danika paused for a few beats on the other end. From the background noise, I could tell she was at work, in the gallery at the Cavendish resort.

"Him who?" she asked.

I winced. It was a fair question. Thus the wince.

"Heath."

"Dayum. So it's not really over between you?"

"It's complicated."

"It always is," she said wryly. "But five times does not sound like it's over."

"It's not. We're back on; it's just, you know, he'll be gone a lot. It's a long story, but the short version is I have to make a very unpleasant phone call to Kevin now."

"Well, hell. I'll bring the wine."

It was a few hours later. I was on my third glass of wine, and I was cooking Danika dinner.

The unpleasant phone call had gone about how I'd expected.

"So what do you do now?" Danika was asking me. "What are the particulars of dating a super spy?"

"I'm not exactly sure. I'll keep you posted. A lot of going about my life as usual and waiting for him, I suppose."

She made a grunt of a noise at that. I looked at her.

"You think I'm a fool," I noted. "That I shouldn't wait for him."

She shook her head, eyes widening like I'd misunderstood her. "I didn't say that. Only *you* can say if it's worth it to wait. I'll tell you one thing I learned the hard way, though. You can't *un*love someone just because you want to. Trust me on this. So if you love him, *really* love him, then of course it's worth waiting."

"Even years?"

"Even your whole life. What's the other option? Settling for Kevin? That wouldn't work. I had a Kevin once, too, you know, back in the years when I thought that Tristan and I were hopeless. And just like you can't *un*love a person, you can't make yourself love somebody, either."

"So I'm not a total fool for this?"

"No. Hell no, you're not. I've taken the foolish route, and it involves going *against* your heart, not following it. You *are* in love with him, aren't you?"

I don't know how it happened, but I didn't even have to think about my answer. "I am."

"Then no wait is too long, if you ask me."

I thought of something, and grinned at her. "God, I'm *terrible* at casual sex."

We both laughed long and hard at that understatement.

"Join the club," she told me.

CHAPTER
THIRTY

I was freaking the hell out. Straight up *tripping*.

I didn't even know whom to call to talk it out with, girlfriend-wise.

This was *embarrassing* and too crazy to be believed.

It was nothing obvious that tipped me off. That's why it took me so long to notice that something was different about me.

It was the smell of pizza that did it.

It was just a few days after Heath had visited me. My boys were over for dinner.

It was Gustave's turn to cook, and he was making his best dish: Margherita pizza.

I'd taught him the recipe. We all knew it by heart. I could pick out by smell and taste every single ingredient he put into the sauce, but as he cooked it, it smelled *off* to me.

Not like anything had gone bad. It wasn't even necessarily a smell I didn't like. It was just *wrong*.

"What's that smell?" I asked Raf. We were in the dining room, setting the table.

"That is the best pizza sauce in the world that you taught us both to memorize at birth," Raf shot back, grinning at me.

He didn't smell it.

I went into the kitchen, looking over Gustave's shoulder at the saucepan. "Did you do something different to the sauce?" I asked him.

He shot me a puzzled look over his shoulder. "Are you kidding? Who messes with perfection?"

Well, hell.

Gus didn't smell it either.

I tried to ignore it, but ended up thinking about it more and more.

The smell of a lot of things had changed to me of late. But it took something that familiar, a family recipe, to make me realize that it wasn't the food that was off.

It was me. I was changing, and that wasn't the only change.

I'd gained a bit of weight, but I'd attributed that to the fact that I'd gone out to eat so much when I'd been dating Kevin.

And so back to me, freaking the hell out, driving to the store after my sons left, in the middle of the night, to grab a home pregnancy test.

It's impossible, I reassured myself, for maybe the thousandth time.

It's at least improbable, I tried telling myself when the impossible didn't work, because it was simply a lie.

My God, what was I going to do? This was not a problem I should be having at this stage of my life. It was ridiculous. Too silly to give any credence to.

Dammit.

I'd always had problems with the pill, and Eduard had gotten a vasectomy after Gustave was born, so it wasn't something I'd had to worry about for a very long time.

Until that one night, months ago, when Heath had decided to show up to my house without condoms.

Dammit.

I couldn't believe it. It was too silly. I was *too damn old* to be dealing with a mistake like this. Okay, *making* a mistake like this.

I bought five home pregnancy tests, brought them home, laid them out on my bed, and just stared at them.

And then I used them each, one by one.

And just stared at them.

Five plus signs.

I was well aware how unlikely it was to get five false positives. The home pregnancy tests were pretty damn accurate these days.

Even so, I made an appointment with my doctor, taking her first available window.

But I knew what I needed to know.

I was pregnant.

Heath had knocked me up.

My first reaction, and it lasted a while, was pure shock.

Heath had left me a number, nothing else, and he'd said very clearly that it was for emergencies only. That's why I waited until after my doctor's appointment to call it. I wanted to be absolutely certain before I freaked him the hell out right along with me.

"Jimmy's Market," an unfamiliar male voice answered the phone.

I thought at first I'd dialed wrong. But I asked anyway. "I need to talk to Heath. It's an emergency."

"No Heath here. Wrong number, lady."

His tone was abrasive, but I checked the card, and the number I'd dialed, and they were the same, so I went on. "Tell him Lourdes needs to talk to him," I tried.

There was a long silence on the other end, and with a curse, I added, "It's an emergency, like I said."

More silence. I hoped the fucker was taking notes. "Tell him— *fuck*—tell him I just found out I'm pregnant."

I hated doing it like this, but I didn't know this system they were using, didn't know if I'd get to talk to him directly at all, and I felt strongly that he needed to be aware that he was going to be a father, the sooner the better.

The other line went dead. Well, hell.

What was I supposed to do now?

CHAPTER
THIRTY-ONE

I t was a few days later. I still hadn't told anyone the big news except
that stranger over the phone.

And I had yet to hear from Heath.

I was just sitting on it. I figured I'd put off telling anyone for as long
as I could, but the fact was, this baby was coming in around six months,
and I couldn't hide it for long.

I was still in the shock phase, and I'd decided to embrace that for a
while.

I was at home, photo-shopping a shoot I'd done recently, trying to
distract myself with work.

My phone rang, and I checked it.

Unknown caller flashed on my cell.

Well, hell. I hated answering unknown numbers, but if Heath were going to call, it would likely be from an unknown line just like this.

I answered.

"Lourdes," a familiar voice said on the other end of the line.

I hung up the phone instantly, cursing at it.

What was *she* doing calling me?

Christie.

I'd blocked her number ages ago.

Right after I'd listened to her having sex with my husband.

My phone started ringing almost instantly.

The worst ex-best friend in the history of time had the *nerve* to call me *again?*

I ignored the call. When she tried three more times, I turned my cell off. No way. There was no reason on this earth I should ever have to speak to her again, for any reason. Women like her, the home-wrecking variety, should be shipped off to their own island in the middle of nowhere as far as I was concerned.

It occurred to me that with my phone off, I might miss a call from Heath, and I switched it back on a few hours later, but it didn't ring again.

It was late afternoon and I was just heading out, literally halfway out the door to run errands, bag in hand, when my doorbell rang.

I wasn't expecting anyone, but sometimes, even though they had keys, Raf or Gus would ring my doorbell, so I went to answer it.

I checked the peephole, because if it was solicitors I was damn well going to ignore it.

It was her. The home-wrecker. Christie. At my *house.*

Was she *demented*, thinking she could come here?

She should know better. I should never have to look at this woman's face again. Never have to hear her voice, or breathe the same air.

Dealing in any way with the bitch who had pretended to be my best friend while she fucked my husband was nothing a woman like me should have to do.

When I say we'd been best friends, I mean *best* friends. Get up every morning and call each other friends. Tell each other our deepest darkest fears and secrets friends. And for over a decade, no less.

I'd never forgive her.

It wasn't even that I was still bitter about the divorce. And it sure as hell wasn't that I wanted my ex-husband back.

This bitch could have him. Hell, anyone could have him, as long as it wasn't me.

It was the betrayal. The kind of betrayal that, to this day, made me feel more alone in the world.

A woman that could do that to a friend, sneak around behind her back for who knew how long, and still smile to her face.

My contempt for her would never change. It was that simple.

I decided pretty quickly that I'd just ignore her. If I opened that door, there'd be some kind of confrontation, and I didn't want to give her the satisfaction of knowing she could get under my skin.

I started to walk away, heading toward my garage.

Her voice, calling out loud enough to be heard through the thick walls of my house, stopped me cold.

"Lourdes! It's about Eduard! He's been killed!"

Well, that did it. One second ago I'd have sworn it was impossible, but she'd found a way to get me to talk to her.

I opened my door, staring at the woman that had tried her best to wreck my home.

Tried, I told myself, and feeling it ring true. My home without Eduard was still intact. My boys and I were doing just great.

Still, the bitch had tried, and I'd never forget it.

I hadn't seen Christie in about a year, but she looked like she'd aged ten in that time.

Her blonde hair was stringy with grease, like she hadn't washed it in days.

She'd always been a thin woman, but she was emaciated now, the lines around her mouth and eyes starkly accentuated by the weight loss.

"What did you say?" I asked her, sure I'd heard wrong or misunderstood, and as soon as she cleared this up, I'd be able to shut the door in her face.

"Eduard. He's been killed. I'm sorry to tell you that way, but I knew you wouldn't open the door otherwise, and I've been trying to call all day."

I studied her some more, trying to process the information, finding it hard to believe, but the signs of grief were evident in her. This wasn't some strange stunt. She was genuinely distraught.

The woman I remembered had been very well put together with a consciousness for the way she dressed that bordered on vain. She'd come to my house in sweat pants and a stained tank top. She was a mess.

My God. *Eduard was dead?* My mind kept jumping around, to her car at my curb, to the yellow patch in my lawn. Anything normal that did not involve death.

"How?" I finally asked her.

She blinked rapidly, and I could see that she was struggling not to weep. "He didn't come home for a few days, and I was really worried. It's not like him to disappear for *that* long. Overnight maybe, but not for more than one night."

I'd learned a lot from that little bit. For one thing, they'd been living together. I hadn't even known, but of course it was salt in the wound that she was likely helping him spend the money he'd gotten out of me in the divorce.

"Still," she continued. "I didn't call the police or anything, even then. I just figured he was off having fun somewhere, and he'd be back, you know, *sometime.*"

I didn't know. Eduard had never done any of his cheating on me out in the open, as he apparently did with her. He'd gone to great pains to hide it well from me.

If he hadn't, I'd have kicked him to the curb ages ago.

I was surprised she seemed accept it, but then, what could *she* expect when he'd been married at the start of their relationship? Hell, maybe that was what made them compatible.

"But the police found him before I could call them," she added tremulously.

A chill ran through me at those words. That sounded ominous.

I blew out a breath. God, she had me feeling sorry for her, that's how pathetic she looked just then.

"Do you want to come in?" I asked her. This did not seem like a conversation we should be having through an open doorway.

She shook her head back and forth rapidly. "No."

Whatever. I nodded at her to go on.

"Someone had called in a tip, a tip about a body in a warehouse somewhere near the strip."

The word body got to me for some reason. Made it more real.

Perhaps it was that I was starting to process that Eduard was not a living person anymore, instead he was a *body.*

Christie was openly crying now, her whole, frail body trembling with it. "Eduard was murdered, Lourdes."

I tensed up. "What?"

"Murdered! The police said—they said—they said he was evic-erated," she pronounced the word like she'd never said it before in her life. And she probably hadn't. "They found his body strung up, tied by his wrists. Even they—the police—were shocked by the way he was killed. They said—they asked me if he had any enemies, Lourdes. They asked me if he was *gang* affiliated."

"My God," I said dully. What else could I say? What did a person say at a time like this? "I'm sorry for your loss," I added, because it was the only appropriate thing I could come up with.

At that, her trembling stopped and her eyes hardened.

She pointed at me. "You know he was about to sue you!"

And then I saw her game. Why she'd been so determined to tell me herself.

Goodbye, sympathy. It was real.

I stood up straighter. She was petite, and I towered over her. "Are you accusing *me* of something?"

"You know he was about to sue you, and he—he said you were dating some huge, young, scary guy that kept threatening him."

I glared at her. "I was aware Eduard was suing me, thanks for the heads-up, by the way, and I couldn't have cared less. As you saw in the divorce, I can afford better lawyers than he can. I wasn't worried. And the only reason my boyfriend ever spoke to Eduard was when he was harassing *me.*"

"Where is he? I want to talk to him myself!"

"He's out of town. He's *been* out of town. And I'm sorry to hear that happened to Eduard, but it had nothing to do with *me.*"

She looked unconvinced, to say the least. She was distraught and grief could quickly morph into rage, and she had clearly settled on a target for her misfiring emotions. There was no reasoning with a person in that state.

"Well, just so you know, I told the cops all about his threats," she said unevenly. "This isn't over. Eduard wasn't in a *gang*." She said the last as though I'd been the one to imply such, when I knew as well as her how ridiculous that was.

"No, he wasn't. That doesn't mean his death had anything to do with my boyfriend."

She waved a hand at me like she was trying to bat the words away. "We'll just see about that, won't we?"

"I guess," I said, my voice as emotionless as hers was emotional. I'd turned off to her. Sympathy, anger, all of it was just gone. I wanted her to leave so I could call my sons about their father. I dreaded that even while I knew I needed to do it before they heard from someone else.

She turned to leave, thank God, but she hadn't taken four steps before she whirled, snarling at me, "Also, I tried to tell your sons. They wouldn't take my calls, either."

"No, they wouldn't," I said coldly. "Did you think they would? I'll tell them myself."

She left.

I called first Raf, and then Gustave, and asked them both to come over.

I didn't want to inform them over the phone that their father was dead.

Eduard's death hit me slow and strange, more of a shock than anything. It was tragic, in its way, as all life cut too short is tragic, but it didn't even feel like a loss to me personally. He'd already been cauterized from my life, and so it was no question that I wouldn't be missing him.

But the way he'd died, that affected me, got to me. It was just so awful.

And the more I thought of it, it struck me.

Murdered.

Eviscerated.

That's what she'd said. That word, that *exact* word was already burned into my mind in a traumatizing way.

Because it was attached to Heath, to that story from his gory past. It was something he'd done to people.

It couldn't be such a common thing to do that it would come up again and be mere coincidence, could it?

But of course it could, and it was, I told myself. Heath hadn't liked Eduard. Well, okay, he'd pretty much hated him. But he'd had no reason to *kill* him. And certainly not like that. He'd had no reason to seek him out at all.

I kept telling myself that, but I would have felt so much better if I could have had just one short conversation with Heath.

More than anything, even Heath's violent past, I worried about how Eduard's death affected my sons.

It was tiresome, how much I checked up on them the first day, calling every hour to see how they were holding up.

It was odd; they both took it the same, at least from what I could see. Their reactions were solemn but stoic, and they emphatically did not want to talk about it.

Sadly, they both took it about how I did, with dull perplexity as though someone they'd known had died, but not anyone they'd had a real relationship with.

CHAPTER
THIRTY-TWO

It was evening, the day after I'd found out about Eduard.

I was just getting home after a shoot that had gone on until the last light fell from the sky. I was tired and ready to crash as I flipped on lights and headed for my bedroom.

I stopped dead about halfway into my room as I caught sight of something through the doorway to my bathroom.

There was something on the counter. Something odd. Something *wrong.*

Heart pounding, I moved into the master bath, eyes staring in disbelief at five objects that should not have been there.

Lined up, a few evenly spaced inches apart, were all five pregnancy tests I'd used.

There was no good explanation for them being back in my house, when I'd emptied my wastebasket, and taken out my trash days ago.

Who would dig them out and put them back in my house, lined up like that?

It scared me. Badly. Shook me up.

Who would go to the trouble to do something so strange?

And. . .

Who would be so interested in my pregnancy tests?

God, could it be Heath?

But no. I dismissed the idea almost instantly.

That woman, the one that had come to visit me? Somehow I'd still never learned her name, but she seemed to me the most likely culprit. She had spied on me and could still be spying on me now, and I knew without having to ask that she would not be happy I was carrying Heath's baby.

Shit.

I stewed on it for a bit while I went through my house, checking every nook and cranny, bolting every door and window.

Finally, I decided to reach out to Heath again.

He'd seemed sure this woman wouldn't bother me anymore when last we'd talked, and so I thought I should let him know that she apparently didn't agree with him, because she *was* bothering me. Badly.

"Jimmy's Market," a neutral male voice answered, sounding bored. I was pretty sure it was a different guy than the last time.

"I need to speak to Heath."

"No one here by that name. Sorry."

"Tell him Lourdes called again. Tell him I need to speak to him, and that his female partner is messing with me."

The man's voice changed from bored to brusque. "How is she messing with you?"

"I think she broke into my house, did some strange things meant to freak me out."

"I'll relay the message," the man said, and hung up.

At least he'd given me some reassurance that my message would go somewhere. It was a vast improvement over the last interaction.

I could be patient if I knew I was at least being heard.

Next I called Raf.

"Hey, Mom," he answered.

"Hey, baby. I need Tato back, if you don't mind. This house is too empty without him."

"Sure thing. I had a long enough turn. I'll bring him over tomorrow."

"Kay," I said absently, eyes darting around nervously. I didn't think I'd sleep a wink all by myself after what I'd found, but I wasn't going to worry Raf with it.

The doorbell rang, and I nearly jumped out of my skin.

"I'll let you go. Sounds like you have company," Raf said on the other end.

"No, no, don't," I said instantly, ears tuned to the front of my house as I inched my way there. "Just stay with me for a minute, okay? I'm feeling jumpy. I need to hear your voice."

There was a long pause on his end, then, "Mom, you sound scared. What's going on?"

"I don't know. But don't hang up just yet, okay?"

"I won't. And I'll do one better. I'm coming over."

I barely heard him. I'd reached the front door. A glance through the peephole was not reassuring.

Some strange man was there, wearing all black, his arms folded across his chest.

After what I'd just found, the last thing I was going to do was open my door to a strange man.

And then he spoke, calling out loudly so I'd hear him through the door. "Lourdes! Open up. Heath sent me."

I started to, then hesitated. How on earth was I supposed to know if that was true?

"I'm Mason," he added.

I did recall the name. I'd heard Heath say it once, only in passing, when he'd told his sister someone named Mason was waiting for her, but it'd left an impression because he talked about so few people.

"I work with him," he continued, his voice even at that volume, like he was used to yelling. "He just barely got your messages, and he'll be here in about eight hours. In the meantime, he wanted me to check to see what was upsetting you. What is it that you found that's freaking you out? He said if you wouldn't let me in to tell you he has something sweet to say to you, just as soon as he gets here. He said that'd mean something to you."

It did. I opened the door slowly, eyeing up the stranger I was about to let into my house.

He was big with dark hair and eyes, tan skin, and a heavy five o'clock shadow on his hard jaw.

He held up his hands in the universal sign for *I'm not a threat.* The thing is, if you're a huge man wearing a gun it just doesn't work.

"You can just tell me from here, if it makes you more comfortable. I was sent because of your call, that's all. I'm here to help you, however you need."

Watching his eyes, which were warm and kind and hearing his voice lowered down from a shout, all helped to put me at ease. I was starting to believe that this guy was who he said he was and began to feel guilty for doubting him.

"I found something in my house that I know for a fact I threw in the trash days ago."

"What is it and where did you find it?" he asked.

I sighed. If he knew about the calls, he probably knew about the pregnancy by now, too. "Five home pregnancy tests, ones that I had used and thrown out in my trashcan, lined up on my bathroom counter."

He whistled. "That's definitely not normal. And you thought it was Lisa?"

"I don't know her name." I described her in detail.

He nodded. "That's Lisa. I can promise you it was not her. She was taken off this detail, now I'm on it. She's nowhere near here, so if this happened today, that's impossible. Can I take a look?"

I grimaced, and let him, stewing as I followed him through my house. If it wasn't *her*, Lisa, than I was fresh out of ideas.

He didn't touch anything when we reached my bathroom, just studied it closely for a long time.

"Heath's the father?" he finally asked, his tone unreadable.

I flushed, but answered, "Yes."

"You're certain?"

I couldn't really blame him for asking, here he was investigating an odd situation for me, and if he'd been the one spying on me recently, he knew that up until mere days ago, I'd been seeing someone else. But still, it smarted a bit.

I tried not to make my voice sharp when I answered, "Absolutely."

He just nodded, like that settled an issue, and went back to studying.

"I guess the whole idea of privacy sort of flies out the window when you date a man like Heath," I said, tone light, though in truth I was still coming to terms with that.

"You guess right. But, you know, it's all for your safety." He waved his hand at the objects on the counter.

Finally he spoke again, "Has anything else in your house been tampered with? Anything been taken or moved?"

I thought about it, glancing around my room. My house was neat enough, it wasn't messy, but it wasn't particularly organized, either. I had a lot of stuff, especially in my master suite—clothes, shoes, jewelry, lingerie that never got to be properly utilized.

"I haven't noticed anything," I said slowly, "but that doesn't mean it hasn't been. I hadn't thought of it. I wasn't looking for anything like that. I only saw this because it stood out."

"Will you look around now? Take inventory? Tell me if anything seems off. Any detail would be helpful."

I nodded and began a meticulous search through my house, starting with my closet.

I didn't even know how many shoes I owned. I only noticed that a pair was missing because they were my favorite.

My black Lady Peep Louboutins were gone, a cubby on my shoe wall empty. Whoever had taken them hadn't even tried to hide it.

"At least one pair of shoes is missing," I called to Mason.

"Okay," he called back. "Keep looking, and tell me if you find anything else, especially if it's something . . . more personal."

I didn't explain to him that my favorite Louboutins missing *were* very personal. That was nothing a man like him would understand.

"A silk robe," I called when I noticed another missing item from the closet. I thought about it and figured I should add, "It was my favorite. I wore it all the time. The shoes were a favorite, too."

He appeared in the doorway of my closet. "So whoever did this knows you well."

"I guess," I said. "Someone could have found that out by spying on me, like you guys do." It was kind of sad how much I'd become resigned to the idea of being stalked.

He cursed. "I just got put on this detail, but I'll have to touch base more thoroughly with the person I relieved. It seems they were slacking on their job."

"Lisa," I said coldly.

"Lisa," he agreed. "If someone else has been stalking you, she should have noticed it."

"She hates me," I pointed out.

"Yes. I'm guessing that's why she did a shitty job keeping an eye on you. Normally she's the best at her job. It's why she was chosen for this, but it was clearly a mistake on our part. My apologies for that."

I just nodded at him.

"Keep looking," he prompted me.

I finished with the closet, but nothing else stood out to me. That didn't mean things weren't missing, though. Courtesy of my retail addiction, I just had too many shoes, bags, and clothes to keep track of.

I started on my bedroom, going through each drawer of my dressers carefully.

"Are any of those missing?" Mason asked as I was going through my panty drawer, sounding about as uncomfortable as I felt.

I shot him a look. "I honestly have no clue. Someone would have to take a lot before I noticed any missing."

He just nodded, then pointedly looked away.

I kept searching, combing through everything.

I saved the most mortifying thing in my room, for last, of course. Mason, at least, was still keeping his gaze averted as I opened my *toy* drawer.

Well, that sounded bad. It wasn't an *entire* drawer of toys, more like a few toys hidden at the bottom of a certain drawer.

I lifted the bit of lingerie that covered the more pertinent contents of the drawer and couldn't hold back a gasp as I saw what'd been done.

I saw Mason moving out of the corner of my eye, gaze glued on the huge serrated blade set amidst my personal things. It wasn't mine. I'd never seen it before.

CHAPTER
THIRTY-THREE

Mason started cursing.

I started shaking.

"I take it that blade isn't yours?"

I shook my head, and he cursed some more, then crouched down next to me and bagged up the knife.

"Anything else odd about this drawer?"

I was so shaken up by the knife that I didn't even feel awkward about the subject matter. I was beyond embarrassment at this point. "A vibrator is missing," I said dully.

There was a long pause then, "Your favorite?"

I grimaced and nodded.

His slew of curses that time went on for a while.

"Anything else?"

It took me a minute more of staring before I caught it. "A set of handcuffs."

He didn't remark on that, and for some reason that made me add, "They were technically Heath's."

By then he was searching the room himself. "Start packing a bag," he told me, standing on my bed to reach my ceiling fan. "You can't stay here right now. This house has been compromised."

I started to pack, my mind spinning.

I thought of something. "My son is on his way over. I need to call him to tell him if we're leaving."

"You do. But you need to pack first."

I complied, but inside I balked at that. I was a mother, first and foremost, and I felt that the first thing I should do was call my son and tell him not to come to my house, which was apparently unsafe now.

Mason started cursing again, and I glanced at him just in time to catch him taking something small out of the light fixture attached to the ceiling fan.

I started to freak the hell out. To the point that I had to tell myself to calm down.

"What was that?" I asked him, unable to hide the unsteady cadence of my voice.

"Camera," he said tersely, getting down from the bed. "This is even more fucked than I thought. I need to call this in, get something out of the car. It will take me exactly five minutes. And you need to pack quick, and I mean *quick*. We have to be out of here in ten minutes."

I nodded that I understood him, but the second he was out of the room, I was dashing for my phone and calling Raf.

A mother, first and foremost.

The other end picked up, but Raf didn't say anything, so I started in.

"Sweetie, you shouldn't come here now. It's a long story, but you and Gustave need to steer clear of my house for the next few days."

I was trying to pack one handed while I rattled that off.

"Hello, Lourdes," a blank voice said in my ear.

I froze, the toothbrush I'd just grabbed fell from my other hand. It was odd; one hand had gone limp, while the other clutched my phone against my ear in a death-grip.

I knew who it was, even while my mind stuttered to a halt at the words.

It was Kevin, I knew his voice, but it was wrong, so off I almost didn't recognize it.

A few realizations came to me then, all at once.

All of the worrisome things about him shifted into focus, all of the contradictions and quirks gaining enough substance to finally get my full attention, at last overwhelming my distracted mind.

Whoever I'd thought Kevin was, he was not. The man on the other end of the phone was a mystery to me, a terrifying one at that.

Kevin was a lie. A myth created to lure me in.

There was no Kevin. He was a stranger.

A stranger who had known me well enough to feign my same interests, to customize himself into a man I'd fall easily into dating.

And all of it, every last bit, had been a lie.

I didn't know him from Adam, but he clearly knew me.

He'd studied me well enough to break me with one short sentence.

"I have little Raffi," said the stranger.

Checkmate.

"Please," I gasped. "Don't hurt him. Don't harm my child. *Please.*"

"That's all up to you, Lourdes."

"What do you want me to do? Whatever you want, Kevin. Just don't hurt him. Please." I was begging.

"First of all, I want you to be *fast*. Drop everything you're doing, leave your phone behind, and go outside. Use the back door. Now. If your bodyguard stops you, your son will pay. Do you understand?"

"Yes."

It wasn't even a decision. Decisions require thought and choice.

I didn't think, and I didn't have a choice. He had my baby. He won. I'd do anything he asked, if there were even a chance it would keep him from harming my son.

I'm a fast runner, faster in a panic, and I was through my house and out the back in under ten seconds.

It was dark out, and the stranger on the phone had given me no instructions for when I was out.

I had one brief moment to wonder what I should do next when something cracked sharply against the back of my head.

I crumbled with a whimper.

An acrid wet cloth covered my nose and mouth.

The world went black.

I came to with a world-class headache.

I was trussed up, gagged, and in the trunk of a lurching vehicle.

It was pitch-black, but I could feel what was around my ankles and wrists.

Fucking zip ties, the psychopath.

I knew it was futile, with no way to maneuver properly, and no sharp objects to aid, but I couldn't seem to help myself. It was instinct. I struggled. Hard and long, until my wrists were bruised and raw, then bloody and torn. Fear kept goading me on, and so I kept struggling.

I wanted out of that damn trunk. I felt that anything would have been better.

But then I was out, moved from the car to a house, and it was not an improvement.

Kevin, or whatever the hell his name was, carried me in through a dark garage, slung over his shoulder like baggage.

He set me on the ground, propped upright against a wall. He wasn't rough about it, was in fact careful, but even that didn't make me feel better, not when I looked at his face.

When he wasn't in character, it inspired the kind of horror that made your hair stand on end, bile rising in your throat.

It wasn't even that he was sinister. It was the lack of anything at all that frightened me. The blankness of him now that he didn't have to act for me.

I didn't know how to deal with him, what to try to get out of this.

Reasoning with him seemed out of the question. Nothing could touch someone so clean of any feeling.

He left the room briefly.

The lights weren't on, but it wasn't completely dark. I could make out a few shapes in the space, enough to see that it was some sort of a den with a TV, a sofa, and a recliner.

I didn't realize I wasn't the only occupant in the room until I heard a low groan several feet in front of me.

I whimpered through my gag.

Rafael. And he was in pain.

The light switched on, and I saw him, a crumbled, beaten mess on the floor.

My glaring, wet gaze flew to the stranger formerly known as Kevin.

He smiled at me.

I wanted to murder him with my bare hands.

"If you scream, your boy will pay," Kevin said, then bent down and tore off my gag.

"You said you wouldn't hurt him," left my mouth the second the cloth was ripped free.

He waved a negligent hand at Raf's limp form. "That was from before. He didn't come with me easily. Your kid's a fighter."

I shut my eyes and whispered dejectedly, "Why? Why are you doing this?"

"I'm sure you've guessed. This is about Heath. I'm flushing him out."

"But why?"

"For one, I was hired. He has some very powerful enemies. But that's a new development, and this is an old beef. I've wanted him for a very long time. You can't imagine how pleased I was to find out that he finally had a weakness, one that he wasn't keeping particularly well protected."

He studied me like he was looking for a response, but I didn't give him one.

"Do you ever look around and think you're the only one who's really there?" he asked me. "Everyone else is a shell. Just *empty*. So *many* people, a sea of bodies, full of nothing but organs and guts and blood. They're all shapeless and colorless. The only time I see them is when I make them bleed, when I slice them up and feel their entrails with my bare hands. Did you know most people's insides have more depth than their so called souls?"

I shook my head that I did not, eyes wide on his dead ones, wondering if I was going to throw up all over him.

"And even then," he continued, "the color only lasts for a short bit of time, gone before a body even cools, and then I'm alone in the world again, the only one that's really here, it seems. That's how I feel almost all of the time. Alone.

But every so often, I *see* somebody else. For one reason or another, they stand out to me. They aren't empty. Heath is one of those. We used to work together, did I tell you? Co-oped some jobs for the government a few years back. He's a rare talent. I've always respected his work, but on a personal note, we don't get along. We don't see eye to eye on the particulars, if that makes any sense. I won't bore you with the details, but the last time we worked together, it ended badly. Would you believe he tried to kill me? He nearly did. Needless to say, I couldn't forget a thing like that. He took a shot at me and missed. It's time I got a chance to shoot back. I'll almost be sad when I kill him. It's a pity to kill one of the real people, but in his case, it has to be done.

And there's a silver lining here."

I shuddered at the thought. It boggled the mind what he'd consider as an upside.

"Do you want to know what it is?" he asked.

I nodded, because when the crazy man asks you a question, you damn well try to play along.

He smiled his sick smile. "I found you. And you know, you aren't empty, either, Lourdes."

Just my fucking luck.

What was I, like, psychopath catnip?

But as I thought about it, I realized that it might be something I could work with.

CHAPTER
THIRTY-FOUR

M y eyes darted to Raf. He hadn't moved or made a noise
since psycho-Kevin had turned on the light.

"Please, Kevin—"

"Call me Earl."

"Please, Earl, let me check on my son. I need to make sure he's okay
and tend to him."

Earl straightened and moved away, leaving the room. I thought
he was just ignoring my request, but he was back a few minutes later, a
black leather bag in his hand.

I tensed when he got near Raf, but he didn't hurt him, at least not
more than he was already hurt.

Instead, he began to tend to him.

"I used to be a doctor, you know," he told me.

His back was to me, and I couldn't see what exactly he was doing. Both of their faces were hidden from me, but I could vaguely make out his movements.

"Is he okay?" I asked, holding my breath as I waited for the answer.

"He's fine. Bruises and superficial cuts, nothing more. And, Lourdes, he'll stay fine, just as long as you cooperate with me."

"I'll cooperate," I assured him, meaning it. "Just don't hurt him again."

He was silent for a long time, and I barely blinked as I watched him. If he'd tried to further harm Raf, there was nothing I could have done about it, but he didn't. Instead, he cleaned and bandaged his cuts, even going so far as to hold an icepack to his head.

When he finished, he came and crouched in front of me again, studying my face with detached curiosity.

"We need to travel again," he told me, like we were discussing it, and I had some kind of say in the matter.

I just stared at him.

"Do you have any more questions for me before I put this back on?" he asked, holding up the cloth he'd used to gag me.

He was using just a touch of his Kevin persona to coax me, I thought, though I didn't see the point. He could obviously do whatever the hell he wanted, whether I agreed or not.

"You killed Eduard, didn't you?" I asked.

"Yes. For you. He was bothersome, wasn't he? And now he won't bother you. And besides that, I didn't like his attitude."

"You didn't have to do that," I said, voice trembling with rage. It was just so senseless.

"No, I didn't, but I *wanted* to. And he wasn't the only one I killed for you."

My life had turned into a nightmare, and so when he said that, my mind flew to the most horrifying possibility.

God, no. Please, no. Not that. Anything but that.

"Gustave?" I managed to sob out. I couldn't handle even the thought.

"No, no, nothing so drastic. Your sons aren't bothersome to you, at least not that I've noticed, though I was a bit perturbed that you never wanted to introduce me. That almost made me lose my temper, which would have caused you a little grief, but lucky for you, I am a man of restraint."

Thank you, God, thank you, God, thank you, God, chanted in my head.

"Who then?" I finally asked.

"Lisa. She was an old colleague of mine, but I must say, I never had much use for her. Another empty vessel. Soulless to her core."

"Why?"

"She was planning something. They'd taken her off her detail. She wasn't supposed to be watching you anymore, but she was, and she was acting erratic, clearly upset. To be honest, I don't know what she was going to do, but it seemed likely she might try to hurt you. So I took care of her. I killed her *for you.*"

It wasn't lost on me, the horrible irony of this man who was going to hurt me, had done worse already by hurting my son, killing someone because they *might* harm me.

I didn't have much time to wonder over it. I thought he was moving to gag me, but instead he covered my nose and mouth again with a cloth that reeked with that same acrid stench.

I lost consciousness.

I don't know if he'd dosed me harder or what, but I must have been out a lot longer that time, because when I came to it was light out, and I was already ensconced in another house, in another room with Raf, who was conscious now, his eyes steady on me.

I took in every bruise and cut I could see, his blackened eyes, his split lip, feeling every bit of it.

I had no clue why, but Dr. Earl the psychopath had gone to the trouble to make us both comfortable, sitting us up, tied, but in recliners placed about six feet apart, facing each other.

And so began our strange captivity.

For the most part, it was tedious. A lot of awful waiting and anxious worrying.

Raf was bound up tight and treated like someone dangerous. The psycho even fed him by hand, not trusting him with so much as a fork and spoon.

He knew that Rafael was a testosterone fueled young man who was extremely overprotective of his mother, just waiting for a chance to break free.

Me, Earl treated drastically different, though it took me some time to catch it. He kept me tied, but he had no caution with me, no thought that I'd try to attack him. He treated me only as a risk for flight.

Because he'd been watching me, stalking me for God only knew how long, and he knew some things about me.

He knew I wasn't violent.

He knew this from watching me and felt confident in his assessment.

He hadn't done enough research.

He might have been a perfect killer, but in this instance, he was an utter fool.

Because I was not violent. In general, no, I did not have the urge to hurt inside of me. For the most part, I did have a pacifist's soul.

To a point. We all have that breaking point. Everyone probably has a few of them, but hands down, my children were the quickest way to snap mine.

How *dare* this sicko drag Raf into this?

I'd kill him with my bare hands. I was just waiting for my chance.

Earl did keep his word about not hurting Raf anymore, as long as I cooperated, and I did, but the same could not be said for me.

It could have been worse. That was an absolute fact. There were a dozen things just off the top of my head that would have been less tolerable to me.

Still, there was some pain to be had. Some torment to be suffered.

Some burdens to be borne that could not be taken back.

I'd carry them forever.

It began, around noon on the first day in that second house and stuck to a rigid pattern.

He started by gagging Raf, then turned to me.

He untied me and took me, without a word, into another room.

I didn't fight him. I knew that this was what he'd meant about me cooperating.

That didn't make it easy.

Raf could be heard screaming helplessly into his gag from the second we left until he saw me again.

When I said that Earl hadn't hurt my son again, I was only referring to physical pain.

The other room was a bedroom, and that first day was the worst with what I thought and feared he'd do when he sat me on that bed.

But he didn't rape me. Thank God at least for that.

"I don't have what you'd call 'normal wiring,'" he explained to me at one point. "I don't *get off* on sex."

I didn't ask. I sincerely did not want to know, but he seemed to feel, as he often did, that he owed me an explanation.

"I'd show you how I do, but I can't, not while you're pregnant. It's not safe. I wouldn't want you to lose the baby. After, though, we'll have some fun, I promise."

I didn't ask him what he planned to do with the baby. I didn't want to draw his attention to it. He was too strange when it came to my baby. Obsessed. Like it was his.

He stripped me, pushed me down, and tied my arms above my head.

I stayed meek as a lamb, knowing that any fight I put up on my part would cause some type of harm to Raf.

It was hard to stay quiet when he took out a blade. It was a small thing, but I didn't let that fool me. Little knives could cut just as surely as big ones, if they were sharp enough. And this one was honed with precision.

I lay there, shaking, while I waited for him to start on me.

I had no notion what he planned, but I knew it wouldn't be pleasant.

"I'd like you to gain some weight," he told me, as he bent down to touch high up on my leg. "And lose some muscle tone. You'll be more fun to play with when you aren't so firm. I like soft flesh."

I shut my eyes and shuddered.

He brushed his free hand over my inner thigh. "Your skin is like velvet, though. I do like that."

And he started to cut, carving at my skin with determined skill.

The pain wasn't unbearable. Pain wasn't what made it so awful. It was the helplessness of it, and the look on his face while he had me at his mercy.

He was quick, though and didn't cut even all that deep. I bled, but he was efficient, and he stopped the bleeding and cleaned the cut in short order.

When he was done, he took pictures. Lots of them.

After that, he untied me and told me to look.

I sat up and studied the spot he'd been working on.

High up on my inner thigh, carved into my flesh, it read: SOFT.

After that, he let me dress, tied me back to my chair, took out Raf's gag, then left the house for a few hours.

This also was a part of the daily pattern.

As soon as Raf and I were alone, our matching eyes would meet, the same desperate, searching fear in each pair.

"You okay?" I mouthed at him.

My son nodded jerkily. "Did he hurt you?" he mouthed back.

I shook my head, the first of many lies I'd be telling him to shelter him from the pain of this.

"Did he—?" Raf couldn't even finish the sentence.

I made solid eye contact and shook my head. "No. That's not his thing."

When Earl returned that first time, he was so full of restless energy that he couldn't stop moving, twitching. He was hyper, excited about something.

"Would you like to take a walk, Lourdes?" he asked me, casually gagging Raf again.

He didn't even look at my son as he did it. In fact, he rarely looked at him. That worried me—that he didn't seem to notice him.

I knew it made him more expendable to the sicko.

Of course it wasn't a real question. I didn't have a choice here, but I had to answer, anyway. "Yes, Earl."

"I changed my mind about you calling me Earl. I'd like for you to call me Doctor."

"Yes, of course, Doctor."

He smiled like he was pleased, then untied me, tugged me to my feet, and pulled me outside.

CHAPTER
THIRTY-FIVE

I t was a bright sunny day out, not a cloud in the sky, but I barely noticed, instead intent on studying my surroundings.

A wave of despair washed over me at what I saw.

We were in the desert. In the middle of freaking nowhere. The small house he had us in had no neighbors to speak of. The only road was a small dirt one, a private road, and it trailed so far off in the distance that I couldn't see where it ended, or where any other roads might intercept it.

We were stranded out here. Even if we managed to get free of our bonds, which was a stretch in itself, there was nowhere for us to go.

"There's no escape here, Lourdes," Earl said quietly, as though he'd read my thoughts and smiled his dead smile right into my soul.

I tried not to glare at him, but a hate the likes of which I'd never known was blossoming inside of me.

It was almost a comfort, how powerful that hate was.

Hatred can become sustenance. This one was growing so huge it felt like it was giving me energy, an energy I could live off, if need be.

He was tormenting my child and torturing me, but it didn't touch him.

None of this touched him. Hurting me, terrorizing my family.

How did you reach a man that couldn't be touched? I needed to reach him.

"If this was all just to hurt Heath, you've made a mistake," I said quietly.

That had him looking at me with something akin to interest at last.

"He's like you," I told him. "Nothing that happens to me will hurt him. I was a job to him, just like I am to you. He only acted territorial because that's who he is, not because the *territory* meant anything to him."

He frowned and shook his head at me, "You're so wrong, Lourdes. I've already won. He agreed to everything I asked, gave in without a fight the first chance he got. He wants to do a trade. Him for you and Raf. He didn't hesitate. You wouldn't believe how he begged me. It was beautiful. You broke my perfect soldier."

I wanted to wretch. Instead, I looked away from him to hide my loathing. It was getting harder and harder to act serene with him.

Something had set him off, a brief glimpse of my unguarded expression, perhaps. He was suddenly angry, gripping my chin and staring into my face.

"That was a *ploy*?" he taunted softly. "You were trying to *play* me? Why, you little liar, you'll pay for that."

That was the first time he beat me, right out in the open, because who would see him out here?

Not a soul.

We'd walked far enough away from the house that the sound of the blows wouldn't carry to Raf. At least he was spared that.

I didn't cry out. I tried to take it quietly, grateful in a way, because he seemed to be avoiding my midsection.

He knocked my legs out from under me and brought me to my knees, scraping them against the jagged ground. Gripping my hair with one hand, he began to hit me with the other, right across the face, small slaps that graduated into open palmed thwacks that progressed into heavy backhanded blows.

He worked me over in a way that was painful enough, but almost superficial, blackening my face, bloodying my knees.

When he was finished he pushed me onto my back, pulled out his camera, and began to snap pictures.

"Pull your knees up to your chin," he instructed me coldly, no anger present, and that's when I realized that he'd done this, not from loss of temper, but as a calculated move.

He was trying to get a rise out of Heath, and I had no doubts it would work.

Sometimes the words he chose to carve into my skin were odd. Random. Words like MOTHER, CALM, PLIANT. Once, randomly, I even received a LOVELY right under my right breast.

But other times, the words weren't random at all. The day after that conversation was one of those.

I received a LIAR in my left underarm, high up into my armpit, right on the most sensitive skin. It hurt like a bitch.

I didn't get a word every time, but words or not, he always carved something on me.

It made it easy, at least, to count the days as they passed.

We were ten days in when he cut a neat little OBEDIENT right on the inside of my wrist.

He was calculated enough to put me in a long sleeved shirt after that one. He was at least trying to hide all of the cutting from Raf. I appreciated that.

He was gone from the house right after, leaving us alone for the usual two-hour stretch.

We were careful when we spoke, I figured he had the room at least bugged, but those two hours were still the highlight of every day.

"Are you okay?" I asked Raf, first thing when we were by ourselves.

His raw eyes hit mine, and I could see that this was taking its toll on him. My poor, sensitive boy. If it wouldn't have done more harm to him, I'd have wept.

"Did he hurt you?" he asked, voice scratchy with the effort to hold everything in.

"No, sweetie. I'm fine."

Raf's bloodshot eyes moved down to a spot on my arm, just below the sleeve of my shirt.

I looked down. Dammit. A bit of blood showed, peeking out through the hem.

I turned my arm, hiding it, but it was too late.

"What's that?" he asked.

"Just a scratch," I assured him.

He shut his eyes, and I could see his lips were quivering.

My poor, sensitive boy.

I'd given up on working at my ropes by then. Earl had noticed the condition of my wrists early on, and calmly threatened to hurt Raf if I continued.

Our situation felt more hopeless than ever. By taking both of us, he had all the leverage he needed to keep us obedient forever.

Just thinking the word had me glancing down at my bloody wrist.

The cuts had leaked just enough to make out the neat OBEDIENT through my white sleeve.

That was the day something wonderful happened.

Earl didn't come back.

Not that day, or the next, or the one after that.

The third day was the day when I began to gain the certainty that we were going to die like this, tied up to soiled chairs and starving.

Each time he'd left, Earl had given us each a large bottle of water, set between our legs. It was tricky, but we'd both picked up swiftly how to drink that way, twisting the cap off with our teeth, and taking small sips.

We each rationed our water as much as we could; taking the tiniest sips when we began to get an inkling that he wasn't coming back anytime soon.

On day three, it was looking dire. Even with the rationing, we were down to the last drops, and soon, sucking at air.

How long could a person live without water? I thought three days. Raf swore it was five, since we were indoors.

I badly did not want to find out which one of us was right.

Another day passed, the water completely gone now.

I had the popcorn ceilings memorized, and I didn't even notice the stench anymore.

We played games, quizzed each other with random trivia to pass the time, but I began to feel my mind getting more sluggish, and we slept longer and longer with each passing day.

Raf was sleeping when I got a sudden desperate burst of energy and began to struggle against my bonds.

I rubbed my wrists and ankles bloody, nearly knocked over my chair, and accomplished nothing at all. Earl'd known what he was doing. He left no weaknesses for us to exploit.

I cried, but no tears came. I was too dehydrated for that.

I woke with a start, and I didn't know why. I sat still for a moment, thinking, listening intently, before I heard it, breaking the great, vast silence of the desert.

A car. A loud one or possibly a few cars.

My eyes met Raf's. We stared at each other, both of us afraid to hope that this might be some improvement in our situation.

Perhaps it was Earl, and he'd just been using a new means to torture us.

His car had never been loud, though. But then it was possible he'd just brought a different one. The man was a stone cold murderer. I doubted he'd have any qualms about stealing a new car.

But no, as the sound grew, getting louder and louder until it felt like it was shaking the house, I became more certain that it wasn't just one car or even a few. It was a lot of cars.

I jumped in my seat when I heard a loud bang on the door, not like a knock, but like a battering ram, accompanied by shouts of, "FBI! Open up!" and more loud bangs, followed by the unmistakable sound of the front door being smashed open.

I thought I might pass out cold, I was so relieved.

Heath was the first one in.

He looked insane. Deranged. He was covered in blood, from his neck to his feet, and his eyes were more animal than human.

I didn't care. I'd take him like that. I'd take him any way at all.

He brought me water, eyes wary on me, but I refused to drink, telling him to get it to Raf first. He moved slightly, letting me see that Raf was being tended to just as quickly as I.

He held the bottle to my lips and as I drank, he bent to kiss the top of my head tenderly, letting me know that he wasn't too far gone. My Heath was still inside there somewhere.

"Are you bleeding?" I asked him as he cut me loose, my eyes running over his bloody form. All of it was dry or nearly so.

"No. None of this is mine."

"Earl's?"

"Yes," he bit out, tone savage. "He's dead."

"Good," I said, just as savagely.

He picked me up and took me out of there.

I couldn't help it, when the outside sun hit my face, I started to cry.

He was holding me to his bloody chest, stroking my hair, over and over, murmuring, "That's my girl. You're good now. Everyone is okay."

His tone was reassuring, but his arms around me were shaking badly. He was trying to convince himself as much as me.

I wasn't the only one that'd been damaged by this ordeal.

I got a few details out of him when we started to drive.

He'd surrendered himself to Earl days ago, but he'd managed to turn the tables. For days, he'd been torturing Earl, trying to get him to give up our whereabouts.

It had taken some time, but he'd broken the doctor. The second Heath laid eyes on me in the house, Mason had been informed, and Earl had been put out of his misery.

Somehow, we'd survived. We were alive. All of us. And Earl, the fucking psychopath doctor, was dead.

CHAPTER
THIRTY-SIX

There were some dark times then, while I recovered and wondered if I'd ever be the same. Ever *feel* the same.

And it was somehow enlightening, because it gave me an insight into what Heath was going through, when you looked around at people living their normal lives and wondered how the hell you'd ever be like them again.

Raf was going through the same. He was changed now, some of his soft spots hardened, some of his sweet traits broken.

But we were alive, and life went on.

Heath had tried his best to let me live a normal life while he protected his sister, but the incident with Earl took that choice out of all of our hands.

My safety was compromised, my connection to Heath had made me a target, and considering that Earl had been a hired hit, there was no reason to think that it wouldn't happen again.

And so, though I wasn't a witness, I went into the program and into hiding with Iris.

My sons came with me. They didn't even complain. We were told upfront that it would likely last years, but none of us could conceive being separated with no contact for so long.

I didn't get to say goodbye to my friends, or even my parents, for fear of putting them in danger, so all of that was handled for me.

I coped with it by telling myself that I'd see them all again in a few years, but it was rough coming to terms with that part of it.

I got some time with Heath after that, a few weeks, while I recovered, time where he didn't leave my side.

I'd been examined by a doctor and put on bedrest for a time to be safe.

Things were strange between Heath and me. Both settled and unsettled.

He was happy about the baby, I could tell. It was obvious by the way he couldn't keep his hands off my belly for more than a few minutes at a time.

Sometimes I'd wake to find him lips pressed to my stomach, a near peaceful look on his face.

But we didn't talk about it much at first. We didn't talk about a lot of things.

There was one thing, though, that Heath *loved* to talk about.

"We're getting married," he told me, bringing it up out of the blue.

"What?"

"You're having my baby. We're getting married."

I couldn't believe what he'd just said, or how he'd said it.

A few pounding heartbeats later, I managed to get out, "I'm forty-one years old, Heath. I don't need to be married to have a baby. This isn't the fucking fifties. We can co-parent without being husband and wife."

"Then don't do it for the baby. Do it for me. I need this. I need to know that when I go out there, I have this to come home to. You're mine, and I *need* to make it legal."

My heart was hammering in my chest, but I just stared at him.

And he kept going. "This isn't negotiable. I let you go once. I went against every instinct I had and walked away from you, because I thought it was the unselfish thing to do. Now you're stuck with me for as long as I'm alive. You're mine, that baby is mine, and we're going to make it legal."

"We don't even have our own identities. It wouldn't mean anything."

His Adam's apple bobbed with a rough swallow as he stared at me, his expression raw, cold eyes stark. "It would mean something to me."

God, he knew how to get to me.

"Tell me something sweet," I urged him with a smile.

"I need you," he rasped, voice weighty with feeling.

"And?" I prompted.

He looked confused, so I made it easy on him.

"Do you love me, Heath?"

"Of course I do. What do you think all this is, if not love?"

That stunned me, stopping my heart, then sending it slamming wildly back into life.

And still, I felt the need to say, "You never would have taken me with you if you weren't forced to by circumstance."

His brows drew together, making him look stern.

Mean and magnificent.

The combination I found most irresistible on him.

"You're absolutely fucking right I wouldn't have. If I hadn't been so careless, because I was *obsessed* with you, you wouldn't be in this situation right now, trapped, confined, in danger. I'd have spared you that. But I'd have done it for you. Not for me. If I were a completely selfish bastard, I'd have chained you to my side from the start.

He stared me down for a solid minute, then continued, "And another thing, I was always planning to come back for you, when it was safe. If you'd moved on, if you hadn't, I didn't give a *damn*, I was going to come, shake up your life, and take you back when this was all over. That's a fucking fact."

"Yes. Yes, I'll marry you," I said suddenly, impulsively, because he'd given me what I needed.

This man loved me how I *deserved* to be loved.

I'd been waiting a long fucking time for that.

EPILOGUE

We were married in a church. Heath, who remained constantly and consistently unexpected, insisted on it.

It was a tiny gathering, just us, Iris, Raf, Gustave, and a few bodyguards standing witness.

Heath's face was unsmiling and serious as he recited his vows solemnly.

I had no doubt in my mind that he meant them.

None of it was anything I could have even pictured a year ago, but I recited mine back with tears in my eyes and joy in my heart.

Life on the run was not as expected.

It was chaotic and a little scary, sure, but there was something unutterably beautiful about it, the living each day like it could be torn from you.

They were rough times, yes, rough years, but roughness was not the nucleus of it. At the center of it all were memories of joyful reunions and meaningful goodbyes, of holding on to the man I loved for dear life and knowing how precious every single moment we had together was.

It taught us to love in a new way, one that we'd never forget. Having a love that was endangered made it all the more precious.

And enlightening, because I learned so much about what love should be, how it should be treated, made me learn to express it as often and elaborately as I could.

Love is all that matters. Every other thing in life is a detail. Love is both your legacy and your salvation. If you have the right kind of love, you can get through anything. That's what those years taught me.

We were a strange little group, with our new names and identities. Heath installed us all in a huge house in the northwest, so it started out as five of us, two pregnant women in different stages of their lives and pregnancies, two college boys, and Heath, who came and went often.

Well, nine of us, if you counted the fact that we each (with the exception of Heath) got our own personal bodyguards.

Iris and I hit it off right away. It was one of those friendships that required no effort at all. It just worked. Our age difference was drastic, but it didn't matter; we got along famously, almost from the beginning.

Like sisters. And, when we were having fun, partners in crime.

It was Iris who told me just who she was testifying against that had made their lives so dangerous.

"The vice president?" I repeated back to her, not quite sure if she was messing with me.

She *loved* to mess with me.

She nodded, biting her lip. "Our grandmother."

My eyes narrowed on her, looking for a lie. "Your grandmother is the VP, and you're testifying against her?"

She nodded again.

"What's the charge?"

"The better question would be: What isn't the charge? I've got so much dirt on that woman I could start a farm."

Now I was pretty sure she was messing with me, but she kept going.

"But the reason I devoted my life to taking her down is that she murdered my parents and my sister. I'd die to bring them justice. They're worthy of that. And even if she kills me, they'll still have a case. My testimony will help, but I gathered so much concrete evidence that it can speak for itself."

The way she spoke, how into it she was, had me finally buying it.

The fucking vice president. Holy shit.

One thing you could never deny about Iris and Heath— they both had enormous balls.

The first house we stayed in was basically in the middle of nowhere, but there was a college nearby, and both of my boys quickly found their own lives and were gone more often than not, which was for the best. They were grown men.

That left me spending more time with Iris than anyone else.

Neither of us ever complained about that.

Powerful bonds were made when women were pregnant together. And we did a hell of a lot of bonding.

Over time, she became like a little sister to me.

With nothing but time on our hands, we got plenty of talking in, and it wasn't long before we were telling each other everything.

I told her all about my strange courtship with her brother.

And she told me all about her enduring obsession with Alasdair Masters.

"Why couldn't you ask Dair to come into hiding with you?" I asked her once.

"He has too much of a public profile. There is simply no way to hide him. The best we could do was to keep him out of it. Also, I don't think he'd want to. I'm pretty sure he hates me now."

I doubted that very much. I didn't know him well, but I did know that Dair was not a man with hate in his heart. Not for anyone, but particularly not for one of the sweetest women I'd ever met, who also happened to be pregnant with his child.

And also, who wouldn't fall for a girl like Iris? She was young and sweet, funny and joyful, and of course, there was her extraordinary beauty. Sure, like her brother, she had some fascinating and troublesome quirks, but I was guessing that a man like Dair would find those quirks well worth the payoff. Hell, with what I knew of him, I thought he'd find most of them endearing.

We had fun together, Iris and I, but always under her bright surface, I could see that something weighed heavy on her, and I knew that it was Dair.

"I wonder if he's moved on. It seems likely. We didn't part on the best of terms, so I doubt he'd even think of waiting for me," Iris lamented.

I didn't know what to say to her. I wanted to reassure her, but I also knew it would be cruel to give her false hope.

"You know, for a while I thought it'd be you he moved onto," she added.

I'd gathered that much, but she wasn't done.

"And then I looked into you."

"You mean Heath did."

She cringed just enough to look guilty as hell. "No, I mean I did, too. Pretty extensively. I just wanted to know what kind of a woman you were, if he was going to end up with you. And everything checked out. *Everything*. You're just good people. You make friends everywhere and treat people well as a rule. Hell, you even give a Christmas bonus to your gardener."

God, she was scary sometimes. How could she have possibly found that out?

"Eventually, I was even kind of okay with the option. I saw you out with your boys—"

"You followed me, too?" For some reason when Iris said she'd checked me out, I'd thought it was all internet dirt. The idea of her following us around just struck me as several shades more crazy.

"Only a little. It didn't take much. I saw you having dinner with your boys, and I knew I'd seen enough. Dair couldn't do better than you. I knew *I* wasn't better. I know I'm as fucked up as Heath, in my own way."

"He couldn't do better than you, either," I told her gently. "Any man would be lucky to have a woman like you."

And she had her pick. Just about every man within ten miles from my sons to her bodyguard were more than a little smitten with her.

But just any man wasn't an option for Iris. She was devoted to Dair, whether he was a lost cause or not. She was a go down with the ship kind of girl.

And it wasn't all pining and sadness for her. We had our share of fun.

We both loved to dance. Whenever we were feeling particularly stir crazy, we'd put on some music, turn it up loud, and have an impromptu dance party.

Her obsession with Beyonce, or as she called her, Bey, was contagious. We drove my boys crazy, randomly singing the lyrics from her latest album.

And we loved to coordinate pranks.

Bubble wrap on the toilet seat, the mayo jar refilled with vanilla yogurt, just to name a few.

The two of us pregnant at the same time was not something anyone would want to mess with.

And we were both obsessed with bad reality television. The worse the better. We'd binge watch it together, though I was pretty sure it lowered both of our IQs.

We kept each other busy, which was good. We both needed to stay busy to stay sane.

My husband was still a mystery to me, one I'd have liked more time to analyze. He was gone more often than not.

"Where does he go?" I asked Iris.

"Heath is taking care of some things that need taking care of," Iris told me solemnly.

"Care to elaborate?"

"I'm so sorry that you were dragged into this, but he's not just doing this for me anymore. We have made enemies that will never let us live in peace, that will use anything to hurt him. You're in as much danger as I am now. Some key targets need to be eliminated if we're ever going to have a shot at making it through this. Long story short: He's making it so we can live a normal life again, someday."

Well, hell, it was darker and scarier than I'd thought, but I *had* asked.

Heath came home whenever he could, and though his visits were erratic, he usually managed to stay for a few weeks at a time.

Those weeks were what I lived for. We even got to squeeze in the occasional date.

Those dates were never dull.

"You make me crazy, and I'll be honest, I'm not sure that's a good thing; I was already crazy enough," Heath told me on our first such date.

We were out to dinner at the only French restaurant within a hundred miles of our remote, temporary home. It was crowded to bursting, but Heath managed to get us a table without a reservation.

"You'll be fine," I assured him.

"Me, maybe. And you, definitely. It's everyone else you should be worried about."

I laughed, though I wasn't sure what he was getting at, I could tell he was being his version of sweet. "How so?"

"You make me want to go around the room and make every fucker in here kiss your feet, just for the privilege of being in a fucking room with you."

God, I loved him. Every screwed up, quirky thing about him got to me in the best way possible. "You do understand you're being romantic right now?" I told him.

"I'm not sure the world can handle my flavor of romantic. Let's hope it doesn't increase my body count."

He wasn't exaggerating all that much. His flavor of romantic was possessive to the point of violence. God help any man that stood too close to me while Heath was watching.

It was definitely a rough edge of his that I had to work hard on softening.

Which was hypocritical of me. I had a jealous streak where he was concerned that was a whacked out mile long. He got as much female attention as I did male, and I *hated* it.

I never had to do anything about it, though. Heath was about as flirtatious as an angry rattlesnake. If some poor woman was crazy enough to approach him, he never hesitated to set them straight.

I fucking loved that.

I secretly got a kick out of watching him shoot these poor girls down. He was rather brutal about it, and the more aggressive they were, the more mean he was when he let them have it.

"I've got no patience for that shit," he told me once, right after a smoking hot blonde had approached him while he was ordering popcorn at the movies. "*None.* What the hell was wrong with that twit?"

He was mean and magnificent and completely oblivious to every woman on the planet but me, and I adored every inch of him.

When I was about six months pregnant, he went off the radar for longer than usual.

Long enough that Iris and I were starting to get nervous. We usually heard *something* from him.

Even the other agents didn't have any word for us.

When he came home, at last, I couldn't help it, I cried like a baby.

I told myself it was the hormones, but he had a hard time keeping his composure, as well.

He came to me first thing when he got to the house, taking me in his arms, face buried in my neck, one big hand rubbing my belly.

He was gasping, fighting for air.

"I didn't think I'd make it back to you this time. I didn't think I'd ever see you again."

That broke me. God, did it hurt. The helplessness was excruciating.

He dropped to his knees, face nuzzling into my belly.

I stroked his hair and tried to comfort him, tried my best to put on a brave face, because this time I could see he needed that from me.

It was long time before he let me go, and when he did, he went straight to Iris.

He wrapped her in those huge arms of his, nearly making her disappear.

She stood stiffly, though it was only because she knew him. He was affectionate with her, and she was an extremely affectionate girl, but she knew better than to touch him back.

"It's okay," he murmured to her. "You can hug me back."

She did, slowly, tentatively, her eyes going straight to me, big fat tears in them and huge helpings of gratitude, like I'd just granted her a long wished for gift.

Later that night in bed I got a look at his body.

"Oh, darling, what have you done to yourself?" I asked him softly.

He'd been shot again. Twice, in the gut. The wounds were still fresh, but from the placement, I assumed that at one point they'd been nearly fatal.

"What I had to, to make it back home to you."

Iris had her baby soon after that. It was a boy that she named Alasdair Cameron after his father.

We called him Cameron, or Cam for short.

And a few short months later, I had my own.

Heath made it home just in time to be there for the birth of our son. We named him Gerard, after my father, who, God willing, he'd someday get to meet.

Fatherhood was good for Heath, I saw right away. It softened some of his rougher edges.

And he was a good father. What he lacked in practice, he made up for in effort. It more than balanced out.

Heath doted on both of the babies, as did Rafael, Gustave, and even Mason.

With all of that adult attention, Cameron and Gerard lacked for nothing.

When little Cam was just a few months old, Iris and Heath had to leave for a long stretch.

It was time for the trial of the century.

It was excruciating for Iris, as it would be for any new mother, to leave her baby for so long, but she knew I'd care for Dair Jr. like he was my own, and so it eased some of that great burden for her.

We watched the trial on TV. It was intense, watching a determined Iris take down one of the most powerful politicians in the country.

Her grandmother wasn't the VP anymore by that time, but it was a technicality. The woman still had pull in Washington.

I knew this because I was glued to the television twenty-four/seven, and all anyone did was talk about her.

Iris didn't get to come back to see us for the duration of the trial, not even for a visit. It was just too dangerous for her, and for us.

Even Heath only came back once, right as the proceedings were coming to a close.

It was a bittersweet reunion, because he'd been gone for months and could only stay for one night.

That goodbye was one of the worst of them all.

He cupped my head in both hands, making me look at him, straight into his eyes. "Listen," he urged in his soft, gravelly way.

I couldn't hold back tears. Something horrible was going to happen on this trip. I just knew it. Something that would break me. I could see it in every line of his tense face.

"Listen," he repeated. "We're going to be separated for a bit. We just are. I can't say for how long." He swallowed, and I watched his throat move, his big Adam's apple bobbing in a way that reminded me just how young he was. "But listen, and I mean this, do *not* turn on the TV. You are not to watch the news, you understand me?"

I nodded that I did and promised that I wouldn't.

That lasted about three days.

It was on every channel. Francis Baker, as Iris was known to the public, had been assassinated in broad daylight, mere days after the trial was over.

The story went that at a stoplight, a van pulled up beside the car she was transported in, and six men in ski masks jumped out of said van.

She was dragged from the car, and her driver and one of her bodyguards, who were both wounded in the attack, witnessed her being shot at point blank in the temple. One of her bodyguards was also reportedly killed, a big blond man, they said, though no name was divulged.

Heath knew this was coming, I told myself. *It has to be fake. It has to be.* How else would he have been so sure it was coming? Why else would he have asked me not to turn on the TV?

I wanted to believe it was all a lie, but it hurt like it was the truth.

I held our babies close and prayed that they would come back to me.

TWO MONTHS LATER

We'd moved again. The second place in as many months.

Raf and Gus took it well, considering that we kept uprooting their lives. I was eternally grateful to them for handling this all with grace, for going so far out of their way to keep from adding to my already vast burden of guilt.

We were somewhere in Arizona, in the middle of freaking nowhere, of course, in a large house, on a huge property with high gates and lots of land.

Our guards had been doubled since the incident with the van. We had men on the perimeter as well as in the house.

I had the babies both in high chairs, feeding them tiny spoonfuls of green mush when I heard the front door open.

This wasn't unusual. With all of the agents roaming around, people were coming in and out at all hours.

Still, I called out, "Hello!" and wondered why no one answered back. The agents assigned to us were usually very good about announcing themselves.

I didn't have to wonder long.

Heath and Iris, looking tired but healthy and whole, came striding into the room.

I started to shake, every bit of me, top to bottom, from the marrow of my bones to the very outer layer of my skin, shaking. Trembling like I had a fever.

But it wasn't a fever, it was a rush of relief so profound and pure that it knocked the breath out of me.

I'd wondered over the last two torturous months what I'd do if I saw him again. If I'd scream and rail at him for putting me through this, or if I'd embrace him and weep, be so relieved to see him that it'd trump all of my anger at the pain and uncertainty he'd put me through.

But after one devastating look at him, it wasn't even a question.

I launched myself at him, running across the room, flinging my arms around his shoulders as I jumped up against him, legs snaking around his hard thighs and gripping.

He grabbed my ass with one hand, my shoulder with the other, pulling me even tighter to him.

I buried my face in his neck and breathed him in. He kissed my temple.

I wanted to say so many things, but none of them seemed as important as this, just touching him, taking him in.

One of his big hands snaked into my hair and angling my face to him, he crushed his mouth against mine.

I pulled back enough to look at him. We stayed like that, panting, breathing each other's air as I stared into his eyes.

They were still cold. They would never be warm. I knew that by now, just as I'd known that they'd never be the windows to his soul.

But it hit me then what was.

His soul was in his touch. His reverent lips, his mastering hands, his seeking body—those were the things that showed his hand and betrayed his true feelings.

His reverent lips told me that he loved me, his trembling hands told me that he needed me, and his seeking body told me he trusted me.

I soothed him, made him feel whole again.

He invigorated me, made me feel alive again.

He was mine and I was his, and no matter how long it took him to make it back to me, I'd be there waiting for him.

THREE YEARS LATER

It was late spring in Vegas. That brief time of year in Sin City where it was actually nice outside; hot out, a perfect day for the pool, but with the temperature still sitting somewhere reasonable in the double digits.

We were enjoying a BBQ at Dair's friend, Turner's, house.

Since we'd returned home, this had become a weekly thing. Turner loved to entertain.

It was good to be home. It had taken years, but at last, here we were.

The running was over, and we were slowly settling back into some semblance of normal a life.

A heavily pregnant Iris sat in the shade on a chaise lounge beside me while our husbands threw the boys around the pool.

She was patting her big belly, proud as punch about it, as she always was these days, when she asked me, "Are you and Heath having any more?"

I was mid sip of sangria, and I nearly spit it out.

I shot her a look, an *are you out of your mind?* look.

"Are you out of your mind?" I asked aloud, when I was done choking.

She laughed, and finally I laughed when I saw that unsurprisingly, she was messing with me.

Gerard was anything but a regret for me. He was one of my four biggest blessings in life, in fact, but it was no question that I was now done with the child-bearing times of my life.

We didn't speak for a time as we watched our boys in the pool.

Heath had a giggling child in each arm and carted them around like they weighed nothing.

Neither boys were small. Gerard was bigger, Cameron taller, but they were both large and heavy for their age. When I picked either of them up, my entire body had to brace itself, and my back bowed with the burden, but they both looked like they weighed about as much as a feather when Heath was holding them.

I don't think anyone quite expected it, but Heath was very good with kids. He was a devoted father and uncle, dedicating a great deal of his time to both boys.

He said they calmed him, which was surely strange as they were both bundles of nonstop energy.

But it was good, because he was retired now from working for the government and taking some time off to stay at home with Gerard while I got back into pursuing my passion for photography.

He talked about different jobs he could do with his vast experience and many specialized skills. He'd likely start up a security firm, sometime down the road.

But he wasn't even worried about it now. Now, he was enjoying some much deserved and hard earned time with his family.

I was distracted briefly from my musings as Cam made a mad dash out of the pool, running for the grassy lawn, Gerard hot on his heels.

Iris and I shared a look. They were at it again.

Our sons were close cousins, near inseparable, so this was a fairly regular occurrence. They had near opposite personalities, but they were still best buddies.

"Gerard!" Heath barked, and our son stopped what he was doing, which happened to be pinning his cousin down for no good reason that I could tell.

"Help, Uncle, help!" Cam called out between giggling fits.

Heath pushed his huge dripping body out of the pool, and my jaw went a little slack with desire.

Iris noticed. "Ew," she said, though she was just giving me shit for fun, because she was surely used to it by now. "You know that's my brother you're ogling, right?"

I ignored her, watching Heath playing with the boys. He made a show of rescuing Cam, but as soon as he got low enough to the ground, the boys both turned on him, tickling, pushing him down, using every dirty trick in the book to try to pin him.

He let them, but only for a moment, straightening when he'd had enough, grabbing a kid in each big arm, striding across the lawn, and throwing them back in the pool, much to their squealing delight.

"He needs help," Iris mused.

I looked at her, and it took me a moment. I followed her stare to see that she wasn't talking about Heath.

She was talking about Dair's friend, Turner.

He was chatting with Dair and my older boys, the four of them huddled together. I couldn't catch any of what they were saying from here, but it had apparently gotten her attention.

I'd known Turner briefly, on a professional basis years ago, and we'd become friendly again recently due to the weekly barbecues, but my knowledge of him was still superficial at best, and mostly came from what Iris shared with me.

Turner was one of Dair's closest friends and colleagues, though they couldn't have been more opposite if it'd been their goal.

Turner was sarcastic, snarky, and arrogant. A total and unapologetic womanizer. He was very vocal about the fact that he never intended to settle down.

Apparently Iris had a problem with that.

"Help with what?" I asked her, just to clarify. Sadly, though, I knew her well enough to guess with some baffled accuracy the strange and gleeful inner workings of her brain.

"Finding the right woman. I have a plan."

I sent her a sideways glance. Her smile was positively diabolical.

Well hell.

I wondered if I should warn Turner, but I quickly decided against it.

When Iris made plans, woe betide any poor soul that got in her path.

BOOKS BY R.K. LILLEY

THE WILD SIDE SERIES
THE WILD SIDE
IRIS
DAIR

THE OTHER MAN
TYRANT - COMING SOON

THE UP IN THE AIR SERIES
IN FLIGHT
MILE HIGH
GROUNDED
MR. BEAUTIFUL

LANA (AN UP IN THE AIR COMPANION NOVELLA)
AUTHORITY - COMING SOON

THE TRISTAN & DANIKA SERIES
BAD THINGS
ROCK BOTTOM
LOVELY TRIGGER

THE HERETIC DAUGHTERS SERIES
BREATHING FIRE
CROSSING FIRE - COMING SOON

THE BISHOP BROTHERS SERIES
BOSS - COMING SOON

JOIN MY EMAIL NEWSLETTER AT RKLILLEY.COM

Twitter: @authorrklilley

Instagram: Authorrklilley

Facebook.com/RkLilley

Email me at Authorrklilley@gmail.com

HERE'S A LITTLE TEASER FOR MY
UPCOMING NOVEL,

BOSS

HAZEL PIPER

I loved Clayton Bishop. Huge love. Hug him tight and never let go love. We were best friends, near inseparable, and had been for years.

He loved me back. He'd have done anything for me. He thought I was the most beautiful girl in the world. I knew it because he told me, but also, I could see it in his eyes. He was in love with me.

I loved Clayton, but I was *in love* with his brother, Declan.

Declan, who hated me.

Declan, who would barely look at me. Who went out of his way to avoid me.

He hadn't always hated me. I used to be as close to him as the rest of the Bishop brothers.

It happened about two years ago, the hate. Came out of nowhere and trampled its way all over my heart.

And to this day, I did not know why.

It didn't matter. I was lovesick. Totally. I couldn't see beyond the agony of my feelings for him, not even for Clayton.

When Declan was nearby, my body knew it. Not just the same

room, but even near that room, and I swear I changed, things in my body started throbbing, I lost brain cells, and became an utter fool.

He, on the other hand, barely seemed to notice me now.

I couldn't have gotten his attention if I stripped down and started dancing naked.

It was so unfair, because he had all of my attention all the time.

It was an obsession that had kept me company for so long that I needed it. Needed it to get through the day.

And as if unrequited love weren't enough, our lives were securely and inevitably entwined. It wasn't even an issue of seeing him daily. This was an *hourly* affliction, with shared car rides, classes, and often, when I went home, even shared dinners between our close-knit families. There was no escape, no relief, no reprieve from the barrage of feelings that I held inside of me for a guy who'd barely given me solid eye contact for nearly two years.

I was so screwed.

This dilemma had been the contentious focal point of my life for so long that a lot of other things slipped my notice.

Significant things.

Important things.

Things I'd soon come to regret.

COMING SOON!

Made in the USA
Coppell, TX
08 March 2024

29901206R00184